Between Love & *Betrayal*

Between Love & *Betrayal*

Mary Clancy

POOLBEG

This book is a work of fiction. The names, characters, places, businesses, organisations and incidents portrayed in it are either the product of the author's imagination or are used fictitiously. Any resemblance to actual persons, living or dead, events or locales is entirely coincidental.

Published 2022
by Poolbeg Press Ltd.
123 Grange Hill, Baldoyle,
Dublin 13, Ireland
Email: poolbeg@poolbeg.com

A catalogue record for this book is available from the British Library.

ISBN 978178199-716-1

www.poolbeg.com

About the Author

Mary Clancy was born and raised in Tipperary Town. Later moving to Cahir, she spent many happy years rearing two of her four children, Denise and Adrian, before settling in County Kildare where she now resides with her husband Michael and her sons Michael and Fionn. She spends much of her time in beautiful Donegal.

Mary is an Honours graduate in Social Studies (BSS) from Trinity College, Dublin. She holds an MA in social work practice from TCD and the National Qualification in Social Work (NQSW). She holds a post-grad in Mediation and Conflict Resolution.

Moving away from her social-work career a few years ago allowed her the opportunity to wind down, finding the perfect distraction: writing.

Her debut novel *The Blue Washing Bag* was published by Poolbeg during lockdown in September 2020.

Between Love and Betrayal is her second novel.

Acknowledgements

Thank you so much, readers, for choosing *Between Love and Betrayal.* I hope you enjoy reading it as much as I enjoyed writing it. Cheesy, I know, but true.

I must firstly acknowledge my daughter Denise and my mother Mary Theresa who have passed, but never from my heart.

To the wonderful Paula Campbell at Poolbeg Press for affording me this great opportunity. *Thank you so much, Paula.*

To Gaye Shortland, my editor, for her keen eye as well as her attention to detail. Engaging with the ever-respectful Gaye is a pleasure. Thank you, Gaye.

To Michael, my darling husband, for proofreading the entire manuscript. I won't include an emoji. I promised. X.

To my sons Michael and Fionn for their continued kind words of support. They mean so much to me. And to Adrian my eldest son. I love you all.

To Maria and Eamon, my friends for over thirty years.

To my dear friends who were my first port of call to

read the book. Marcella, Rosemary, and Mel. Thank you so much for being there for me.

To my friends Anne and Rita for their continued support.

For the many conversations I have had with my friends – you know who you are.

To my siblings Adrian, Anne, and Gerard for your kind words of support.

To the one and only Coco, my canine pal of fifteen years.

Dedication

For Michael X

PART ONE

Chapter 1

London

1926

Connie Stapleton wasn't at all conscious that she was inclined towards women, until the very moment she laid eyes on Lucrezia Romano. The Italian girl was wearing a full-length white-lace dress, with a sash of wide lemon ribbon emphasising her waist. She wore the longest strand of cream pearls that Connie had ever seen.

Walking through the hotel foyer, she approached Connie who was standing at the front desk. When she spoke, her voice suited her perfectly. Pronouncing each word precisely, she spoke with an accent.

"Good evening. I'm afraid I'm lost. Can you tell me how to get to the Queen's Theatre, please?"

"You're a bit away from it, I'm afraid – it's over on Shaftesbury Avenue. But I'll be going there myself once I've cleared up a few things here. If you'd like to take a seat and wait?" She suddenly didn't want to lose sight of the girl.

"Oh, I will, thank you."

"You can sit over there by the window so. I'm Connie, by the way, Connie Stapleton. Front of house manager here at the Strand Palace Hotel."

"Lucrezia Elena Romano – soon to be student at the Heatherley School of Fine Art. So very pleased to meet you." The girl stepped forward. Placing her hands gently on Connie's shoulders, she planted an unexpected kiss on each of her cheeks.

Feeling Lucrezia's skin brush against her face, Connie blushed. The goose bumps were rising on the back of her neck. Inhaling the scent of Lucrezia's dark curls as they fell towards her, she had never experienced such a sensation.

Ballygore, Ireland
1924

Connie's world had crashed around her when her father was killed two years before, back in Ballygore. Struck in the head by a bolting horse on the main street during the fair. One sharp kick to the temple. "It was the iron shoe that did the main damage," they said. "And not another mark on him." He died on the street, leaving a traumatised Connie staring down at him, frozen in shock. Layla, Connie's mother, who had never been strong, took to the bed after the funeral. In no shape to care for herself, let alone run a public house and look after her family, she lost all interest. The youngest child, Johanna, was six, the twin boys almost ten years old.

Connie, who had just turned seventeen, had little choice but to take on the role of carer and provider, now that her father was no longer around to earn an income outside of the pub. He had worked as a rates collector in the town.

The public house, which had been in the family for three generations, was at the side of the street on Mill Road, just off the main street in Ballygore. Small and local, certainly not profitable enough to provide a decent living for the family, as had been evident since her father died.

The shop front had been painted in various shades of green for as long as Connie could remember. "A testimony to the past," her father had insisted, pointing out the two bullet holes left permanently on display on the front window. Outside, the lower half of the window had been covered with a painted wooden panel, protecting the cracked glass behind it from the prying eyes of Peelers, and those who felt no shame in snooping and reporting. Evidence to all that the Black and Tans had fired their guns – banging on doors up and down the street – searching for men hidden behind closed doors in darker times. Black and Tans – temporary reinforcements in the Royal Irish Constabulary during the War of Independence, who weren't afforded a good word, held instead in contempt and disgrace. Wearing uniforms which were pieced together from British army and police stores. Half of one man's uniform and half of another's. Men without shame, shouting with unfamiliar accents, firing indiscriminately from guns which gave power to men of questionable standing. Bullets through glass panes, carving perfectly formed holes well over an inch wide. Memories of men hidden on old horsehair mattresses, balanced high on beams in dark outhouses, in ivy-ridden back yards. Men who had a war to fight. And the pride of ordinary people who sheltered their countrymen. And public houses such as Stapleton's, where customers told stories. Stories of cowards and braver souls, stories which would carry through the generations, lest anyone forget.

After her father died, Connie had taken whatever work was on offer at the local hotel, rushing home to open the pub door in the evenings.

Layla remained upstairs, leaving Connie to get on with things. The shock, her mother maintained, would never leave her, rendering her incapable of managing the household.

Connie did her best to fit into her new role, caught between the loss she was feeling on the death of her father and her mother's constant complaining, casting a guilt-ridden shadow onto her eldest girl. Chastising her daughter with little cause, losing patience, undermining her. Connie felt overburdened with her mother's constant whining.

"Could you not have helped your father, Connie? Or warned him in time? Or run home to get me the minute you saw him fall down? But no – standing there more interested in what was going on around you, no doubt."

Connie, already consumed with guilt, had reached a point where she could take no more. She loved her mother. But she felt trapped.

It had been in the back of her mind for some time to run away. To lose herself. To get lost. But where would she go?

Her interest had been piqued when she'd heard that a number of men in the town had left for London to work on the tunnels. And the women were leaving just as fast as the men – finding work in the thriving clubs and pubs around England. Many working as maids in the big houses and hotels, word filtering back to Ballygore that there were plenty of jobs to be had across the water.

Having read in the papers about the opportunities in Canada and America, Connie dismissed the notion of travelling so far away. She'd be near enough in London to appease her mother, if she let her go in the first place. And far away enough to be gone. Free to be herself. Free to laugh out loud if she felt like it, without feeling guilty for being happy. Free to meet new people, lighthearted people, who might enjoy her company.

Connie set her sights on the West End of London.

Initially, her mother had cited her anxieties and ailments as being all too debilitating to contemplate such a change for the family. Spending days at a time locked in her bedroom at the back of the house, refusing to consider the implications of losing Connie. Good days, bad days. If Layla were to be believed, things were nowhere near as bad as her eldest was making them out to be.

"*Aaah*, for God's sake, Connie, will you just give over? You're depressing me with all that talk of leaving home. It'll settle down in time. You'll see. And aren't we managing fine as we are?"

Her mother, she feared, would never shake herself out of it, as long as she had her there to do everything for her. Biddable Connie.

Yes, they had the business, but it was only viable as long as the doors remained open and the customers were leaving their money behind the counter.

As Connie's urge to leave Ireland grew stronger, she began to nudge her mother towards taking on more responsibility, doing her best to coax her out of her malaise.

Business in the pub had declined since the shoe factory in town had closed its doors, with many of the unemployed joining the queues at the docks to leave. Those who had remained on in Ballygore had enough to be doing to be looking after their families rather than leaving their shillings in Stapleton's public house.

The finer establishments in the town played host to the moneyed people, those unaffected by hard times, many of whom would not frequent the small public house at the side of the street with the name *Stapleton* painted over the door. Unless they were drunk enough to be refused a drink in whatever establishment they had left.

Connie reminded her mother that it hadn't been too long ago since the workhouses were full to capacity with decent people like themselves – people who were no longer able to put food on the table. If they still had a table. It had been at least enough for Layla to entertain the notion of her eldest leaving home, Connie insisting that if she didn't make a move soon, they would all be in trouble.

"Mammy, the twins are nearly twelve, and Johanna is eight – surely to God she can do a bit more for herself? She's expected to do little enough as it is. And you'll have the three of them here to help out after school. And why not think about selling tea and bread and a few other bits from the snug counter, keeping it separate from the bar? That way you won't have to stay open late if you don't feel up to it."

Seeing no other choice in the end, Layla gave nineteen-year-old Connie her blessing of sorts.

"Off you go then, if you must. Maybe we *will* open up during the day, and the boys can stay on in school that bit longer, now that you'll be earning. 'Tis young Johanna that worries me the most – she's not made like you, Connie. She doesn't have the *brawn* that you have."

Relieved that her plan to leave for London was finally becoming a reality, Connie set about leaving the place spotless for her departure – cleaning and polishing until she was satisfied that she was leaving little for her mother to complain about.

Connie would choose her own way of providing for her family. But at a distance, no longer smothered and confined, no longer the dependable daughter, running the small familiar public house on Mill Road that she had grown to detest so much. The place which had lost its very soul the day her father had last walked out of it. Whistling.

Once she had coaxed her mother out of the bed, down the stairs, Layla's form improved. Stocking the pub with mixed items to entice a regular day-trade seemed like a good idea. With the snug cleaned out, the counter waxed, the floor polished, Connie placed soft red cushions at either corner of the benches, where the women could enjoy a glass of stout and a chat with Layla, away from the prying eyes of the pure.

Starting out with a half chest of loose tea, eggs, currant buns and soda bread, made upstairs by Layla, this new venture seemed to entice her mother enough to take an interest in life outside of herself, leaving Connie to get on with her plan.

No man had ever turned Connie's head, least of all Mattie Grogan of Black Post Inn, a friend of her father's. He hadn't so much proposed as taken a notion to offer her what he considered was a fair option for her to remain on in Ireland.

Quietly measured and calculated, Mattie hadn't been taken too seriously around Ballygore. Ever since he'd moved to town, he'd been on the lookout for a wife. At least he said he was.

People had been listening to the same old story for so long they were tired of hearing it. They had tried to set him up with girls from neighbouring farms – before they realised it was pointless. He was chancing his arm, they maintained.

"All in the mind with Mattie Grogan – he's more bloody suspicious than interested," they said.

Mattie believed that the townies were after his land and the fine house that went with it. They were all put in their place by an ever-tactful Mattie, who had mastered the art of ignoring people – avoiding confrontation.

When a less than sober Mattie had enquired of Connie what her answer might be, if he was likely to offer her a proposal of marriage, she had immediately interrupted his flow.

"No, Mattie. Let me stop you right there. The answer would be no. I will not be considering any proposal from you, or indeed anyone else here in Ballygore. That's of course if you were to ask me, which you haven't really, have you? And you know well I'm off to London next week. So … say no more."

Putting her finger to her lips, she had quickly pulled her wool jacket across her chest with her free hand, warding off any further intrusion to her person. Mattie had smiled, adding that his well-meaning gesture had been out of respect for her late father. Adding that outside of his deep regard for James Stapleton, she was the only woman he could safely say wasn't a gold-digger, after his money, even if she was a townie with little to bring to Black Post Inn, apart from her fine self. And to let him know if she ever changed her mind. But Connie sensed that he felt relieved at her rejection.

Once settled in West London, Connie worked as many hours as time allowed. Starting with what she was most familiar with, she served behind the bar at the Strand Palace Hotel, working evenings at the ticket office at the Queen's Theatre on Shaftsbury Avenue, a fifteen-minute walk away.

Mesmerised by the glitz around Soho, Connie was comfortable with her anonymity as she went about her business, smiling to herself. The London lifestyle suited her perfectly. Connie Grogan from Ballygore could breathe at last.

Becoming known as a grafter to all she encountered through her work, she was not shy of taking on responsibility. Everyone seemed to like the low-sized Irish girl with the long step, whose sense of humour and raucous wit could match any man's.

Within two years she had worked her way up to manage the front of house at the hotel, availing of the accommodation in the one-bedroom flat in the basement. At twenty-two years old, Connie had no regrets.

She was happy to be sending a steady sum of money home every fortnight. The boys could remain on in school until they were old enough to work. And young Johanna, who was not shy in her expectations of what Connie should do for her, would want for nothing. Connie was confident in knowing that life for her family back at home was as good as she could make it for them. Her father would have been proud of her.

She missed him terribly, particularly when she needed sound advice. Her closeness to him kept her going. Never allowing herself to accept that she was less than capable, she spoke to her father when things played on her mind. And things *did* play on her mind. The familiar thoughts taunting her, over and over again. "Overthinking" her father had called it.

Her short stocky frame was just like his own, in stark contrast to her mother's slim figure, which was more like young Johanna's. It was her father who had shortened her name from Cornelia to Connie. He said it suited her better.

Reading the letters coming from home, there was little in terms of gratitude – just enquiries as to when the next parcel would be arriving. Her mother would mention items she had seen advertised in the newspaper, items she insisted were not available in Ballygore. "Argyle socks would look smashing on the twins." Or, "A cloche hat, if you don't mind," she'd hinted. "Oh ... wouldn't our Johanna just love a new bonnet for Easter ..." Point taken. Not that Connie expected much, but an acknowledgement of her hard work would have been nice.

Mattie Grogan would continue to lend a hand, even though there had been no real commitment offered before she'd left. Mattie wasn't the type to be tied down by expectations. Had she remained in Ballygore much longer, no doubt her mother would have found out that he had shown an interest in her, and expected her to marry the man she had regarded as "an awful bloody nuisance" in the earlier years, but "a pure godsend to the family" since Connie's father had died. He had called in most nights of the week since her father had died, preferring to spend his evenings in the pub where he would meet people, rather than sitting at home on his own. Offering to help out in whatever way he could, taking on the heavier jobs without hesitation, doing the dirty jobs, which otherwise would be left for Connie to deal with. There was an awkwardness about Mattie which didn't appeal to Connie. She knew she'd had a lucky escape.

Chapter 2

The Inheritance

1919

Mattie Grogan's fortune had changed on receiving a letter from Thornton Solicitors, Ballygore, on the morning of his twenty-first birthday. A man Mattie had never heard of had died, leaving his house and land to him.

He had inherited a modest-sized farm, thirty acres of prime land at a place called Black Post Inn, on the outskirts of Ballygore.

Mattie moved down from Kintown to Ballygore three weeks after getting the letter – the first envelope he had ever seen with his name written on it. His mother's name. Grogan. He had refused to move until he had completed the work he had undertaken. Mattie Grogan was a man of his word.

Nobody seemed to know much about the unobtrusive stranger when he landed in town to take up his inheritance. Dressed in heavy brown-wool trousers and a rough linen shirt, wearing boots that had seen better days, he looked more like a labourer to the locals than a landowner.

Mattie had chosen to declare that he was an orphan. That was the end of it. Not up for discussion. And no mention of a mother, making it clear from the outset that he'd be keeping his business to himself. Rumour got about that he had been born in the poorhouse hospital in Kintown, up the country.

Once they'd set eyes on him, there was little doubt amongst those who cared to comment as to who his father was. The locals swore he was the spit of Robert Hyland, back in the day. The same height, the same straight back, hooked nose, the wild bushy eyebrows. He wasn't a bad-looking young man, tall and thin, strong at the same time, with a full head of dark hair and a long neck. He had played it cool. Remaining composed, making no-one the wiser. People surmised that the newcomer must be worth a fortune, given what was known about the previous owner of Black Post Inn, Robert Hyland, who was widely regarded as a miser.

Mattie didn't share that he had just found out that he was indeed Hyland's illegitimate son. A rude and arrogant man by all accounts. Mattie bore no such arrogance, having spent the first three years of his life in the workhouse.

Mattie had been boarded out to a family after his mother died. Taken out of school at the age of twelve, reaching six feet standing in his bare feet by the time he was fourteen, he could read and write and not much more when it came to academic achievements.

Never shy about work, he had been seldom idle. Working for the local carpenter, he had learned the trade as he went. Accepting whatever work he was offered from local farmers, he took full advantage of whatever sleeping arrangements were on offer, anywhere to lay his head other than where he'd been brought up.

No-one would ever know for sure how he felt on laying eyes on the impressive Black Post Inn, sitting on the finest of land in the county – not even John Thornton the solicitor, who had delivered the new owner to the property once the papers had been signed in his office. Thornton, who wasn't known for his discretion in such matters, had little to offer in terms of reading Mattie's reaction. He had just disclosed that Mattie had played it cool. Too cool. Never flinched, or allowed Thornton to see how he was feeling inside.

Thornton did let it be known in certain circles that Mattie's foster family in Kintown hadn't been shy about voicing their disgust at being left the scant sum of twenty-five pounds by Hyland. An insult, they'd said, after the man had promised not to forget them in his will. They had been taken aback to learn that the lad had not alone been left the farm, but every last shilling that old Hyland had amassed over his lifetime. And all they'd got from the State for taking the boy in had been a meagre allowance. They had been further incensed on realising that Mattie was keeping his mouth shut. The ungrateful lad had hidden every scrap of correspondence about the will, without showing one sign of gratitude for all they had done for him.

Matthew Grogan was just being himself, taking it all in, deliberating, offering no explanations where he felt none were needed. He had asked Thornton only the questions he needed to ask, pertaining to the practical issues facing him, before accepting the keys to his new abode.

Later, exploring the place on his own, Mattie found the lodge at the front gate to be far less daunting than the big house, which he reckoned was a full half mile up the fir-lined avenue. That same evening, as he stood in the courtyard in front of the main house, he counted more windows than he had ever seen in a country house. Standing there in the centre of the courtyard was a large black metal post with the words '*Welcome to Black Post Inn,*' forged into a circular sign at the top. Mattie couldn't help but snigger – wondering why the sign wasn't out at the main gate.

Moving his few belongings into the small cottage by the black iron gates, he thought about what his poor mother might say if she could see her son all set up with his own farm of land, and the grand house that he was half afraid to call his own. All that space was far too much for a young country fellow. Too much to take in, for a man who had never known a home life outside of the deprivation he had suffered from the very people who'd claimed to care for him.

Once he had settled in the lodge, the new owner of

Black Post walked back up the avenue, sitting himself down on the low circular wall surrounding the sign – laughing as loud as he'd ever laughed before. Laughing at his luck as the soft rain fell on him. Soaking him. Laughing at Robert Hyland, the man who could have made his mother's life bearable, had he only acknowledged her. Black Post Inn would be well looked after. He'd spend as much money as he wanted to spend. And more along with it. Money that Hyland had begrudged his mother years before. Money that would have changed their lives. Crying.

As his mother had no choice but to enter the poorhouse, he felt strongly that he wouldn't be compliant in easing a dead man's conscience. Checking the house each day, going from room to room, keeping it aired in the summer and warm in the winter, deliberate in his intent to look after his fine house, Mattie Grogan became the curator of his own home. He had no inclination towards moving in.

Gradually making himself known around Ballygore, he greeted people with caution. Being raised by people who'd paid more attention to the swine in the pigsty than they did him, had made him wary.

Wearing the best of fine suits, along with the same hat that Hyland had worn, a tweed coat resting on his shoulders or folded under his arm, Mattie dressed each day as if he were going somewhere. Standing out from the other farmers around Ballygore, and more so again once it became known that he had no notion of farming what had been Hyland's land. "He didn't need to," the locals said. His inheritance had been substantial enough for him never to know a lean day.

Some said Mattie must be a bit slow on the uptake by remaining in the lodge, leaving the big house empty. Treating it like a museum.

Once Mattie had full access to his new-found wealth, the deliveries to Black Post Inn became a source of envy and inquisitiveness for many.

There were those who figured he was planning to open up Black Post Inn as the fine guest house that it had once been. Some said he was far too crafty to be showing his hand, calling him a "'cute hoor". While others contended that Mattie had more intelligence than many gave him credit for. There were those who coveted Mattie's inheritance. Mean people, who couldn't find it in themselves to be pleased that he had made a better life for himself, having come from nothing. The thinkers amongst them reckoned that the trappings of a childhood raised with people who didn't want him had left him feeling undeserving. Rejected.

A man visiting from Kintown, who recognised Mattie, let it slip that he had worked like a slave for people who wouldn't let him share the bedroom along with their own children. Leaving him to sleep under a blanket in a makeshift bed at the back of the old farmhouse, in the alcove of a disused fireplace, where a sow about to give birth would often be housed in the winter time. Half the time riddled with fleas and crawling with lice, the boy had known little else.

The new owner of Black Post had never experienced what it was like to be truly comfortable with people, until the day he walked into Stapleton's pub on Mill Road, a week after he moved to Ballygore. James the owner had taken an immediate liking to the tall pleasant young man, whom he said was "the grandest young chap he'd ever met in his whole life". From that first evening, Mattie was always made to feel welcome at Stapleton's public house.

There was a simplicity about Mattie that appealed to people, a non-threatening yet guarded approach. And he was never shy about buying a round of drinks at the bar counter. "A gentleman," was how he was largely described by the customers at Stapleton's.

Once people got to know him, they accepted him as he was. Awkward and shy at times, rarely showing anger even when confronted. "A decent fellow," they said. Mattie Grogan settled in well, three miles outside of the town of Ballygore.

Taking full advantage of the sound advice he received from James Stapleton, Mattie found out who to trust, and who to avoid having any dealings with. He swore that he would never again be under a compliment to anyone. It wasn't in his nature to hold a grudge, or to speak untoward, or to pull a punch, even where one might be well deserved. It was in his nature to walk away, rather than getting involved in a dispute.

Once James had established that Mattie was not cut out for farming, and had no notion of working the land, he guided him towards those he knew would rent the land from him. Mattie trusted the older man's word without hesitation, knowing that he had his best interests at heart. He felt a sense of belonging around Ballygore, a sense of pride that he had never known as a youngster. Acting on James' advice he leased out most of the land, keeping a couple of acres aside for his own use, but that was it. Mattie would not be farming the land that Robert Hyland had held so precious.

His foster brother Eddie could come down from Kintown and stay with him on the farm, if it suited him, once he was old enough. He wanted to offer something back to Eddie, for being the one who made him laugh, on days when they had little to laugh about.

When he heard the news that James Stapleton had been killed on the street just over three years later, Mattie had got the shock of his life – immediately stepping in to help Layla out with the arrangements. And paying for them.

At James' removal, Mattie stood shoulder to shoulder with the deceased man's brothers from Westmeath, as they carried the coffin of the man who had been like a father to him, a man he would honour for the rest of his days.

Chapter 3

The Neapolitan Rebel

1926

Lucrezia Elena Romano, a confident eighteen-year-old Italian arrived in West London in August 1926, having skilfully avoided the advances of a balding tenor from the northern city of Bologna. Arriving by boat from Naples, she was relieved to be free from the annoying chaperone who had been hired to deliver her to the door of her boarding house. On her departure, her father Abramo had wasted no time in booking his return passage to Chicago. Back to the architectural project he had abandoned when summoned home to Naples to deal with his wayward daughter.

Having been introduced by her aunts to the tenor from Bologna, Lucrezia had told her father in no uncertain terms that she was having none of it, insisting that the tenor had been pompous and arrogant, full of himself, rude. Relaying the event to her father, she had demonstrated for him, arms flailing, mimicking the Bolognan's reaction towards her when she had politely told him that she would not be party to any arrangements concerning her, made without her express consent.

She had rejected the tenor's advances which made her feel most uncomfortable, once alerted to the quickening pace of his breathing when he caught her off guard, moving close to her, much too close. Close enough for her to smell the pungent garlic from his breath. She told her father that the sound of the tenor's heavy breathing had alarmed her, forcing her to back up against the wall. She had pleaded with Abramo, her voice animated and high-pitched.

"Papa, you should have been here. He was furious with me. More than furious. His nose was twitching, and I could barely understand a word he was saying, he was speaking so fast. He said he had travelled all the way south to Naples, to meet a stupid, silly girl, who showed no appreciation of his talent, never mind be grateful for his expression of interest." Lucrezia insisted that the belligerent tenor would have punched her straight into the face, only that she was in her own home, with her aunts listening in the next room.

"Papa, he stormed out of the house – shouting insults back at Auntie Rosa and Fiorella. They were shouting back at him, cursing, and they were fuming with me. Fiorella was by far the worst. You should have seen her face. She called me a disrespectful *stronza!* She said I have every one of my mother's ways. Rosa shouted at me too.

She said that they had full control over me while you were away and, if I didn't do as they said, they had every right to punish me in your absence. And my brother Roberto was no better."

"I trust you advised your aunts otherwise," her father said, trying to keep his temper under control.

Abramo had found it difficult to conceal the rage he felt building up inside him. Lucrezia's aunts had overstepped the mark this time. Since his late wife, their sister Vittoria, had died giving birth to Giovani eight years before, they had sought to control their rebellious niece, using every opportunity to enforce order on her. But like her mother before her, Lucrezia had resisted their persistent meddling in her life. Her aunts had been stubborn in their determination to succeed with Lucrezia, where they had failed miserably with Vittoria, who had humiliated them by laughing in their faces when they had tried to prevent her from marrying Abramo. He had expected them to lose interest over the years, but the sisters had instead held on tight, refusing to let Lucrezia out of their grip, keeping track of her movements, overriding the governance of the housekeeper in Abramo's absence.

Lucrezia had refused to be controlled, ignoring her aunts when they called over to the house to have another go at her over her refusal to entertain the tenor from Bologna.

"I refused to discuss the matter any further, Papa, until you returned from Chicago. Fiorella is really furious with me, and Rosa won't speak to me. She refuses to even look at me. They are all about my brothers. Why can't they just leave me alone?"

Abramo had never been forceful in this regard. Lucrezia had designs on her own future, which did not include being married off to a man she maintained would rule her with his fist. Abramo missed his wife Vittoria so much. She would have known how to deal with her overbearing sisters, having spent her own life resisting what was expected of her. Standing against tradition. Against control.

Vittoria had been regarded as a rebel within her own family. Refusing to accept that a woman's primary role in society was to procreate, she would not be subjected to the authority of a husband. She abhorred the idea that women attained true fruition only through motherhood, defying the notion that women were possessions, mere chattels, owned by their men. Vittoria had overtly involved herself in situations where it was obvious she was not welcome. Inviting herself to take part in discussions considered to be outside the realm of a woman's brain. She had aggravated men and annoyed women.

Just like her daughter Lucrezia had been doing ever since she was old enough to question.

Abramo, a third-generation Italian-American, had been born and raised in the States, to parents who had never themselves set foot in Italy. Vittoria had been intrigued by his creative flamboyance when introduced to him at a concert in Naples. Having spent time in

America herself, she wanted to hear all about Chicago. All about him.

Speaking a mixture of poor Italian and English, the couple communicated well enough. Abramo told her how he had left Chicago to further his architectural studies under a renowned Neapolitan master. He had not been convinced that she understood what he was saying, but she appeared to hang on his every word. He told her about his passion for Italian fourteenth and fifteenth-century buildings. Listening attentively, without interrupting him, she said very little. He was in love. Deciding to base himself in Naples with Vittoria had taken little consideration.

She had agreed to marry her handsome Abramo, on the condition that societal expectations would not be respectfully followed within the confines of their marriage. She had quite rightly observed that he was far less interested in maintaining societal male and female roles than he was in avoiding conflict with headstrong traditional Italian women.

Over the years, Vittoria's English had improved well enough for her to communicate in English. Inside of their house Abramo spoke only in English, his first language. Whether Vittoria replied in English or not, he felt was up to her, his one insistence being that he would continue to speak English when they had children.

As his genius was recognised, Abramo was commissioned for projects that he had only dreamt of back in America. Gaining first-hand experience working with the experts, restoring ancient Renaissance buildings in Rome, Abramo Romano became a master in his own right.

His wife had given birth to Roberto, their first son, prematurely, a year after they married while he was working in Florence. The birth had been difficult for Vittoria, who took some time to recover. Roberto, a docile pleasant child, rarely demanded attention, allowing his mother to recover her strength without duress.

Their daughter Lucrezia arrived two years later, the direct opposite of her brother before her. She came into the world screaming, louder than the midwife had ever heard a new-born scream. She proved to be a handful, refusing to sleep, difficult to wake, wanting to be held at every waking moment. Demanding attention. Abramo, who had paced the hallway awaiting the delivery of his second-born, had bonded with his daughter from the very moment he'd laid eyes on her. Rising during the night to bring Lucrezia to her mother, he never complained. But the birth had weakened Vittoria. They were warned to avoid having more children.

Lucrezia had been eight years old when Abramo was offered the opportunity to travel back to Chicago, to design and oversee the construction of an ostentatious Renaissance-style hotel. He had immediately accepted, excited by the scale of the project which had been commissioned by wealthy Italian Americans who were more than willing to pay the price for an Abramo Romano creation. Being away from his family for weeks at a time was a price he was willing to pay.

Vittoria loved being a mother. She was devoted to her family, watching her children develop their own personalities, careful not to have their heads filled with the stereotyping of women.

Vittoria became pregnant again as Roberto turned eleven. The couple had dismissed the obstetrician's warning. Their longing for each other had intensified beyond any rational thought on Abramo's homecoming. Lucrezia was nine years old when Giovanni arrived. Abramo hired a wet nurse from the locality, leaving Vittoria to recover after the birth, while her sisters Rosa and Fiorella took over the running of the household.

Three weeks after Giovanni's birth, Abramo made the decision to return to Chicago, satisfied that Vittoria had all the help she needed. His project had been entering a critical stage.

The day he received the telegram from Naples was the worst day of his life. Vittoria's heart had given up. She had died suddenly on Christmas Day at the age of thirty. Giovani was two months old. It was two weeks before he could get back to Naples, by which time Vittoria had been laid to rest in the graveyard at Poggioreale.

Abramo's world collapsed.

Coming home to face his life without his beloved Vittoria had been the most painful time in his life. Surreal. Holding the infant boy, Giovanni, had done little to ease him out of his misery. The feeling he got when he held the baby was one of regret. Overcome with intense pain, he was incensed with grief. The shock of losing Vittoria had sent him into a pitiful state, distancing him from what was going on around him. Seeing his ten-year-old daughter Lucrezia in such a state of grief finally shook him from his torment. He blamed himself for abandoning his family.

Having idolised her mama, Lucrezia was inconsolable. Refusing food, she became sullen and disengaged, vowing that as long as she lived she would never celebrate Christmas again. She had become older than her years. She insisted on wearing her deceased mother's flowing gowns in gold and silver lamé as she slept, a white feather boa draped around her neck, laden with as many of her mother's colourful beads as could fit. Her father feared she would choke. Abramo was demented, watching his daughter fade before his eyes, along with the light that had shone around her wherever she went. He feared for the child who reminded him so much of his darling Vittoria. Giovani was thriving, largely undemanding, fed by the wet nurse. Twelve-year old Roberto, silently grieving for his beloved mama, had become surly and distant.

The unspoken expectation within Vittoria's family, was that Fiorella, the younger of the sisters, as yet unmarried, would marry Abramo. Quietly and without fuss. Taking over Vittoria's duties, in every sense, allowing Abramo to travel back overseas without restriction, back to overseeing the projects which had been yielding more than enough money to secure a great future for his family.

But the spirit of Vittoria had been much too close for Abramo to consider lying with another woman. He could never replace his wife, regardless of the urges which consumed him during the curse of darkness. Tempting him. Making him turn the framed photo of Vittoria down on its face, disowning her for a time. It had not been without shame. Demented at times by images of likeable creatures on whom he lusted during the dark moody hours. Harlots and plump fleshy whores, who paraded their goods openly. Accepting. Afterwards retreating under the blanket. Relieved. Chastising himself for succumbing to the seduction of lewd imagery. His sister-in-law Fiorella had never appealed to his senses.

The opportunity to halt any impending notions, before it was too late not to offend and create conflict, came just a week after Fiorella had taken over the running of the household, instilling in the children from the start the very traditions which her late sister had refused to condone, negating the feminist ideations which she had been so supportive of. Ideations which were frowned upon in many households within their own community, outside of some brave academics, writers and free spirits.

Fiorella had been forced to abandon any hope for her future as Abramo's wife after she was caught beating Lucrezia for refusing to clear away her brother's dishes from the dinner table, while Roberto sat watching her … expectant.

Fiorella had shouted in Neapolitan dialect, insisting that her niece reply only in their local tongue. "*English is not to be spoken under this roof!"* she roared. She was not only in defiance of her dead sister's wishes, she was going against Abramo's clear instructions. Dialect had rarely, if ever, been spoken in his household.

Vittoria had been filled with pride to be Italian, all the while supporting her husband in his quest to rear the children bilingually.

Abramo physically pushed his sister-in-law out the front door when he saw the red-raw finger-marks on Lucrezia's face,

Fiorella had fallen to her knees in the lemon grove. Incensed that she had set out purposely to undermine Abramo's position as head of the household but had taken a step too far. Abramo was tired of Vittoria's sisters.

It was not a wife he needed, he decided, but a housekeeper – someone from outside of the family who would follow his direction without question. An educated woman, who would encourage the children to speak English, enabling them to connect as adults with the wider world. His wife's older sister, Rosa, could take over, but only until a suitable woman could be hired.

Realising how tenuous the situation had become between Abramo and her family, Rosa had tentatively agreed to step in, doting on her two nephews, Roberto and the baby Giovanni, who clearly adored her in return. She avoided conflict with Lucrezia, being of the mind that the girl would never settle as long as her father allowed himself to be taken in by her childish impudence. Rosa was covertly opposed to Abramo's interference in his daughter's upbringing, a role she felt strongly should be left to women. But she held her tongue. Her family would not be losing hold of her niece, even if Fiorella had been cast aside like an old shoe, while Abramo continued to give in to the theatrical protestations of his favourite child. A spoilt brat.

Three months after his wife's death, having almost succumbed to Rosa's insistence that she would raise five-month-old Giovanni at home with her own children, Abramo travelled thirty miles to meet with Madalina, a childless woman of forty who had returned from teaching in England after her husband had run off, leaving her destitute. Abramo had heard of her through a teacher he knew, who had come across her in Sorrento. Madalina spoke fluent English. She certainly wasn't shy in voicing her eagerness to move away from her own village. Abramo was suitably impressed and hired her. Expressing her willingness to move to Naples, to take up her duties as live-in housekeeper in the Romano household, she pledged her commitment to the family, leaving Abramo free to travel back to Chicago to his work.

Eleven-year-old Lucrezia had been relieved to be finally free from the hard-handed ways of her aunt. She loved being under the care of the gentle housekeeper Madalina, who became skilled at handling the spirited girl.

Surrounded by the arts, Lucrezia attended concerts in the theatres around her home, often accompanied by

Madalina, who proved to be popular amongst her friends. Visiting galleries around Naples delighted the young girl, filling her with interest in expressing herself through art.

Strolling around museums in Rome with her father on his return from abroad excited Lucrezia, allowing her spend time with the one member of her family who encouraged her love of the arts.

Marvelling at the craftsmanship of the baroque master Bernini, the sheer enormity of his marble sculptures around the city never failed to impress her. Playing games. Rushing ahead of her father, running to the next street corner, thrilled to find another miniature Madonna, high up on the walls above their heads. "*Madonnelle stradarole!*" she would cry, pointing to the piece of art.

While Lucrezia marvelled at the work of the old Italian painters, soaking up much of what was on offer in the cultural hubs, she became intrigued with more modern trends – the Art Nouveau style, which she had been hearing so much about of late. Abramo, eager to support his daughter's emerging talent, hired a private tutor for her in Naples when she was fourteen.

Chapter 4

Get Her Out

1926

Having studied under the tutor, a former master of the avant-garde movement in Rome, for four years, Lucrezia was hungry for more. When he mentioned to her father that a few years in the School of Art in London would be all that he could wish for eighteen-year-old Lucrezia, Abramo agreed, recalling the most recent disruption in the house not so long before. The tutor had not alone been thinking of Lucrezia's development in the arts – he was offering her a way out of Naples.

Her growing tendency to speak out against Mussolini's government had not gone unnoticed amongst those who supported fascism. Lucrezia had boldly refused to conform, voicing her strong disapproval of the fascists. The time had come to get her out of Italy. Fast.

Abramo had had enough. His social standing could only protect his daughter for so long, now that she was an adult. Given the rumblings of discontent towards those who opposed Mussolini, he could do little to protect his daughter while engaged in a work project thousands of miles away.

Encouraged by his aunts, Giovanni loved to attend his after-school activities in uniform, running home afterwards to Madalina, who had become attached to the boy.

Having fully embraced fascism, in keeping with the growing trend towards order and compliance, Roberto had been happy to be conscripted into the Italian army when the time came, becoming a staunch advocate of the totalitarian government. By the age of twenty he had become an organiser of regular military-style choreographed marches, promoting the indoctrination of youth, exalting duty and physical exercise above intellectual abilities.

Lucrezia held no such views. She strongly opposed Mussolini and all he stood for, refusing to accept that the primary aim of all young women was to provide a clean fascist population for the future, allowing men to do what was natural to them: enlist and fight.

Lucrezia held on to the view that life was for living one's own life. For being true to oneself, and not up for sale to the highest bidder, or indeed any bidder, spending a lifetime organising domestic arrangements, and in time preparing one's own daughters in line with what was expected of them. Motherhood.

Roberto had forewarned his father that Lucrezia's name had been mentioned more than once amongst members of his party, who sought to out traitors and oppressors of the regime.

Lucrezia would, he warned, come to the attention of those who would not hesitate in chastising her. The manifesto coming from their leader was intent on allowing Italians little control over their own lives as individuals. And it was fast being enforced.

The Black Shirts, armed ex-soldiers, known for the cruel punishments they inflicted on those whom they believed to be critical of their leader, were not short on punishing those who opposed the state.

Roberto had banged his two fists on the dining table, angrily shouting that his sister had become nothing less than an embarrassment to the family. A disgrace. As tensions were rising in the house, Abramo was becoming more fearful for his daughter, who refused to be intimidated by threats coming from the regime.

Hearing of people who had been tied to trees, with pints of castor oil forced down their throats, had horrified Abramo. Others he'd heard had been forced to swallow live toads. Allowing Lucrezia to remain in Italy as an unprotected female who was not fearful in vocalising her objection to fascist rule, was to throw her to the wolves. She would, as Roberto insisted, be held in contempt. A traitor.

Abramo had tried scolding his daughter, but to no avail. She had laughed and sneered, poking fun at those who held the view that a woman's primary role in society was to bear children. And lots of them.

Abramo couldn't trust that members of her own

family would be opposed to having her silenced if she continued to bad-mouth the regime which they supported. Least of all Roberto, who had become increasingly infuriated by his sister's refusal to keep her mouth shut, and knew that it could only be a matter of time before Lucrezia would be formally reported, particularly once word had reached him that secret police were being formed to infiltrate communities.

Mussolini had declared himself Dictator of Italy. He talked about bringing back the death penalty for serious offenders. All too much to consider for Abramo. With the help of the Neapolitan tutor, who had connections in England, Abramo arranged for his daughter to spend the following two years studying modern art in London.

Trusting that London would offer her the space to mature, he was of the belief that time and travel would settle her, along with freeing himself from the burden of having to constantly worry about her. Not being around to protect his adored girl, he had seized the opportunity, insisting to all that he was sending his daughter abroad to advance her studies, before returning her to her mother country to fulfil her womanly duties.

Lucrezia herself was likely to resist should she become aware of her father's main aim in removing her from Italy.

Fiorella and Rosa, themselves supporters of the regime, accepted Abramo's decision that Lucrezia should go to London to advance her artistic endeavours, affording her the opportunity to mature. In the meantime, they would be on the lookout for a suitable husband for her. Someone who would be well equipped to manage the girl. Finally.

Lucrezia had been more than willing to leave Naples when the time came, relieved to be distanced from the constant scrutiny of her mother's sisters.

Arriving amongst the hustle and bustle of the West End, she immersed herself in the vibrancy of the city. Eager to become part of the bohemian world which awaited her, she engrossed herself in her studies.

She was finally free to study the work of the avant-garde leaders, excited to learn more about the radical and unorthodox artists who made bold social statements through their work, such as French artist Gustav Courbet. Lucrezia concentrated on portraiture, figurative painting. She was relieved to have escaped from the art scene in Italy where artists were being encouraged to focus on the work of the old Renaissance painters, steering them away from modern trends. Lucrezia wanted above all to sketch and paint what she could see. Fascinated also with the drawings of French artist Degas, Lucrezia immersed herself in sketching scenes of contemporary life, capturing fleeting moments in the lives of real people.

Falling for the fair-skinned Irish girl with the wide smile and the bright blue eyes had been unexpected. Lucrezia Romano would never want another. And she knew it instantly.

She had not been uncomfortable with her instant attraction towards the girl. Her first encounter with the female pleasures of another woman had occurred while posing in a studio in Naples. She had spent a leisurely afternoon lying on a worn leather sofa, posing with the artist's muse, a deer hide underneath her, irritating her skin. The girls had flirtatiously giggled their way through the sitting, while the deep-breathing artist captured the fluency of their sensuous energy on his canvas.

Chapter 5

London Town

1926

During their first year together, secure in their love, Lucrezia and Connie sought no more than to enjoy their lives in the bustling city. The post-war years had brought a renewed sense of excitement around West London, as people moved around, openly indulging in life free from the lingering distrust and suspicion of earlier years.

Lucrezia diligently attended her classes in the college, excited to expand her knowledge. Often walking for an hour across the city in the evening, to meet with Connie, to accompany her over to her shift on Shaftsbury Avenue, eagerly telling her all that had excited her about her day. Outside of their commitments, the couple enjoyed what the West End of London had to offer.

Connie's ears were quick to pick up the Irish accents, all the while cautious in case someone would recognise her, and carry news of her love-interest back to Ballygore, a scandal she knew would destroy her mother.

Lucrezia dismissed her fears, "*Puh*, Connie, if that old photograph of you wearing the flat black cap is anything to go by, no-one will recognise you anymore. So stop worrying."

All the same, Connie urged Lucrezia to be less demonstrative towards her when out in public. Lucrezia would laugh at her lover, dancing around her, teasing her, until Connie relaxed, leaving her guard down enough to enjoy herself.

The couple lost themselves in the busy streets in the thriving West End of London. Trucks being loaded and offloaded. Smells wafting up and down the street from crowded restaurants. Workmen hammering, mischievously cat-whistling at the ladies as they passed. London, by night, lit up in all its glory, glitz and colour, becoming busier as the night unfolded. The sounds of jazz and blues coming from every other nightclub, enticing the girls to enter the smoky dimly lit bars, allowing the rhythm of the blues to flow through them, without a care for the world outside, where revellers were rushing about, whistling, calling to each other, the sweet aromas of their cigars lingering behind them on the street.

Fur stoles on ladies who showed their ankles through the sheerest of silk stockings. Modern hair styles sculpted into shape at the nape of their necks, having left the London fashions of past years behind. Pleated dresses with waists that dropped below the hips of women who wore them well. Clean-shaven men in their peaked caps and heavy suits by day, switching to lighter suits and homburg hats by night, in preparation for the London night scene. London was awash with life and laughter. And Lucrezia and Connie fitted right in.

The couple made no demands on each other that first year as they got to know each other, no declarations or plans for the future, fulfilled by the passion of their togetherness. There was no need for the testing of feelings, neither one was affected by insecurities. They loved each other. Each finding in the other that which was missing in themselves, they had found completion, dismissing any thoughts that might distract them from their harmony.

Lucrezia, keeping in mind the need to satisfy the curiosity of her landlady, lied to cover herself for the many nights she lay with Connie, before she realised that as long as the landlady had her money on time, she couldn't care less where the art student from Italy laid her head.

The girls became an integral part of a wild colourful set in West London.

Lucrezia introduced Connie to a world to which she had never been exposed. A world of pleasures. Advising Connie to trust her space, to use her senses, to close her eyes and feel the music of the Italian greats. Vivaldi. Puccini. To find her soul and, when she did, to recognise it, and not deny it. To value who she was. To be receptive to the pleasure of taste. To breathe in the sweet aroma of ripe tomatoes and salami on fresh bread which they bought from the Italian bakery on Regent Street. The joy in eating crusty bread dripping with hot oil infused with garlic.

"Oh, breathe it, Connie, and stay with the aroma. Don't just touch it, feel it! Sense it. Close your eyes. Turn off the sound in your ears. Now open your eyes and look!"

Connie wasn't tuned into much of what Lucrezia was showing her, but all the while was smiling inside, enjoying the dramatic displays over a crust of bread. She would never allow Lucrezia know that much of what was being said was going over her head. Connie never interrupted nor scolded her love – she adored her. And that was enough.

Lucrezia had a liking for strong coffee taken without milk served in tiny cups, with just the perfect amount of sugar. A new world for Connie, who had never tasted coffee, being used to cups of strong tea, which reminded her too much of home.

She, in turn, guided Lucrezia around the London that she had come to know and love. Introducing her to people she knew – to artists and thespians, partygoers with free spirits and light hearts. To fearless people, who involved themselves in shady dealings, people with smiling faces that could turn. People who were not to be crossed.

The couple felt secure within the madness of it all, protected by those who had grown to respect the no-nonsense Irishwoman and her feisty Italian girlfriend.

Towards the end of their second year together, conversation between the two had become more meaningful. Both of the mind that any thoughts of being separated were to be laughed at. London within its confines had given them the most wonderful sense of freedom over the past two years.

They liked to mingle with the masquerading set, hidden behind powder and paint, feathers and fur, tuxedos, part of the flourishing London homosexual scene. It was easy to believe that they had no worries. Attending parties, drag balls, excitedly travelling at short notice to attend covert events, driven by the need for secrecy. Often raided by police. Those unlucky enough to be arrested faced charges of indecency, accused of corrupting public morals.

Abramo had visited London on one occasion, the trip being well planned in advance, allowing Lucrezia time to make herself available at the boarding house. Lucrezia's father had returned to Naples, openly satisfied that his daughter's artistic gains were progressing. Impressed by her growing maturity, her commitment to her course, he urged her to write letters home more often. She agreed, showing not a hint of the defiance inside her.

But London was beginning to feel smaller and overfamiliar, it had begun to close in on Connie and Lucrezia. When a distant cousin of Lucrezia's turned up outside the art college on Lots Road unannounced, they realised that their world was nowhere as safe as they had imagined it to be. It was time to work harder and plan.

Lucrezia was excelling in college, painting miniature portraits, embracing the Art Deco style which had been spear-headed in Paris some years before. Learning from the work of Tamara de Lempicka, a Polish bohemian, who, with her clean linear depictions brought colourful glamour to life, Lucrezia began showing her work through contacts in the West End. She experimented with charcoal, drawing minimalist female nude figures, using glass and tile as a medium, fixed to black wooden templates by Connie. Her miniature portraits became much sought after.

Nearing the end of her studies at the college, commissions for her work were fast coming in. Securing an outlet for her work to be sold in a prestigious department store on the High Street had been a huge bonus. One which she chose not to expand on with her family back in Naples. By the end of her two years in the school of art, Lucrezia's mini-portraits were hanging in the homes of many of the rich and famous in London.

Avoiding any thoughts of her promise to return home, dragging one month into the next, preying on her father's weakness as well as his bank account, Lucrezia saved her money. Unsettled by her father's burdening suggestion that she leave London to progress her studies in Paris, she sensed that her father was luring her back, bringing her closer to home.

She avoided committing herself, acknowledging her promise to return, but not just yet, insisting that she wished to travel to New York with a female companion, having been invited to showcase her latest work in a private gallery. Six months, she insisted. Just six months. After which she falsely assured her father that she would return to Naples. For good.

Letters from her mother back in Ireland gave Connie reason to suspect that she was expected to be making plans to return home to Ballygore. According to her mother, she no longer opened up during the day. She said it had all become too much for her. She was fine with the few regulars coming in the evenings, now that the shoe factory was up and running again. The twins, she had written, would soon be seventeen, and were both leaving for Canada.

It had been over four years since Connie had left Ballygore, and any thoughts she may have had about returning to Ireland had long since passed. And soon she would be free from the burden of sending money home. It would be her brothers' turn to send their dollars home once they got set up in Canada, leaving Connie guilt-free to secure a life for herself and Lucrezia.

Being accepted living with her Italian lover in the small town of Ballygore could never be an option. And she would never subject Lucrezia to being treated like an outcast. Up to now, life in London had been trouble-free, even if their relationship was unacceptable in society.

Hearing that Abramo had purchased Lucrezia's passage from Liverpool to New York had been the news they were waiting for. There would be no turning back. Abramo had agreed to fund Lucrezia's travel to New York, on the understanding that she would return directly from New York to Naples, no later than in six months' time. After which time, he insisted, there would be no more pandering to his daughter's demands.

Connie and Lucrezia sailed from Liverpool bound for New York City in April 1929, having worked hard, saving every shilling, selling what paintings they could, using whatever money they could syphon off from Lucrezia's allowance. Lucrezia had left the boarding house, sneaking into the room at night with Connie, saving the money her father had sent to cover her expenses.

No longer sending money home to Ireland now that the twins were earning, Connie used every resource she could think of to make extra money to fund her passage. Normally honest to a fault, it wasn't in her nature to involve herself in crooked dealings. Desperate times. Through her contacts, she made fast money. Holding packages. Passing them on. Collecting bulky envelopes. Risky business. No questions asked.

Relentless in forging ahead with their plan, they were leaving London for good. Neither had any intention of returning back across the Atlantic once their feet touched American soil.

The timing was perfect for them to explore the opportunities waiting for them. Accommodation on

Broadway was plentiful, now that many of the occupants were leaving for Hollywood, to work on the new motion movies with sound.

The women had a soulful connection that neither felt the need to explain. They were determined to break away from the clutches of their past. Writing a short letter to Ballygore, Connie advised her mother that a move to New York for six months was forthcoming, as part of her job. No need to explain anymore for now, she thought. She posted a small parcel home to Mill Road before leaving on the steamer bound for America.

Chapter 6

New York

1926

New York excited both women. A place far enough away from London where they would not be looking over their shoulders. Travelling on the subway to the last stop at 42nd Street, they held hands as they walked together through Times Square, their eyes gazing upwards, marvelling at the Times Tower looming towards the sky like a giant skeleton. Standing at the junction of Broadway and Seventh Avenue, they had arrived.

Connie secured a job as stage attendant in a theatre two blocks down from the apartment which they rented on Broadway. Lucrezia, giddy with delight, took a job washing dishes in the Italian restaurant underneath, until she changed her mind a week later. Too hot in the kitchen. Caged. She couldn't bear to be so confined. She would concentrate instead on selling her glamour portraits.

Taking their place amongst the thespian community,

the couple enjoyed the experience of living amongst the theatrical set. Taking the bus to Greenwich village – frequenting places without fear – attending parties in Harlem in the early hours, full to the neck of bathtub gin, which was easily available in defiance of prohibition, they couldn't have been happier. Attending stage productions where beautiful men made even more beautiful women. Where straight patrons eager to experience the lively culture of the flamboyant, dressed accordingly. Under cover. Others losing themselves without inhibition, being who they were, amidst those who didn't care.

Enjoying the best of the musicals on Broadway, where last-minute empty seats would be made available for theatre staff to fill at minimum cost, they enjoyed life to the full. Connie with her long confident stride, arm bent at the elbow, walking on the outside of the pavement, accommodating the slender arm of her lover, as they moved through the busy streets of New York city.

Lucrezia painted her glamour miniatures from early morning, prompted by the New York street fashion, attaching her work to finely sanded wooden templates, before delivering them to their new homes. Her flair for creating the most striking pieces, on six-by-four-inch frames, was evident. Her drawings sold as fast as she could sketch them.

Within two months of her moving to New York, Lucrezia was mentioned in a top glamour magazine, allowing her to charge more for her individual pieces. Connie and Lucrezia had more than enough to fund their lifestyle. The couple were without restraint. Each was stylish to a fault as the months passed, spending their money as quickly as they earned it. Connie in her wine-coloured silk pants suit, one of three she ordered in the Chinese area of the city. Multicoloured silk cravats. White cotton shirts. Always white. Waistcoats made from silk jacquard, designed and hand-stitched by the best that New York's Indian tailors had to offer. Her bright blonde hair short and sculpted. Her fair Irish skin prone to blushing. Her blue eyes dancing with the happiness she felt in her heart.

Lucrezia, a vision of colour in her long flowing kaftans, fur stoles, luxurious fabrics, sparkling accessories, embraced the New York way of life. Her hair worn loosely, falling down her back. Her dark eyes opening wide with delight at the simplest of things, her skin bronzed by the American sunshine. The couple cut a dash wherever they went.

Connie and Lucrezia had avoided deeper conversations about the practicalities, apart from believing that they would always be together. The fact that Lucrezia was expected back in Italy in two months' time went over their heads.

Connie felt far removed from Ballygore. The letters home had stopped. The couple spend every free moment exploring the city, languishing in the company of the other. Visiting the Hamptons and the Jersey shore, they took advantage of their free time to explore. Time was passing.

Connie suggested taking a week off to visit Cape Cod, to give them a much-needed break away from the stagnant heat of the city. She had heard so much about the Cape since arriving in New York – shaped like a bent arm with a clenched fist and miles and miles of sand on both its sides. It sounded heavenly. The trip would take them from New York up to Provincetown where they booked into a hotel for the duration of their stay.

Eager to find out as much as they could about the area, they stayed for six nights, meeting people who had settled there amongst the farmers and fishermen, setting up businesses, selling their artefacts, proud to be part of the growing artisan colony. Hand in hand, arm in arm, the lovers strolled the streets, charmed by the atmosphere. The sense of freedom, acceptance, amongst people who didn't judge. An eclectic mix of people. Romantics, writers, poets, dramatists, who savoured the sea-scented weather, along with the natural beauty of the place. And journalists who spread the word.

It was the end of July – the streets were filled with people, many who like themselves wanted no more than to taste the life on offer at the tip of Cape Cod.

They met a couple who were not ashamed to admit that they had long since cut all ties with their families, choosing instead to live in their white-painted wooden house, surrounded by others who wanted the same thing. Freedom. To be themselves. And accepted as such.

The atmosphere in Provincetown had drawn them in. Lucrezia and Connie walked around, smiling. A place where the sun shone most days from May to October. Where people, mostly from Boston and New York, spend their vacations, along with those who had come from farther away wanting to be part of the growing community they had heard so much about.

The couple heard stories about people being spat at on the streets of their home towns, stories of those who were beaten for daring to be who they were. Not knowing how to be anyone else.

Locals in Provincetown appeared to extend no such prejudice, living alongside the newcomers, appreciative of those who brought life and gaiety to their town, making the place come alive, bringing tourists who had money to spend, giving fishermen and farmers a market for their produce. Provincetown had become a place where homosexual couples could live openly without fear of reprisal.

It was without question where they would settle.

On their return to New York, they would plan for their future together in Provincetown. And this time Lucrezia would not be so foolish as to disclose her address to her family. They would take their leave from the lives they were expected to live and live their own lives.

Connie would have no difficulty in finding employment, there would always be tourists on the Cape. Testing ideas, the couple talked excitedly about their future. They would rent a shop on Commercial Street, just like the one they had passed with the 'For Rent' sign outside. The shop would be perfect for them. Connie would open her tea room at the front Lucrezia would work in a studio at the back, showcasing her work on the walls of the shop. They would hang a piece of driftwood above the front door. They would recognise the piece when it came to them. And it would. They wouldn't need much. They could get lost and live their lives. Both agreed. Nothing would keep them apart. They were full of hope and excitement returning to the city.

Connie sent a picture postcard home to Ballygore, on her return to New York. Whatever about the growing sense of guilt, which she chose to dismiss, she would let her mother know of her plan to live permanently in America. But all in good time. In the meantime, she busied herself organising the stage sets for the forthcoming productions, while Lucrezia concentrated on her painting and taking orders for her work.

Lucrezia, who had never succumbed to order, knew that her refusal to return to Naples would be seen as undermining her family's name – an insult to her father who had always stood by her. She chose not to entertain the anger she knew would be building up amongst her family back in Naples.

If the telegrams she was receiving were to be believed, it was not only her aunts Fiorella and Rosa who were at boiling point, but her brother Roberto was becoming vocal in insisting that she return home. Challenging his father's authority, he seemed intent on taking control of the loose rein that Abramo used when it came to his daughter. Lucrezia ignored Roberto's rumbling of dissatisfaction with her. But they needed to move fast. And disappear back to Provincetown.

Chapter 7

Crash

1929

By September, Connie and Lucrezia had finalised their plans to move to Provincetown, far beyond the reach of Lucrezia's family in Naples. Connie dismissed any feeling of guilt that crept in on her as soon as her guard was down. They would move to the Cape in the spring.

By October, news of weakening stock markets had brought the economy to its knees. The economy had collapsed.

Crash!

News of the Wall Street Crash spread, leaving people in shock, wondering what had hit them. People rushed to the banks to get their money back. Those who had borrowed heavily to fund stocks and shares were left with nothing.

Jobs in the city became harder to hold as money became scarce. The frenzy on the streets was palpable.

Broadway was no longer the centre of a bustling night life, as people's spending power was decimated. The owners of the apartment that the girls were renting rushed ahead with a plan to sell up, before the value of their property declined further. Connie and Lucrezia had no choice but to resort to staying in the dressing rooms of the theatre where she worked.

Lucrezia said nothing to Connie at first, having received a telegram from Naples ordering her to return home immediately. Sent not by her father, whose work in Chicago had been suspended as a result of the Crash, but by Roberto, who was now issuing demands. Threats. For the first time Lucrezia felt fear. Being used to her father's gentler way, her brother's authoritarian tone was jumping at her from the page. Threatening to bring her back to Naples by force if necessary. Her ticket had been purchased.

Lucrezia, No more money. You are to return to Naples on October 14th. Refuse and I will come for you myself. Your ticket will be waiting for you at the ship's office by the docks. Details to follow. Reply immediately or you will be most sorry. No more excuses!

Your brother, Roberto Romano

Lucrezia had hidden the telegram from Connie, not wanting to upset her.

As the economy continued to crumble, Connie struggled to hold on to her job at the theatre, finding herself for the first time in years facing unemployment. The long-running productions on Broadway had fallen drastically, as Hollywood continued to absorb many of the producers and stage actors. Broadway productions had become a casualty of the times. It was no longer the thriving district of the years before.

The girls would soon be homeless, a predicament far too dismal for either to consider. Lucrezia finally told a disheartened Connie that she had been ordered home, producing the latest telegram from Roberto.

Connie, ever-practical, pondered the reality of their situation. The cash they had tucked away was in no way enough for them to leave New York and set up elsewhere. And if they remained, they would be out on the streets before long. Destitute. The situation was dire. At least if Lucrezia was back in Naples she would be looked after by her family. Connie deliberated before convincing her lover to return to Italy. For the time being.

"You must go, Lucrezia. At least you'll have a roof over your head and food to eat. We can't remain here in New York with nothing. We'll figure out something after all this calms down. And it will. But for now we need to be practical."

"Connie, I knew all along that it was only a matter of time before Roberto took control. I won't be treated like a possession. I'll go back for now if you insist. But I'll be back – I'll find a way, you know I will. But surely there is something we can do? We could still go to Provincetown? No?"

"Lucrezia, we can forget about Provincetown for now. There are no tourists there. No market. I heard that the stored fish has been thrown back into the sea – there's no one there to buy it. We have to be realistic."

Connie, practical to the core, listened to the cries from her lover, comforting her, reassuring her that returning to Naples would be in her best interest for now. There was nothing in New York for them. And there was no way of knowing what would face them back in London were they to return together. But it would not be forever.

Putting her own vulnerability aside, Connie decided their fate. Soon they would be out on the streets and penniless. Refusing to contemplate any measure of misery for her Lucrezia, there was no other way out this time.

Connie encouraged Lucrezia to reply to the telegram, agreeing to return to Naples. Dying inside, pretending to be strong and capable, she would figure something out for herself, as long as Lucrezia was safe. Remaining outwardly strong wasn't difficult for Connie, who'd had many years of practice.

Inside, she was sinking.

Then she heard that London's West End theatres were anxious to arrange the return of expensive sets and extravagant costumes back to Liverpool by steamship – the risk of losing the merchandise was too great now that Broadway was no longer a stronghold. She volunteered immediately to organise and oversee the safe passage of the merchandise, in return for the price of her passage on the steamship.

Connie and Lucrezia were to be parted.

Between the tears and the swearing of their commitment to each other, the contentment they had experienced over their three years together was fast eroding.

They were engulfed in loss.

Lucrezia proclaimed that she could not survive a life without Connie in it. Connie tried with all her might to remain firm. In control. The decision had been made. Until they could find a way to be together again, they had no other option for now. Chastising herself when she felt less than strong, knowing that Lucrezia was just one step away from refusing to comply with the order from Naples, Connie remained steadfast in her determination.

Lucrezia expressed her love, using words that Connie loved to hear but was unable to express in return. "Wherever we are, my love, life cannot separate us. We may be separated physically, but close your eyes and think of me and I will be forever there in your heart. Ours is not a love that needs to be stoked. Our love is beyond that. We will find a way."

Connie had wiped the tears from Lucrezia's eyes, unable to find the words to respond. She kissed her lover, uttering the only words she could muster, her eyes a watery red, her voice slow and measured. "You are my very soul, Lucrezia Elena Romano. For the rest of my life my heart will beat only for you."

It would take at least three weeks for Connie to gain access to the merchandise which had to be prepared for shipping and delivered to the dock. Connie would accompany the lot back to Liverpool.

Fearful, anxious that nothing would go wrong, she engrossed herself in the job at hand, pacing the streets of Broadway, searching for the right people, demented at times, issuing idle threats on deaf ears, before finally taking hold of the precious cargo.

They had four days left to languish in their pain, before Lucrezia was due to collect her paperwork from the ship's office, returning to Naples on the following day.

Connie had little time to reflect on her reality. Given her record, she was hopeful of a job back in Soho at the Strand Palace. She would take whatever they offered her. She would take a bed wherever one was offered. From there she would wait until the economy had settled, after which time they would plan their escape back across the Atlantic, to Provincetown.

Standing on the docks, Connie was traumatised, desperately wanting to put an end to this nightmare, wanting to call Lucrezia back, to tell her how wrong she'd been to insist that she return to Naples. That they'd manage. Somehow. As long as they had each other they'd find a way.

Unable to express the emotion she was feeling inside, beyond the tears that fell unashamedly down her face, Connie remained as she was.

Lucrezia, high above her on the deck, was frantically searching Connie out amongst the crowd. Seeing her. Calling to her, using words that got lost in the noise.

"Cornelia, amore mio! Do not give up! I will keep you with me as long as we are apart!" Too upset to continue, she slid to the floor of the deck.

Passengers were waving frantically to the crowd below – caught up in their own thoughts, calling out to their loved ones, too engrossed in their own lives to take any notice of the broken-hearted Italian down on her knees. Wailing. And the sad-looking Irishwoman, in the green silk suit, holding her trilby in one hand, blowing awkward kisses with the other.

Three weeks later, once Connie had organised the collection and transport of the stage merchandise, she boarded the steamer bound for Liverpool. This time there were no tears. No great shows of emotion extended towards her. Nobody left behind to miss her.

Broken-hearted Connie did as she had always done, immersed herself in the work at hand, refusing to acknowledge the pain.

Chapter 8

Connie Go Home

1929

The letter addressed to Miss Cornelia Stapleton arrived at the Strand Palace at the beginning of December 1929. Connie had secured a job back at the hotel. Aware of a distinct sinking feeling in the pit of her stomach, she had opened it tentatively on seeing the Irish postmark. Reading the letter, she slapped the palm of her left hand against her chest.

Parochial House,
Ballygore,
9th December 1929
Re: Mrs. Layla Stapleton

Dear Cornelia,

My name is Father Jeremiah MacNulty. I'm the new curate

in the parish of Ballygore. I'm here to take over from Father Furlong (God rest his soul).

I am writing to request that you make whatever arrangements necessary to return to Ballygore immediately. Your mother has been admitted to Peamount Sanatorium in County Dublin with tuberculosis (TB). She's not in great shape, according to the medical people. It's expected that she will be there for some time. In fact, it could take a year or two before she'll be strong enough to come home (God willing, of course). Your sister Johanna has been staying in Mary Cullen's, who by all accounts is grateful for the remuneration sent by your brothers from Canada. I believe they're well settled there, so there's no point in bringing them back. The public house has been closed for some time, awaiting your return.

I assume you will comply with your mother's wish for you to return home in the coming weeks. Mrs Cullen is more than willing for young Johanna to remain with her until after the Christmas, giving you time to sort yourself out over there.

Contact me on your return, if there is anything I can do to help. Dr Nolan will have more detail on your mother's condition and will be happy to talk to you on your return. I enclose a scapular of Saint Christopher to grant you a safe trip.

God bless you,

Fr. JJ MacNulty CC

Connie could do nothing but stare blankly at the page in front of her. She had but one thought in her head. She was being dragged back to the place she thought she'd never get away from. Back to where she started.

But, having persuaded Lucrezia to return to her family in Naples, little else mattered.

Refusing to return to the life she had run away from was not in her make-up. Connie's mind went into overdrive. If she ignored the letter, the chances were that fourteen-year-old Johanna could be taken into the care of the State. Or worse still, end up in rags on the street. There was no guarantee that the twins would hold onto their jobs as Canada had been hit badly by the Crash, and Mary Cullen mightn't be too keen on holding on to Johanna if that were the case. Until her mother was well on the mend, there was no option for her, other than return to Ballygore to do her duty.

Dialling the telephone operator from the front desk at the hotel, she asked to be put through to the sanatorium in County Dublin, Ireland.

She was told that her mother had tuberculosis and was in a serious state. Allowed no visitors for fear of contagion, relying on rest and medication to keep her lungs from failing altogether. There was no cure for the disease.

Connie was bereft, wishing that she could talk to her father, whom she knew would expect her to return home. Praying silently. *Daddy, what should I do? I'm returning to a life that I don't want to live.* Knowing what he might have answered was all it took for Connie Stapleton to make up her mind: *"Connie, go home."*

She would return to Ballygore until such time as her mother was well enough to leave the sanatorium. Until Johanna was old enough to look after herself. Writing a letter to Lucrezia, she explained the situation, not allowing herself to admit that the future that she and Lucrezia had talked about was being put on hold. Telling Lucrezia to stay strong, that as soon as her mother was well, she would return to London and get a place for them to be together, until they could organise themselves to head back to America. Back to their shop in Provincetown.

Arriving back in Ballygore two weeks from the day she had received the letter from Father MacNulty, Connie's mood was low. Seeing the Stapleton family name above the door made her eyes water.

Sniffling for a brief moment, she steadied herself before walking down Mill Road towards Mary Cullen's house, to collect Johanna, whom she hadn't seen for five years.

Connie, who was usually one to hold tight to her emotions, couldn't wait to see her sister as she approached the door. To hug her. To tell her she had no worries. That her big sister Connie had come home to look after her. That she would take care of everything.

After an awkward encounter at Cullen's front door,

Connie's heart sank. Barely greeting her older sister, beyond asking what she had for her in her suitcase, Johanna had refused to return home with her, saying she was quite happy to remain with the Cullens.

"I don't know what all the fuss is about. What made you think I'd just up and leave to go home with you? I hardly recognise you anymore, Connie."

Mary Cullen broke the awkwardness by suggesting that Connie sort the place out at home before removing Johanna. "The place above is in a bit of a state I'd say, Connie. From what I hear it may take you a while to sort it out. We've had young Johanna here for some time now. Layla just wasn't able. She was great for the first couple of years after you went, but she seemed to give up after the boys left. And when she got sick with the TB, 'twas the finish of her. People started avoiding her and crossing the road if they saw her standing at the door, afraid to go near her in case they'd pick the dirty thing up."

Connie felt ashamed at what she was hearing. She had been so consumed by organising her life with Lucrezia, it had never dawned on her that her mother might be seriously ill. She had always complained about having one ailment or another. Connie hadn't seen it coming.

"And we couldn't leave Johanna back up there, in case she brought the bloody thing down here – 'tis rampant, you know, so be careful. Why don't you go up and have a look around the place? And we'll keep Her Majesty here over the Christmas 'til you get it sorted. There's no rush at all. The boys have been great to send on the few bob."

Connie turned the key in the front door of her childhood home. It was smaller than she'd remembered. Darker than she'd had imagined. The day she'd left, five years before, the fire had been blazing in the grate, the place as clean as a whistle, smelling of lavender wax polish. Connie hadn't known what to expect. But certainly not this.

What she saw in front of her made her heart sink. She'd had to put her full weight against the heavy swollen door, which once open made her gag. The heavy stench of damp turf, mingled with the acrid smell left behind by whatever tomcats had been roaming about after dark, leaving evidence of their visits behind them.

The glass panels on the back door had been broken, allowing easy access to whatever was small enough to fit through. The smell of pig slurry from the neighbouring back yards sickened her stomach. The snug looked as if it had been used as a bedroom.

Connie's reality was a far cry from what she had left behind her in London. She felt furious with her mother for allowing the place to get into such a state. And where had the ever-helpful Mattie been? How had he not seen to it? The least he could have done was fix the door. And why had he not taken it on himself to contact her in London to warn her, before things got this bad?

The living quarters upstairs were no better. Dirty bedclothes. The sight of a stained chamber pot made her stomach turn. Her old bedroom was much the same as her mother's room. Damp and dreary. Johanna's room was no better. She hadn't helped, that much was obvious. Connie sighed heavily at the daunting task in front of her.

Having seen enough, she went straight to the shed and roughly pulled out her father's old bike. Tears of frustration came to her eyes then, when she saw the dirty oil-stain on the leg of her raw-silk trousers.

She cycled three miles out to Black Post, the cold December wind beating the rain against her. She didn't know what else to do.

Matthew was closing the front gate. He leant forward to offer his cold hand to welcome her back. It had been over five years since she had laid eyes on the man who greeted her with the familiar unassuming smile.

"Connie Stapleton, but you're a sight for sore eyes! Look at you! Fair play to you. Come in, Come in out of the cold. You're drenched to the skin."

The low-sized woman in her wet silk suit, her sculpted blonde hair stuck to her head, looked astonished as she took in her surroundings once inside the gate lodge. Shocked. Everything in its place. Warm and inviting.

"Two bedrooms," he told her. "And a dry toilet at the back. Everything new."

Once she got over the surprise of seeing how he lived, she wished it was to the lodge at Black Post she was returning, and not the cold dirty damp place in town which awaited her.

"Have you been in there yet, Connie? Let me hazard a guess that a brush wasn't taken to the floor since the day you left on the bus. I stopped going in there myself this long time, with the state of the place. Well before the rumours started about Layla having the TB. People stayed away, Connie. And hearing that you were doing so well in London, I didn't want to be upsetting you, knowing well what was in store for you if you were dragged back. But I'd no idea that Layla was as sick as she was."

"She never told me things were as bad as they are in her letters, Mattie. Apart from her hinting some time ago that I come back to Ballygore."

"In your mother's eyes, Connie, it was all going great. She couldn't see it. Layla wanted the money you sent her and, once she had that she was fine, but when the boys left she lost all interest in the place. And in fairness she was never going to keep it right, was she? And young Johanna was nearly living with the Cullens anyway, before they took her on fully. I see her the odd time. And sure, they don't mind as long as the boys keep sending the Canadian dollars for her keep. Once your mother had closed the front door of the pub, I didn't see sight nor sign of her. And I didn't want to be calling in where I didn't feel wanted. Banging at the back door when she had the bolt on, and I looking in the windows, like a criminal. Some of the neighbours were in and out to her in the beginning, but once they knew what she had, and they avoided her like the plague." Mattie looked away. "I feel bad now, Connie, but what could I do? You're welcome to stay here for as long as it takes. You know the gossips will have a field day but the offer is there."

Connie was grateful to Mattie, knowing that the impropriety of her staying in the lodge with a single man would be the talk of the town. She had no intention of drawing that kind of attention on herself.

Expressing her gratitude, bold in the manner in which she looked at him, aware of her impertinence, she asked if there was any chance of a bed in the big house.

"That way there would be no slur on either of us, Mattie. I can sleep on a mattress on the floor. Just until I get the home place sorted out."

"You'll do no such thing, Connie Stapleton, as sleep on any mattress. Wait 'til you see what I've done with the place above. 'Tis all kitted out up there, and you're dead right in your thinking. We won't be under the same roof, so that'll keep them quiet. Though they'll find something to talk about at any rate."

Mattie was eager to show Connie around Black Post Inn so up they went.

Seeing her eyes light up as she walked around there pleased him. The house seemed to have that effect on people.

"Connie, stay here for as long as it takes to clear your head. The fire is set and there's plenty of wood in the barn. I had it rented out, you know, for a time. But you know, when the tenants left, I was as well pleased. 'Tis vacant now this long time. And it suits me fine to keep it that way, until I move in there myself. 'Tis just a house after all. Maybe what it needs is a woman's touch."

Connie cut straight in.

"Mattie, I'd be delighted to take you up on your kind offer. There is something about this place. It feels strangely familiar for some reason. Reminds me of London with the high ceilings. And I'm weary after the travelling. I need to sort out in my head what needs to be done about the pub. Johanna is out with me – she all but slapped the door in my face."

"Don't mind her, Connie. It's her age, and in fairness she hasn't had it easy either. Layla mollycoddling her all these years, and she not allowed to lift a brush. Or make a cup of tea. Layla wouldn't let her go near the kettle, in case she burned herself. Now, I'll bring you back in to get your bag and straight back here. I won't be intruding on you while you're here, and you can leave Johanna where she is until she calms down. You can have your Christmas dinner right here with myself, if it suits? There's a fine goose wandering around out there waiting for the oven."

Connie stayed at Black Post Inn far longer than she intended. She felt at home there. Picturing Lucrezia beside her there was not difficult. Two parts of one. A sense of peace enveloped her as she wandered through the house. Sleeping soundly under its roof, she dreamt of Lucrezia. Connie loved her surroundings. The house drew her in, luring her, calming her. Whatever happened in the future, she sensed she would be together with Lucrezia Romano at Black Post Inn.

She loved it all. The large comfortable front room with decorative coved ceilings. Two brass oil lamps, one at either side, casting a warming glow in the room. The deep windowsills on which she placed jugs of holly. The sash windows, complete with brass fittings. Heavy brocade curtains in wine and cream, complementing the rich wallpaper. The richness of the dark golden-brown teak furniture, tempting her to glide her hand along the large dining table as she passed. The oak doors solid and inviting. An old burgundy Chesterfield sofa taking pride of place in front of the fire. No wonder he had wanted to bring a wife out here, she thought. A place most suitable for dreams and pleasant conversations. Connie hadn't felt such contentment in a long time.

With Mattie's help, Connie had the home place in order before the first week of March. The job had been even bigger than she had anticipated. She had spent over two months at Black Post Inn.

Mattie had kept his word. He respected her privacy enough to leave her alone – apart from Christmas Day when they had dinner together, one at each end of the oblong dining table. Johanna had declined their offer to join them.

Connie had bought him a tie. He gave her a pair of gloves.

"Lord and Lady!" they had joked.

Convincing a reluctant Johanna to move back home with her after Christmas had been trying. She had refused to budge until Connie had wallpapered the front bedroom for her. She wanted new curtains. A new quilt. Clashing with Connie at every opportunity.

"I'd love to know who you think you are, Connie Stapleton, ordering me about. You're my sister, not my mother. So don't think I'll be taking any orders from you. And where were you all along when we needed you here? Mother wouldn't be so sick if you'd been here doing your job, instead of enjoying yourself in England or America or wherever you were. And the get-up of you – I'm ashamed of my life to admit you're my sister."

Connie thought about the life she had given up to come back to this. Johanna was lazy and self-centred. Spoilt by their mother. She was growing up to be quite a madam. Doing her best to ignore the insults, she bit her tongue and said little. But the resentment she had refused to allow set in when she turned her back on London was fast reappearing.

Down on her hands and knees scrubbing the black stone floor, Connie was no stranger to hard work. She aimed to have the doors of the public house open in time for Saint Patrick's Day, once it had been cleaned and painted to her satisfaction. Having spent five years working in London and New York, she wasn't willing to settle for less than she had become accustomed to.

With money borrowed from Mattie, she succeeded in making Stapleton's public house a fine establishment, a decent home for Johanna and herself. She would have to continue to work hard to make a go of it, but she would give it her all. Johanna would come around in time.

She stocked the shelves behind the counter with a small assortment of whiskeys. Jugs of draught porter. A row of syphons brought back to their former glory. Plug tobacco and cigarettes kept in the small varnished drawers on the wall behind the counter, as well as cloves and tins of snuff. Mattie proved to be a dab hand at carpentry, restoring the snug to accommodate those who preferred privacy.

Money might be short around Ballygore, but there was always the few who had it to spend. Always the few who should be handing up their full wage packets at home. But didn't.

Packing away the best of her London clothes into her suitcase under the bed, Connie walked down the main street to the draper's to purchase more suitable attire.

She would make a plan that would take her back to her Lucrezia, once her mother was healthy enough.

The pub was better than it had ever been, the upstairs quarters freshly painted, the wooden floors polished to the last by a reluctant Johanna, by slipping and sliding around the floor in multiple pairs of woollen socks.

In Connie's head was the idea that once the business was up and running, she would teach Johanna everything she knew. Until then, she would keep the business going herself. Johanna, by the age of seventeen, would surely be old enough to take care of herself, and run the bar – though it might be necessary to hire a lad to lend a hand and back her up if there was any trouble with drunken customers – leaving Connie free to reunite with Lucrezia.

It would take a year, maybe two, for her mother to be well enough. She could manage that. But once she left again to be with Lucrezia, she would not be coming back.

Lucrezia had written every other week in the earlier months of their separation. Late at night by the light of the oil lamp, Connie would hold the pages to her heart, yearning for connection. Closing her eyes, breathing in the scent of the paper to bring her closer. The letters, written in Lucrezia's flowing style comforted Connie, who used the side of her hand to wipe her tears from the page.

News from the sanatorium hadn't been good over the months that followed. By November, of 1930, Layla's health had deteriorated too much to hope for a good outcome. Her lungs had failed to heal. Connie was given no hope for her mother.

Working harder than ever, keeping her mind occupied, making sure that Johanna was well looked after, Connie was told that her mother wouldn't survive the Christmas. She told her sister as gently as she could, resigning herself to the fact that her mother was going to die.

Nine days later Connie's mother was laid to rest beside her husband in Ballygore. Mattie had stepped in to help. The boys sent a telegram.

Layla had faded so much in the months leading up to her death, Connie had felt it an ease for her to go. Her mother would be united with her father, on whom she had depended so much.

Johanna held her own, insisting she was fine. Slapping Connie's hand away when she went to put her arm around her in the church. But Connie could see it in her eyes. The same blaming look that she had seen in her mother's eyes. Johanna stepped away from her sister's side at the graveside, in the bitter cold. Mattie took his place between the sisters.

Connie resigned herself to the fact that life with Lucrezia would have to be put on hold once again. It would take longer than they had planned to be together. Writing to Lucrezia, whose letters had been slow in coming of late, had been difficult. Without Lucrezia by her side to encourage her, she felt she was losing her way. Time and space had come between them. The raw energy that had consumed them both had waned. Connie's head was filled with the practicalities of keeping the home place going. Teaching Johanna to look after herself was frustrating. Her sister remained on the pedestal she had made for herself.

Keeping the letters to Lucrezia as casual as she could, Connie explained the situation.

Her heart was broken, her life had changed so much in the year since she had returned. Dwelling on the past, she knew, would bring her no nearer to Lucrezia.

Lucrezia wrote back to a broken Connie. She was to be married in Naples, in the spring of 1931, to Marco, a widower with two sons. She could hold out no longer. She said she was not strong enough to stand up to her brother. And she did not trust that her family would protect her if she refused to marry, now that Roberto had taken full control of the family. She had agreed to marry, after many months of pressure. But it would not be forever. As she did not and never could love her husband-to-be, it did not feel like cheating.

Asking Connie to be mindful in writing to her.

I accept that while we cannot be with one another, we are one another. Sharing the same soul. So don't despair for me, amore, as I am yours to love forever as you are mine. Time has no bearing on us, Cornelia. Our love is infinite. While we cannot be together in our senses, there is nothing preventing us from being together in our souls. And we will figure it out eventually. I promise you. I will marry for convenience only – never for love. So trust me when I tell you not to be sad for me. Believe in us, Connie.

Connie cried as she reread the letter many times, accepting what could not be. But Lucrezia had not given up on her, for that she was grateful. Lucrezia had refused to accept that their love was over – that in itself had to mean something. Connie felt loved. In her heart it would remain so for as long as they both would live. Each resigned to the reality of where they were at, it would be a long time before the two women would see each other again.

Lucrezia had winced at the way Roberto had grabbed her arm as she stepped off the ship in Naples. No one had ever handled her in such a rough manner. The look in his eyes told her there would be little point in resisting. Her attempts to do so had aggravated him more. Lucrezia would no longer be free to suit herself. She was under her brother's control.

Her father was out of the picture, spending most of his time in America. The atmosphere at home was very different to the freedom she had become used to with Connie. Quietly she resigned herself to the fact that she had no choice for now, other than follow orders.

Roberto, along with their aunts, had arranged the marriage. A wine-merchant. Marco Rossi, a widower. Sensing from the first introduction, that Marco, whose late wife had tragically drowned off the Island of Capri, was far from the typical Italian husband, Lucrezia guessed that he too had a secret. Marco Rossi wanted no more from her than to live a lie.

The wedding was a society affair held in the Church of Santa Chiara, attended by some of the most influential people around Naples. Lucrezia, wearing a white ornate wedding gown with voluminous underskirts, the opposite of what she would have chosen for herself. In another time.

Abramo had returned for the wedding, expressing relief that his daughter was finally over her wanderlust – settling down with Marco Rossi. He didn't ask for details as to how his eldest son had convinced Lucrezia to return from New York without protest. It pleased his pride that he was no longer responsible for his daughter. He had found himself a young love interest in Chicago – his head was giddy – leaving room for little else outside of his work.

Chapter 9

Stapleton's Pub

By the summer of 1931, Stapleton's public house had become a welcoming place. Connie had used the experience gained working in the hotel in London to great effect. Customers returned and new customers came through the doors, on hearing that the place was being run by the ever-efficient Connie Stapleton, "back from managing some grand hotel in London".

Mattie, pleased to be back in the old familiar surroundings, became a frequent visitor once again, pulling the heavy bolt across the door last thing at night, putting up the shutters on the window outside, coaxing those who were less inclined to leave to drink up and head for home. Quenching the oil lamps, before heading out the back gate to where his pony and trap were waiting.

Sixteen-year-old Johanna showed little interest in the place at first, leaving Connie to get on with it. Having watched Mary Cullen baking bread in the bastible pot over the fire, Johanna began to spend time in the kitchen upstairs, pleased to be out of Connie's way. She experimented, producing bread and scones which were mostly edible, the failed batches offered to Mattie for the fowl out at Black Post. Or fed to the neighbour's pigs, providing entertainment for Connie and Mattie, who couldn't but laugh at the state of some of Johanna's efforts. Johanna had jumped up off the chair on one occasion, running down the stairs, calling back at them, *"Laugh all ye want! I will show ye what I'm made of one of these fine days! Mark my words!"*

The second year of Connie's return proved to be a turnaround for the business. Johanna's baking skills improved beyond what they had expected. Once again they were selling fresh bread, along with duck eggs and whatever vegetables Mattie brought in from the plot he kept on the farm. Tempting passers-by with the smell of baking floating out the front door onto the street, Johanna began to take it on herself to serve customers, anxious to soak up the compliments for her bread, which they said was as light as air, all the while gaining popularity for the jolly disposition she presented to them.

The two sisters came to an understanding that Connie would manage the orders, and run the bar in the evenings until closing time. Johanna would open up in the morning and take over the day trade from the snug counter. Connie was relieved to see Johanna stepping up to the mark.

Mattie continued to play an active part in the lives of the Stapleton sisters over the coming years as Connie did all she could to encourage her sister towards fending for herself. Impressed by their efforts to make a success of the business in trying times, he supported them where he could. It had been young Johanna who had surprised him the most. Small and dainty, pointed features, her curly auburn hair pinned back from her face, her sharp eyes never missing a trick, her skin clear and unblemished, she reminded him of Layla. She had grown into a self-assured young woman who at twenty made clear her intention to remain single, proclaiming to Mattie that she had seen too many married women tormented by their own children. "And, in the end, you're back to square one, on your own." She insisted that she'd be happy as a spinster, living a stress-free life. "And all the better if Connie remains true to her constant threat of moving away."

Mattie had been taken aback. He had watched her as the boyfriends came and went. None of them good enough for Johanna Stapleton who dismissed all attempts to charm her. Giving them the eye at the same time. Just enough for them to wonder. Drawing them towards the counter – to spend their money.

Mattie felt that Johanna had proved herself to be tougher than her sister, whom he suspected was taking a step back, losing her spark.

The memory that Mattie had in his head, of Connie, dressed in her finery, staying at Black Post Inn, was a far cry from how she had been looking of late. He now found it hard to see the youth in her. Getting her hair cut at the barber's shop on Spring Street hadn't helped. Short back and sides. Wearing clothes which were loose-fitting and dark. No shape. The years hadn't been kind to her. And Connie most certainly hadn't been kind to herself.

As Johanna celebrated her twenty-first birthday, Connie presented her sister with a key to the front door – the key that she had been given by her father many years before. It meant nothing to Connie anymore. She had all but lost interest in the place.

Continuing to scribe carefully worded letters to each other, words written with love and sincerity, Lucrezia and Connie never lost sight of their feelings for each other. Letters of hope. Promising that when the time was right they would be together. Plans made became plans cancelled. Ideas which seemed credible on paper during the hours of darkness by lamplight, became silly notions in the light of day. Notions without substance. Dreams belonging to another time.

Connie didn't purposely decide to allow her sister to take over from her. It just happened.

Holding her own in the bar, Johanna continued to prove her worth with the customers, who were more than willing to deal with the more cordial of the two sisters, leaving Connie on the side-line. The dogsbody. Johanna ran her business with pride, never faltering in her determination to keep a good clean house.

Mattie continued to help out in every way he could, carrying the turf from the back shed, any carpentry work that needed doing. Repairs, plumbing jobs, all seen to by Mattie. He came to the pub most nights, as he had done over the years. On the nights he didn't appear, he was missed, more so for his willingness to sort out whatever needed doing. When tempers were frayed, or patrons under the influence struggled to leave, Mattie's presence made the difference. As Johanna became less tolerant of her older sister, Mattie felt for Connie, whom he suspected had no idea that Johanna's plans for the future did not include her.

The atmosphere between the sisters took a turn for the worst. Rather than address her sister directly at a tense moment, Johanna had taken to talking over Connie's head, overriding her deliberately, directing her requests towards Mattie instead. Smiling and laughing with the customers, who enjoyed her light-hearted banter, she could turn abruptly on Connie, showing her other side. "Connie, take yourself outside, will you? There's no room for the two of us behind the counter."

Sitting pretty on her stool behind the bar, reading her book, Johanna liked to sip weak tea from a dainty bone-china cup, part of a mixed set that Mattie had given to Connie years before. "You better take these yokes home with you, Connie," he'd said. "I've broken a good few already. A cup is a cup, but they're far too weak for me to be handling, with my big awkward hands. I'll stick to my enamel mug, that I can take outside with me, without fear of it shattering." Making use of the hand-embroidered linen which had been stored in the attic, hiring a local woman to do her laundry once a week, Johanna Stapleton had standards.

Connie felt unwanted in the public house for which she had sacrificed so much. Johanna wanted a dogsbody, someone to bring in the turf, clean out the grate, wash down the outside toilet, empty the slop, anything that she herself was not inclined towards.

Feeling her self-esteem erode as her sister's infectious laughter continued to draw in the customers, Connie's mood darkened.

Demeaned by Johanna's growing intolerance of her, her confidence ebbed away. Knocking off the corner of one of her front teeth held little distress for her when it happened. Her hair was streaked with grey. Her smile seldom on show. The misery of a life lost had left its mark on her. Inwardly she yearned for the soft caresses of years before, in the bedsit in the basement of the Strand Palace hotel in Soho, in the apartment on Broadway, in the hotel room in Provincetown. A world away.

Summoning up the image of Lucrezia, remembering her light sensual touch as she massaged her skin with a lightly scented cream, comforted her as she lay in her bed, doubting the future.

Taking Mattie up on his offer of the use of a plot at Black Post for planting had been a turning point for her. He had coaxed her over the weeks until she reluctantly accepted.

Out in Black Post, she slowly found her way back. Whatever the season, Connie had purpose. The freshness of the spring air revitalised her. Clearing the plot, loosening the damp earth with her hands, setting seeds, watching the tiny plants peep through the soil, settled her, giving her hope. Seeing the tulip bulbs she had buried underneath the cold soil in November shove their noses through the surface in February made her smile. Spending much of her time on her new-found interest, Connie healed. Sitting on a rusty iron chair drinking tea, she felt grounded. No longer caught up in a hazy gloom. She had purpose. Cycling out to Black Post each day, looking forward to the day ahead, calmed her. Buying day-old chicks to rear, watching their tiny bodies running around the pen, flapping their wings, brought her joy – leaving the running of the pub on Mill Road to the ever-smiling Johanna, who was in her element sitting pretty on her stool behind the counter. Connie left her get on with it.

Johanna Stapleton had ousted her sister Connie.

Chapter 10

The Invitation

1939

The telegram from Dublin arrived to Mill Road in June 1939, briefly explaining that as a result of last-minute events, Lucrezia would be joining her husband Marco for a short stay in the Gresham Hotel in Dublin on the following day. She invited Connie to join her.

Connie got the shock of her life. Was she seeing things?

Lucrezia in Ireland!

What?

Her heart thumping in her chest. Her mouth bone dry. Connie panicked. Mattie was beside her, lighting the lamp on the counter. Handing him the telegram, unable to speak, her mouth dropped open with the shock. She reached for the brandy bottle.

It had been nine years since she had seen Lucrezia last. The letters between them had become less frequent. Promises made. Promises broken. Lucrezia had written about the marriage she had entered into. Grudgingly. A marriage she would remain in until the time was right. Ever hopeful. But she loved her stepsons.

She had told Connie about the rise of the fascist government in Italy, which had made her businessman husband Marco an important man. She insisted that she had no other choice but to keep many of her opinions to herself. No longer free to paint her avant-garde expressionist portraits of women, she had been spending much less time in her studio – enabling the false image of domesticity, allowing her husband to soak up the notoriety he craved, expanding his business. The prosperous wine merchant. At the expense of her own life. "My darling stepsons," she said, "are at an age where they still need to be cared for."

And here she was in Dublin. Staying at the Gresham Hotel.

Connie swallowed the brandy in one gulp. Pouring another.

Ignoring Mattie's advice to the contrary, she went straight to the post office to send a telegram to the Gresham, saying that unfortunately due to last-minute complications she would be unable to travel. She would be in touch.

Simpler to keep memories of better times in her heart, than expose her reality. The Connie who managed the hotel in London and the stage sets on Broadway was a far cry from the Connie looking back at her in the mirror. The Connie who had proudly walked the streets of New York city with the woman she loved at her side, the Connie who had sworn to love Lucrezia for the rest of her days, had gone.

Her teeth needed fixing, the raised blemishes on her face had flared up with the shock … too many reasons not to be seen. And her clothes were certainly not of the style that Lucrezia would remember. Connie was far too distressed to think about travelling to the Gresham, never mind presenting herself to Lucrezia.

Four days later, on a warm sunny evening, Matthew Grogan collected Lucrezia Romano from the train station in Ballygore. It hadn't been difficult to pick out his Italian guest from the others. Lucrezia had an air about her, dressed in her expensive city clothes, her dark curls stylishly pinned back, her cream-leather elbow-gloves matching her fancy shoes. Quite a looker. Standing there on the platform, floral weekend bag by her side, Lucrezia looked every bit the lady, her striking features setting her apart from the others on the platform. She was the very opposite of her dear friend Connie Stapleton.

Mattie immediately scolded himself for his recklessness in inviting Lucrezia down to Ballygore to surprise Connie. He had made the call in an attempt to cheer her up. To put a smile on her face. Finally understanding Connie's shock, he realised he had just made the situation a whole lot worse.

Making up his mind not to bring Lucrezia anywhere

near the public house to add to Connie's distress, he could have kicked himself for being so quick to act. But the two women would be just fine out in Black Post Inn for the two nights, after which he would return the fancy Italian to the train station.

Mattie had found it difficult enough to understand half of what the woman was saying to him. He had never met anyone like her. Her voice was sharp and strong, but entertaining. She explained that she had left her husband Marco free to explore Dublin city with his businessmen friends. She had convinced her husband to agree to her travelling to Ballygore to spend the weekend with her old friend. Worlds apart. Mattie knew he had been tactless, acting out of pity for Connie. He continued to scold himself on the short journey back to Black Post Inn, where he knew Connie would be waiting.

It was to be a surprise for her 35th birthday, but when he had seen the state of her, he had thought it best to prepare her, to give her notice. Connie had not taken it well.

"What have you done?"

Red in the face, her eyes open wide with alarm. Mattie had been unprepared for her response. She had been horrified.

"Are you a fool, Mattie Grogan? A complete fool? I confided in you that Lucrezia had invited me to the Gresham – it didn't give you the bloody right to go behind my back and bring her here."

"But I thought you were great friends with her,

Connie. I only asked her cos I thought 'twould bring you out of yourself on your birthday."

"I cannot believe you've invited Lucrezia here. To Ballygore. I only told you she was in Dublin because of the shock I got when I read the telegram." Connie had marched straight out the front door and down the street.

Mattie didn't know how to react. Caught unaware by her outburst, which he felt was uncalled for, far removed from what he'd expected.

He later confided in Johanna, saying he thought Connie would have been more appreciative of his efforts to cheer her up.

"Mattie, are you soft in the head? You couldn't cheer that one up in a million years. I remember Mammy saying that she was like an old aunt of my father's. Grumpy as hell. She'd better stay well away from me, until your woman goes back on the train. The last thing I want is her creating talk around the place."

Mattie didn't ask what she meant.

Connie, excited but nervous once she calmed down later in the evening, had thanked Mattie for his kind gesture. There had been something blocking her from making arrangements to see Lucrezia, she told him. But the decision had been made outside of her.

"But so what, Connie? She's your friend, isn't she? If she's sincere, she won't be looking at you like that. She's coming to spend a few days with you, not to be judging how you look."

Knowing that her sister would be well pleased to be

rid of Connie for the few days, he felt rather pleased to be on the good side of Johanna. He was happy to leave Connie and her friend, whose name he could hardly muster, avail of Black Post Inn.

And Connie seemed in better form.

Connie had realised that being alone in Black Post Inn, for three days with Lucrezia, uninterrupted, was a dream come true, even if she was less than pleased about her appearance.

The two women laid eyes on each other in the front room of Black Post Inn. Immediately responding to the strong connection between them, nothing else mattered. No need to explain. No room for awkwardness. Or embarrassment. Only the need to love and awaken. To nurture and unfold. To toss aside the layers of uncertainty and pain. To wade through the years of sadness and longing, revealing the feelings within. Each relaxed by the presence of the other. Complete.

Over the three days, the two became as they were. No obstacles between their souls. Lucrezia admitting that her arranged marriage to Marco had been a cruel twist of fate. Explaining that her husband was living his own best life. Meeting young men. Covertly. How she had never felt deceived by his philandering ways. She feigned contentment by choice, which she insisted was easier by far. He had told her he would never agree to dissolve their marriage, or indeed allow her to do so.

Connie listened as Lucrezia described her life. The couple lived in Naples, with a summer villa which she adored clinging to a cliff in Positano, overlooking the ocean below. They were the essence of respectability, supposedly supportive of the fascist regime, which Lucrezia detested. Marco the prosperous merchant, Lucrezia his wife, the dutiful housekeeper, whose bold modern statements on canvas had long been replaced by landscapes, keeping in the traditions of the old Italian masters. And two doting stepsons, unaware that their parents were each living lives wished for by neither.

Connie talked about Mattie, how kind he had been to Joanna and herself. How he'd given her the use of the plot to tend, and built the chicken coup for her. Laughing that he had turned her into a country girl. Saying that Mattie had more or less proposed to her before she'd left for London years before.

"Imagine, I could have been the mistress here. But then I would never have met you, would I? But I wouldn't swap the three years we had together for a lifetime in this place."

The tears slipped easily down Lucrezia's face as she tried to comfort Connie, asking had she at any time considered becoming Mattie's wife.

"Connie, surely a life here in Black Post Inn would be far better for you than remaining in town, where you are obviously not wanted?"

"In some ways, yes, it would."

"Then at least think about it, Connie. Please." She

could not bear to think of Connie living in Ballygore without support. "I have no right, Connie, to expect you to wait for me. I don't know how, but I tell you we will be together. Above or below ground. I had little choice other than to marry Marco, they made sure of that. In the end I couldn't have cared less, to be honest. But, as I told you years ago, our love will endure through many lifetimes – we don't have to be together to feel it. From what I have seen, Mattie does care about you. And you *are* out here most days as it is."

"Lucrezia, you can get that right out of your mind. I have no intention of marrying a man I cannot love. I do know Mattie better than most. And, yes, he cares about me. But is it enough? Anyway, of late he seems to have set his sights on our Johanna. He thinks I haven't noticed. But I have."

Changing the subject, she asked Lucrezia if she'd like to meet Johanna before she returned to Dublin. Lucrezia declined, saying that she would fear what she might say to her. What she might do to her.

Chapter 11

The Proposal

1939

Lucrezia left Ballygore on the train to join her husband in Dublin. Connie returned to Mill Road, later resting on the bench in the snug, sleeping off the ill-effects of the malt whiskey she had downed earlier. Hearing voices coming from the bar through the open hatch, she lifted her head to listen, while swallowing the dregs left in the glass in front of her.

Tuning in to the conversation at the other end of the dimly lit bar, she turned her head sideways to listen. Peeping through the hatch, barely making out the faces of the only two people left in the bar in the candlelight, it still wasn't difficult to make out who they were. The main oil lamp had been turned off, the shutters put up, to avoid a knock on the door from the Peeler who did his rounds by bicycle each night. She recognised the voices. Cocking her ear, she soon realised who the two were laughing at.

Her. They were laughing at her.

Johanna was vilifying her, maligning her, laughing at her expense, calling her an old fool, while Mattie stood listening to her. Close to her.

"The get-up of her! And the dirt under her nails from digging outside at your place or whatever she's at out there. Mattie, the customers don't want her here at all. They tell me every day. They're only laughing at her. She has a face on her that'd stop a clock, and you're worse for pandering to her."

"*Aaah*, come on, Johanna, is she as bad as you're making her out to be? She's done good by you, hasn't she? Coming home to take on this place when it was gone to pot. She's had a rough time these last years with whatever it was that got in on her. She's not the same Connie she was, that's for sure. But as long as she's abroad in my place with the garden and the fowl she's contented enough."

"And she coming back here smelling just like the fowl. But I won't complain. At least when she's out at Black Post she's not in here tormenting me. Oh, I'd be far better off without her. I don't know why she stays on here at all."

"Johanna, I know it can't be easy on you. That's what I had in mind when I gave her the use of the place."

"Mattie, come on, she's a joke, and you know it only too well. When she's not depressed, she's giving out. She could stay in bed half the day when it suits her, and then be up all night mooching around the place. She's a bloody martyr, is all she is. She should have stayed away altogether and left me with the Cullens. Instead, I've had to put up with her bloody moods. The sooner she moves on out of here the better for us all. I'd run it blindfolded, if I didn't have to keep an eye on her. I wish someone would take her off my hands, but I suppose that's highly unlikely, isn't it?"

"I suppose you've a point there all right."

Hearing Mattie's reply sickened Connie. And, though Johanna had often had a go at her in the past, to hear her talk about her with such venom in her voice shook her to the core. And with Mattie of all people. Recalling all the years she had put herself last, to provide for the ungrateful brat. All she had given up in London to come back to Johanna. All in vain.

What a fool she had been! Having spent these wasted years back in Ballygore. But biggest mistake of all was forsaking her plans to be with Lucrezia. Enough was enough.

Connie got up. Straightening her clothes, picking up her glass, she walked towards them. Unsteady at first, swaying a little, she came into view. Johanna's mouth fell open as she realised that Connie might have been listening to her conversation with Mattie. Trying to backtrack, changing the subject, seeking to undo the damage.

"So that's it all so, Mattie. All locked up for the night." All too late.

Mattie, looking embarrassed, cleared his throat, saying nothing. Doing what he did best. Avoiding confrontation.

Connie banged her glass on the counter to show her fury.

"Connie, I thought you'd gone upstairs. What were you doing skulking around there in the snug, listening to a private conversation between Mattie and myself? Well, you know what they say. No good is to be had from eavesdropping. Aren't I right, Mattie?"

"Leave me out of it now, Johanna. I'm away home."

Connie spoke with a confidence she had long since lost.

"Don't you move, Mattie Grogan. Stay right where you are. You were in the thick of it up to now with this ungrateful wretch. You can chat away. I'm off to my bed."

Connie heard the latch fall on the back door as she climbed the stairs. Mattie had left.

The look on Johanna's face had said it all. She couldn't have cared less how hurt Connie was. She was using Mattie, and would continue to do so until he was no use to her. Connie had arrived back in Ballygore ten years before to do her duty. Her father wouldn't have expected less of her. But she had been thrown to the wolves by Johanna, who looked on her as no more than a workhorse. Had she stayed where she was, Johanna would have survived after all. The twins had continued to send their dollars to Mary Cullen for her keep, right up until she moved back home with Connie. Her brothers had honoured their promise. The brothers who had barely sent a Christmas card home since.

Mattie hadn't said as much, but in Connie's mind lingered the thought that he indeed had Johanna in his sights, as she had told Lucrezia. Marriage material.

Watching him hanging on her every word earlier, inches away from her sister's face, had convinced her. Johanna had Mattie exactly where she wanted him. At her service.

Connie had enough of being used, being trampled on by a sister who had shown no compassion during times when she needed someone to understand, times when she was not feeling the best. Times when a kind word coming her way would have helped. Johanna cared about no-one. Everyone would get what they wanted in the end, except her. Dependable Connie.

Staying awake for most of the night, Connie devised her plan. This time there would be no going back. No change of heart.

Connie felt a rage building up inside of her, a rage kept hidden for far too long. Time to take a stand. Or allow Johanna free rein over her. Pleasing others had got her nowhere. It had been to her detriment.

Connie Stapleton was done with playing the fool.

She would do as Lucrezia suggested. She would marry Mattie. And live her life where she had been happy, where Lucrezia had rested easily beside her.

Give him a child, an heir to his precious Black Post, if that's what he wanted. She might even open the Inn to guests again, and no reason why Lucrezia couldn't visit her every now and then. Worth thinking about. As thoughts of the future visited her mind, Connie felt her old determination creeping back. She had been happy staying at Black Post Inn. Why not make it permanent? But first she had some work to do on herself.

Mattie had been decent to her these past years. Marrying him would secure her future. And he had all but proposed to her in the past. The way things were going there wasn't much facing her unless she left Ballygore. And where would she go, having given her best years taking care of Johanna? She didn't have the energy to start over again. Forcing Johanna to sell up was not an option for her. So where would she be best placed? The answer to her question made her mind up for her. She'd be best placed in Matthew Grogan's iron bed outside in Black Post Inn, the bed she had shared with Lucrezia the very night before, in the house she loved above any other. Instead of thrown on the scrapheap by her selfish and insensitive sister.

Lucrezia had been right.

Offering her hand to the room in front of her, speaking in the most affected accent she could muster, she said: "My name is Mrs Matthew Grogan, if you please. That would be the Grogans of Black Post Inn. Very pleased to make your acquaintance."

Connie had never been more determined about anything in all her life.

Three weeks later, Connie set her plan in motion. She felt less than comfortable in what she was wearing. All too tight. The band on her new skirt was cutting her waist, her sheer white blouse displaying more than she was comfortable with. A visit to the hairdresser's on the main street had made a huge difference. She was on a mission, and had no intention of failing. Checking to make sure that her cleavage was on display for the unsuspecting Mattie, she put any despairing thoughts aside. Powdering down her high colour, before rubbing a touch of rouge to her cheeks, she was ready.

Connie confidently lifted the counter, leaving herself in behind the bar where Johanna was busy chatting to a customer. Ignoring the look her sister gave her, she poured herself a small whiskey before handing a generous one to Mattie, who was standing at the other side of the counter, his back to the wall.

Everything that needed doing had been done earlier, leaving Johanna free to serve her customers. Connie joined Mattie outside the counter. She stood facing him, a narrow stained-glass partition separating her from the customers behind her. Mattie was in his usual spot at the end of the bar, his back to the wall, where he had full view of the bar.

Throwing an odd glance at the suspicious Johanna, Connie was determined to succeed. She soon went back in to refill their glasses.

"Mattie paid for it, in case you think we're drinking the profits!" she spat at her sister the third time she went to do so.

The look on Johanna's face said it all. She continued serving the customers, throwing a sideward glance over towards Mattie and Connie every now and then. The bar was busy. Noisy. People raised their voices to be heard.

The evening went on and Connie saw the whiskey

gradually take effect on Mattie. At last she turned in to face the counter, side-stepping closer to him, placing her right hand briefly on his inside thigh. But she soon realised that Mattie was more intent on following Johanna with his eyes. Brave with the whiskey.

"Look at Johanna, Connie. Isn't she looking great? I've had my eye on her this while, you know. I know, I know. 'Tis all in the mind with me."

So her hunch had been correct.

"And if I may say so you're looking very well yourself tonight, Connie. Good to see you cheering up." His eyes falling downwards from her face.

"Mattie, are you half mad? You're wasting your precious time with our Johanna. Half the parish have been after her, and she's turned them all down. You know that. She's a spinster by choice."

Seeing the look on his face, she almost felt sorry for him.

"Right you are, Connie. No fool like an old fool, they say."

Connie acted quickly, before she lost her nerve. The memory of Johanna's voice berating her behind her back, and Mattie looking at her like a lapdog, spurred her on.

"Mattie, you're forty-one, not eighty-one for God's sake. And there was I thinking 'twas me you were after all these years," she whispered. Words that she had never uttered before. Words that she knew she would never utter again. Words that sickened her. Words that she knew she had to say. "You could do what you want with me,

Mattie. Every night if you wanted." She decided to go one step further.

Confident she wouldn't be seen by the customers behind her, she leaned forward towards him, displaying her cleavage, and saw his eyes widen.

Mattie ran his tongue across the side of his lip. "You turned me down years ago, Connie. Or had you forgotten?"

"Well, you didn't exactly propose to me, Mattie. And didn't you say to let you know if I ever changed my mind? Well, I have, Mattie Grogan."

She felt sick in her stomach at what she was doing. But no point in stopping now, she thought. Now that she had humiliated herself to the point of no return.

Moving closer, she whispered, "And I'll give you a child, Mattie, if that's what you're after. I'm still available, ready and waiting. All you have to do is ask."

"Ah, Connie, give over, I'm well drunk and you're not too far behind me yourself. Stop now," said Mattie, turning in to face the counter, calling to Johanna for one for the road.

But she wasn't about to give up now she had gone so far. Past the point. Degrading herself.

"Stay here with me upstairs tonight, Mattie, and I'll give you a little taste of what you'll be missing. Leave our Johanna off to her bed."

Johanna pulled Connie aside the day after the engagement was announced. Unable to hide her disgust.

"I knew you were up to something, Connie Stapleton, when I saw the get-up of you. But I never thought for one moment you'd go after Mattie."

"Does it really bother you, Johanna? You're hardly interested in him yourself, are you?"

"Don't be ridiculous, Connie. Mattie Grogan is a dear friend."

"Johanna, let me tell *you* something. That night I overheard your little conversation with Mattie finished me – those awful things you said about me, and the names you called me. So … seeing as you thought you'd never see the back of me, you will now. I'll never spend a night under this roof again. That I promise you. You can stick the whole lot all the way up your griping arse, Johanna Stapleton. As far as it'll go."

Johanna's mouth opened wide, shocked at her sister's outburst.

Connie continued. "And you're right … I should have left them take you years ago, instead of giving up my life in London for you. I would have been living in America this long time, were it not for you. *Yes, you.* You selfish insensitive wretch! And what have I to show for all the years I gave taking care of you? Not one thing. You ungrateful sniping bitch of a sister!"

"Listen to the gutter language coming out of your mouth now, Connie Stapleton. Yes, you gave up your exciting life for me. So what? And, yes, maybe you should have sent me off to a home. And maybe Mammy did spoil me. Maybe this and maybe bloody that! But I've had to listen to your bullshit, making out like it's all my fault. And I've had to look at you going around with a puss on you. Every opportunity you get, you remind me of all you've given up for me. I'm sick of you. And you certainly don't want Mattie or any other fella for that matter. Be honest with yourself for once. It's Black Post Inn you want to get your hands on – you've been raving about the place for years."

"Indeed," answered Connie, before calmly informing her sister that Mattie and herself would be married in Limerick the very next Saturday, once they had their letters of freedom from Father Mac. Mattie's cousin Eddie would be coming down from Kintown. He would be the witness along with Josie who had just moved in two doors down from the pub.

Then off with the married couple to Salthill for a few days and back to Black Post Inn to begin their married lives.

Chapter 12

1940-1952

Finding out she was pregnant three months after getting married had been a relief for Connie, who had begun to doubt her own fertility. The pregnancy was without complication for the expectant mother who worked as hard as she ever had, keeping her head down, staying away from her sister. She wrote to Lucrezia telling her the news.

Any thoughts she'd had previously about opening the house to guests were put on hold.

Paul James Grogan was born in the bedroom at Black Post Inn on January 7th 1940. Connie sent a card to Naples. Mattie had moved into a room across the landing, on the advice of the attending midwife, allowing Connie to take care of the child. He never returned to his wife's bed, moving to a bedroom at the far side of the landing.

Connie had felt the melancholy creep up on her slowly. It started with a sadness that she couldn't find cause for. Weeping. A feeling in the pit of her stomach that she couldn't let go of. A physical pain. Tears that she had never been able to cry now rolled unashamedly down her face in the weeks and months after Paul's birth. She sank into that dark familiar place, where she had been in the past. Unable to rouse herself out of it, she functioned as best she could. Coping. A visit to the doctor confirmed that Connie was suffering from post-partum melancholy, which he said would dissipate in time. No intervention needed.

Chastising herself for not being the mother she had promised herself to be, dark thoughts remained with her. Unable to give her baby the attention he deserved made her feel worse about herself. Thoughts coming into her head dragging her further down, believing herself to be a failure, non-deserving. Connie believed herself to be worthless.

Mattie would come home to find the baby lying in wet clothes, his nappy damp and heavy.

Connie rarely left Black Post, except to push the pram down the avenue, turning around towards the house well before she reached the front gate. She was seldom seen outside the gates. They said Connie Grogan had lost her mind.

Mattie, having little to do with the running of the house since he had married Connie, had little choice but to involve himself in caring for the baby. Having never known a father himself, he did what he could for Paul, leaving Connie to suffer her own hell. He complained little, though feeling helpless and frustrated. He accepted his lot. Allowing Johanna to help with the baby was a relief. He couldn't manage everything.

As Hitler's army decimated Europe, there was little sign of a war in Ballygore, apart from the shortages. People got on with their lives.

Mattie spent his days milking the rambling goats, whose numbers were increasing beyond his control, killing two kid goats for Easter Sunday – one for Black Post Inn, the other bound for Joanna's table – wringing the neck of two geese at Christmas. Goose wings saved for use as feather dusters for the pub in town. Mattie used every part of his kills, making black pudding with the pig's blood. Feet, head and tail all thrown in the pot. Keeping himself busy. Always busy. A three-legged wooden stool made for Paul. One extra for Johanna to rest her feet on.

Availing of every opportunity to go into town in his truck, Mattie continued to call on Johanna, bringing her whatever he had loaded on the back of the truck. Including Paul, once he was old enough to sit beside him. Mattie looked forward to seeing her bright eyes. To breathing in her scent.

Paul, delighted in the attention he was receiving from his Auntie Jo. The squeals of laughter in Stapleton's kitchen became a welcome distraction for Mattie from the sombre atmosphere at home in Black Post Inn.

Mattie had no time for thinking of what might have been. Using the gate lodge during the day, with Paul by his side, Mattie began to spend less time at home with Connie, leaving her to potter around. By night he roamed the land, lamping rabbits, stunning them with the light of his torch. Dazed enough to kill them. Bringing the rabbits to town, legs tied together, handing them into houses where people were delighted to receive them, keeping the tails for luck. Or handing them out, delighting the children. Taking care of his son, who showed great affection for his aunt in town.

As the war affected supplies coming into Ireland, Johanna worked hard to keep her business open. Spirits and tobacco had become scarce, driving up black market activities, making many goods out of the reach of ordinary people. Trade dwindled as people no longer had the earning power of years before. Raw materials were in short supply, as dependence on imports had left Ireland with a severe shortage of coal, impacting on energy. Tea, sugar and other items became scarce. Some left the country, to join the allied forces fighting against Hitler's army – regardless – while others looked down their noses at those who left Ireland to fight for the Crown.

As ration books became the norm, people in Ballygore did their best to survive, growing vegetables in small plots in their back yards, alongside rearing pigs in the smallest of spaces, next door to other pigs. Turf was burned in fires that had only ever seen coal.

Johanna had a struggle to keep the door open, but she

did, selling what she could make money on from the snug during the day, jugs of loose porter in the pub in the evenings. Mattie was full of admiration for his wife's sister, who never waned in her determination to keep going. She proved herself to be resilient, far stronger than Mattie would have expected. The scarcity of items and fuel barely seemed to affect the ever-resourceful young woman. Mattie would bring her in sods of turf that he had cut from the bog. Eggs and meat were not included in the ration books. Pork products were easy enough to find. Offal became a staple in most homes. No part of an animal was wasted. People showed their resourcefulness by bartering whatever they could get their hands on. Rabbit meat stewed in a pot became a staple in many houses. Mattie's goats provided meat as well as milk. Anything that could be grown in the ground, Mattie and Connie planted in the garden at Black Post. With no shortage of vegetables during the growing season, Johanna took full advantage of Mattie's kindness.

Connie's depression had lifted by the time Paul had started school in the small country schoolhouse two miles from Black Post Inn. Her insistence on driving him to school herself, now that petrol was available again, had come as a shock to Mattie. An intrusion. He had become resigned to her ways. But slowly she had begun to take her place again within the household, showing an interest, leaving the dark days of the past behind her.

Asking questions, expecting answers. Complaining about the amount of time that Paul was spending with his father in town, she accused Mattie of deliberately trying to displace her by taking Paul in to visit Johanna. Mattie had expected little from her during times when she was barely able to function. Nothing at all. Only to be there for Paul who had become used to his mother's ways, saving his stories and most of his smiles for his Aunty Jo, who didn't hold back on showering the boy with attention. Paul had more time for his aunt in town than he did for his own mother.

"I can see what you're at, Mattie. I'm not entirely clueless, you know. Paul seems to talk of nothing else, apart from his Auntie Jo."

Mattie couldn't hold his frustration. "Who do think was there for Paul, when you were stuck to the bed, Connie? He's almost four years old, and I'd safely say this is the very best you've been in all that time. Now, all of a sudden you want to know every step we take, whereas before you couldn't give a damn where we were. Johanna has been there for the boy, and I won't take that away from her."

It was obvious to him that Connie was hurt by his words, but he felt entitled to let off steam. Steam that had been building up inside of him for years. She was well aware of how she'd been since Paul was born. Aware that it was he who had done everything for the boy, everything for her, while she sat chain-smoking cigarettes or lying in the bed listening to the wireless for news of the Allies landing in war-torn Europe.

The relationship between herself and Mattie hadn't been satisfying for either, each respecting the other but not enough. Manipulating each other. Each in their own minds accepting that the marriage had been a mistake. Neither willing to face up to the reality. Mattie continued to visit Johanna in the pub every evening, leaving Connie confused as to how she felt. He had disconnected from Black Post Inn. From her.

"Why do you continuously go in to Mill Road, undermining me every opportunity you get, when it's here alongside me you should be? She's using you, you know. And trying to put a divide between me and Paul. Oh, she's succeeded there all right. But I'm the boy's mother, Mattie. Not Johanna. Remember that."

"I'd say you've got it all wrong there, Connie. I'm only doing as I've always done – looked out for James Stapleton's daughters. I married one, and will look out for the other, and that's all there is to it. And what's wrong with the boy having a soft spot for his aunt? His only aunt for that matter. She spoils the lad."

"How do you think it feels that my own son runs in to my sister with his cut knee and his tears? Never to me, Mattie. And you have never once taken my side in all this."

"The lad is seven years old, Connie. He's reached the age of reason. What did you expect?"

Fearing further rejection, she avoided addressing the issue with Paul, whom she knew wouldn't hear a word spoken against his Auntie Jo. Connie continued to invest all that she had in Black Post Inn. She didn't have the attention of her husband and was at a loss as to why she craved it in the first place. They became apathetic towards each other as the years passed.

Tending to the garden, growing food for the kitchen table, fulfilled Connie as her spirits lifted. Experimenting. Nettle leaves cooked with cabbage. Dandelion leaves served with wild mushrooms which were in abundance in the fields. Wild spinach on her doorstep, full of iron. Tea made with the flowers of St John's Wort, growing in her garden – an age-old remedy. Connie concentrated on healing herself. Trial and error.

Accepting that she had a tendency towards depression had been a milestone. Naming it.

Her mother had no time for gardening. She preferred plastic flowers. Horrible plastic flowers and others made from crepe paper, which her father used to buy from a traveller woman at the front door. After her mother died, Connie had binned every dust-ridden flower in the place and the vases with them.

Connie had not heard from Lucrezia much since Paul was born. A brief note to congratulate her in the early years of the war and after that correspondence had been almost non-existent. But she had heard enough about war-torn Naples on the wireless to upset her.

Taking the old stained letters from her hiding place, of a winter's night, reading them over and over again, alone in the dark evenings, was all she could do to recover her sense of belonging. To Lucrezia.

Connie had no idea what was going on for Lucrezia after the war. If indeed she was alive. Waiting to hear that she had survived the war years became a constant source of anxiety.

The war had changed everything.

Receiving a letter from Lucrezia in November 1947 had re-ignited her, filling her with hope.

Lucrezia had survived the war.

Dearest Connie,

It's been a long time coming. I do hope that you are well and contented with your life in Black Post Inn. I did write several letters to you but it was impossible to get them out. I am not going to dwell on those times. I haven't heard from you in so long and how could I? The house is Naples was flattened to the ground along with most of the neighbourhood. Even the church we were married in was bombed. Nothing was spared. I could tell you about the poverty, the violence, the devastation – but I won't. Marco and I were lucky. So lucky that we could flee. Now I want to escape for a while and think about you. Leave all that behind.

I heard that Ireland remained neutral and then I heard about the bombing in Dublin in '41. So I don't know enough to comment.

How are you, Connie? And Paul? He must be seven by now. I hope he is a joy to you as my stepsons have been for me. And Mattie? So much time has passed.

Marco and I are here in the summerhouse in Positano. Safe. You would simply adore the masses of bougainvillea dripping over the balcony. Although I doubt you would survive the hundreds of steps to the beach. The villa is tucked securely, high in the mountain, on a cliff edge. Little point in complaining. No great damage here. We had the British soldiers here. They came to rest so that will tell you a lot. Marco has since been injured, so I am the dutiful wife, as his sight was damaged by shrapnel. But we are fine. The boys have grown up fast and have their own lives in America. Connie, write to me. Tell me that you're OK.

I will wait for your letter, amore.

Lucrezia

Connie had received the news that she had been waiting for. Lucrezia was safe. It was all that she wanted to hear. She wrote back to Positano immediately, telling Lucrezia about life in Black Post. Now that she had knew Lucrezia had survived she could concentrate on the future.

By the following summer, the courtyard at Black Post Inn had become a testament to the hours she spent coaxing the plants to yield their offerings. Connie felt better than she had in years.

Making the decision to take in paying guests as soon as she was ready hadn't been difficult. As the economy improved, requests had been coming from salesmen travelling through Ballygore, looking for overnight accommodation. She would keep it to a minimum. One or two. And, in time, invite Lucrezia over.

Chapter 13

The Italian Couple

1942

Marco and Lucrezia had fled with the children who were eleven and twelve years old, to their country house south of Naples, in Positano, at the first rumblings of the Occupation. High up in the hills, up countless steps, then up some more, the family felt as safe as they could be amongst the small community, for whom survival became an everyday chore. Away from the devastation in the city where people were starving, eating whatever they could scrounge in order to stay alive, many forced to net birds if starvation didn't get them first. Lucrezia and her family survived on fish and whatever they could grow or forage from the wild, buying what they could on the black market, through connections of Marco's. Their boys were doted on by their stepmother, who did her utmost to protect them in a country that had suffered beyond recognition. The ports, rails and industrial areas on the eastern side of Naples had been the prime targets for the bombers.

After the war, people began to travel in all directions, for many reasons. Some fleeing their homeland for a better life. Those who had openly supported Mussolini's government were now desperately fleeing to avoid being lynched on the streets by anti-fascists who had grouped together, finding and punishing those they believed to be fascist collaborators.

For Lucrezia there had always been a reason to prevent her from fleeing her marriage, as had been her plan from the outset. From the moment her heart had grown fond of the two boys, she was determined to take care of them until they were old enough to do without her. With the war, her days and nights became consumed with staying alive, protecting the boys.

Marco had grown irritated and restless, refusing to stay cooped up in the mountains, regularly leaving the security of the safe house, abandoning his family for days on end, telling Lucrezia that he had business to settle. Always business. No discussion.

Having no time for pondering on what might have been, the reality became all-consuming for Lucrezia. Neighbours shared what they had with each other. Others refused, afraid to let go, in case they would starve. Lucrezia knew how fortunate they had been to survive, seeing entire families wiped out. The war had devastated her country. Entire families had spent weeks at a time, hiding in air-raid shelters in the city, scrambling around the old aqueducts, through miles of underground passages, previously used to ferry water around the highly populated cities.

Not long after the war, Marco had been attacked in Naples, where he had gone under cover of darkness to meet with others like him who were engaged in shady dealings. The underworld. He hadn't paid up. He had been lured to a building where he had been beaten, shot, and left for dead. His face had been burned, his sight badly damaged. Lucrezia patiently tended to his wounds, refusing to allow the boys suffer for their father's poor choices. Determinedly she accepted her lot. Marco losing his sight had affected her more than she could have imagined. Minding him, she had become his eyes. Having long since given up resisting the life which had been forced upon her, she had resigned herself to her marriage, and grown to care for the man who had taunted her so much in the earlier years. He had proven to be a decent husband toward the end. Spending years together in the village of Positano had brought the couple closer together, closer than either could have expected.

Spending their summer evenings outside under vines of scented Jasmine, picking lemons and oranges from the grove, rummaging for wild mushrooms, eating whatever edibles they could forage from the ground. Winter evenings spent by the fire, opening up to one another. Liking each other. Laughing together. Crying at the misfortunes of the war. Laughing at themselves, two people marooned together in a life neither would have chosen, had times been different. The best of friends. Speaking openly to each other as close friends do. He speaking of his confusion as a younger man, the raw desire which had taken over his life after his first wife died. The confusion that he had felt as a teenager, had suddenly come back to excite him. Seeking out young men to satisfy the lust in him. The misguided passion, which had left him a long time since, had been replaced with love of a different sort. Love for Lucrezia. Unconsummated love. "Wild Lucrezia" he called her, filled with admiration for the woman who had raised his sons with such great love and commitment. The woman he had felt envious of at times, knowing she could never love him unconditionally – as she had loved her Irishwoman.

"Yes, I have known this all these years. And when I am gone, you must go to her. Find her. Find the Irishwoman with whom you have shared your soul. The woman whom I have competed with and been envious of all these years. I am sorry."

Marco died with Lucrezia by his side, where she had remained for almost twenty years.

Having communicated by letter to Connie, she left for Ireland, to stay as a paying guest at Black Post Inn Ballygore.

Leaving prematurely three days later. Her heart in pieces.

Connie's son Paul had walked in on them in the bedroom and fled, distressed.

Lucrezia had wanted to follow him. To try to explain.

"Let him go." Connie watched Paul through the bedroom window as he ran across the yard, carrying his shoes. "Maybe it's time he learned the truth," she said dryly. "He can go straight in to his aunt in town now and tell her what he saw. He might as well be living there anyway."

Lucrezia had risen from the bed to put her arms around Connie, who stood watching her son as he rode his bicycle furiously down the avenue.

The bravado Connie was showing was a lie, Lucrezia knew instinctively. Inside she was crushed.

Things had never been the same afterwards. Connie's letters to Lucrezia had stopped. Lucrezia herself had eased off writing to Ballygore, not wanting to add to Connie's difficulties. She decided to go ahead and accept her stepson's suggestion and move to Boston, where he had settled. Her feelings towards Connie never waned – if anything they were deeper – but time had taken its toll, draining the energy from her soul. The war had changed her.

Lucrezia was forty-three when she moved to the west coast of America in 1952, having left her husband's body lying on top of his first wife's, in her family crypt in Sorrento. Her stepsons were pleased to see her getting on with her life, appreciative of the efforts she had made for them.

Renting an apartment in South Boston, she lived alone

for six years, taking time to heal, to paint, to live her own life, before setting out to find the home that had been in her head for almost thirty years.

There had been no mistaking it once she found it. She had recognised it instantly. In Provincetown. Where two young lovers, full of promises and dreams, had once made a pact to return and settle there. But the trials of life had instead distanced them. Kept them apart. But in body only. Lucrezia would fulfil the dream for both of them.

With the large window facing the main tourist area, it was perfect to showcase the many drawings that she had worked on since coming to America. A studio at the back of the shop with a white painted kitchen, a back door opening onto the splendours of the harbour. One bedroom, a small bathroom, bright and airy, painted in nautical blues. And fond memories of Connie Stapleton, and a dream that had been snatched away from them. Time and space no longer a factor. Lucrezia was content.

Opening the shop doors on Commercial Street each morning became a joy for the artist. She became familiar with her neighbours who warmed to the petite outspoken bohemian. Taking out a ten-year lease, she nailed a length of driftwood above the front door, a piece that she had salvaged from an incoming tide. The names '*Lucrezia and Connie*' she had inscribed across the wood.

Life was easy to live amongst like-minded people. People without an agenda. No room for condescension. Spending pleasant evenings in the company of friends, or alone with her music.

It had been nine years since she had visited Connie in Ireland. She had written to her on a number of occasions since moving to Provincetown, choosing her words carefully. Connie had responded, vaguely at times, giving little away, giving Lucrezia reason to believe that she was not in a good place – that she had little fight left in her. But Lucrezia refused to falter in her belief that one day they would be together. She had lived through the hardest years. As long as she had her health, age would be no barrier.

PART TWO

1964–1978

Chapter 14

Aggie Foley

1964

The girl on the black bicycle could hear people laughing as she cycled down Mill Road, down past Stapleton's pub. The bike was ancient – it had belonged to her mother – with its wicker basket attached to the handlebars. The saddle was set far too high for Agnes Foley to sit on comfortably – her feet could barely touch the pedals. The nut under the saddle was too rusty to loosen, to adjust the seat. But she hadn't a notion of walking the whole way as far as the post office, so the bike would have to do. Cycling on the footpath without sitting, made it easier for her to brake and jump off in an emergency, without breaking her neck.

She heard laughter for the second time as she reached the main street. Looking back, she saw a group of boys pointing at her, two fingers in their mouths, whistling at her.

"Go on, Aggie! Give us a gawk! Show us more!"

"Eejits!" she called back at them and cycled on, before hearing her name being called again – this time a girl's voice.

"Aggie! Aggie! Your dress is caught up! Aggie, stop! Agnes Foley!"

She turned her head again and spotted a girl at the far side of the road, shouting at her, waving frantically, trying to get her attention. It was Norah Gorman. What the feck did that young one want? She pressed the brakes as gently as she could, before jumping off the bike. It took her a few seconds to realise what all the commotion was about.

Agnes had cycled from her house, down Mill Road and onto the main street, with the back of her dress tucked inside her baby-blue knickers. Jerking her dress back into place, her face red but defiant, she parked the bicycle against the wall of the post office. Fuming, she turned around and, bending her arm, gave the lads the two fingers.

Norah Gorman was nearly tripping over herself crossing the road towards her.

"Are you all right, Aggie? I was trying to catch your attention there."

"Of course I'm all right, Norah Gorman. And why wouldn't I be? Wouldn't you be just fine too, if you'd cycled the whole way from my house, past your shop, and down the length of the main street, with your own big blue arse on display? And every fecking eejit in the town laughing at you!" Aggie was raging with herself.

"Well, at least they're clean, Aggie. And they're your own."

The two girls burst into laughter. Norah was thirteen. Agnes a year older.

Walking back up the main street towards home, they formed an unlikely friendship.

When Aggie got home, she told her mother what had happened.

"You and your letter, Mam! They were laughing their heads off at me. And that eejit of the Mackeys in the middle of them."

Aggie felt annoyed at her mother who turned her back on her youngest daughter to hide the laughter as she bent over in two, crossing her legs at the same time.

"Mam, stop it! I see you! I said stop it! Only for Norah Gorman from the shop warning me, I'd have cycled the whole way back up home again, not knowing a thing."

Her mother straightened herself. "Ah, come on now, Aggie, that could happen to a saint. Next time you'll check, before you go parading your underwear around the town. I hope 'twas your good knickers you had on and not them old faded pair." Her mother was goading her. "Did you say Norah? The quiet young one from the shop? Hilda's daughter? Isn't she a year behind you in school? According to Hilda, she's off to join some order of nuns in America. Her mother does be raving about her. I suppose there's hope for us all yet, Aggie. Maybe you'll find a vocation yourself and make us all more respectable."

Agnes knew when her mother was getting it up for her. Teasing her.

"Well, I'll tell you something, Mammy Foley – you'll be joining the nuns yourself before I ever do. But they don't take married women, do they? I think you have to be pure. A virgin like." Aggie had a similar sense of humour to her mother's. "But, Mam, Norah's great fun and we got on really well. I was surprised myself. I'd never even spoken to her before. She's awful quiet in school – she keeps to herself. Me and her had a great laugh on the way home. She was roaring laughing at me, Mam. Roaring laughing."

Aggie's mother, Josie, did her best to hold her tongue. But she couldn't. Up their own arses, they were. The Hilda one, full of her own importance since she married Francis Gorman. Just because he had two sisters in the nuns, and their eldest young fella was a Brother in the foreign missions.

"Oh, I know all about Hilda's pedigree. A crowd of cadgers that'd take the eye out of your head. Every single one of them. And that Francis Gorman, an oddity, full of bullshit, going around like he owns the place. Well matched the two of them. Her trying to pretend she's someone. And him leering at anything in a skirt. The dirty eye of him, and he gaping at all the young ones coming into the shop. Pretending to be all holy and pious, and he as randy as an old goat. That poor young one, Norah –

sure the whole town knows since the day she was born that they have her earmarked for the nuns."

From that day forward, the two girls were firm friends. Linking each other everywhere they went. A symbol of their closeness.

Aggie would call to the side door of the shop for Norah on her way to school. If she went into the shop without buying something, she would be told by Hilda to go back out and ring once at the side door.

Odd people, who weren't shy about letting Aggie know what they thought of her. When she rang the bell at the side door, she'd be told to wait outside, or to stand in the hallway but only if 'twas raining. She was never invited past the hallway into the kitchen, unless Norah brought her in.

Agnes didn't take it personally. Or let it upset her. She carried on being herself. Bursting in the front door of the shop. "Morning, Hilda, is Norah ready?"

"It'll be Missus Gorman to you, Agnes Foley."

Aggie guessed they didn't like her. She wasn't good enough for their Norah. It didn't bother her, and she continued to get on the wrong side of them.

"How'ya, Francie? Oh! I mean Mr Gorman. Is Her Ladyship ready?"

Breaking into a laugh, Agnes Foley was as cheeky as she could be to her best friend's parents.

Aggie couldn't help herself, especially when Norah's

mother was boasting about something. Inclined towards exaggeration, Aggie made things up. "I'm off home now for my dinner, Hilda. Roast pork, I'd say, that's if Mammy didn't forget to take it out of the deep freezer."

There would be no roast pork or roast anything. Aggie's mother didn't use the oven much. She loved her chip pan. And there was no freezer. Not because they couldn't afford to buy one. Her mother said there were more important things in life to be spending their money on.

They had a television. Her sister in England had sent a pack of plastic sheets to stick to the screen. But they got sick of changing them from yellow to blue to green to red. Her father had put them in the bin in the end. "Those yokes are pure stupid, Josie. Whoever said they made a black-and-white television look like a colour one was pulling your leg."

Her father worked in the shoe factory, along with most of the men on the street.

Aggie was the only one of the Foley children still at home. Her sisters had left for Birmingham at sixteen. Arriving home only once a year, usually at Christmas. White high heels, fur coats, with permed heads backcombed to the last and big handbags. Red lips and small Hamlet cigars. But they were good to Aggie, sending presents home for her birthday. And parcels of hand-me-down clothes.

Norah's parents, Hilda and Francis Gorman, ran the shop on Mill Road. It sold most things you could think of, and if they didn't have it in stock, they'd order it in from the local Cash and Carry – the locals knew that was to stop them spending their money elsewhere. From hammers to hair-curlers. From pipe tobacco to rosary beads. The shop sold everything – bulky items like four-stone bags of loose potatoes and toilet paper kept in the back of the shop, along with the turnips and whatever other large veg they had in stock.

The front of the shop stocked everything else, with the sausages and bacon held in the small glass case at one side of the counter. Half the time sour. Turned. Or well on the way. Sweets and chocolate kept at the other side, with cigarettes and tobacco on high shelves on the wall behind. Anything that wouldn't be stolen, or ruined by a shower of rain was kept outside, high enough off the ground to prevent it being urinated on by a passing dog.

The shop was busy from the time it opened its doors at quarter past seven sharp to catch the factory workers on their way to work. Closed at half past six in the evening once they had passed again on their way home.

Norah's future in the religious had been mapped out for her by her parents. Just as Damian her brother's had been before her. All according to plan, with Damian joining the foreign missions as a Christian brother, teaching in the Philippines. The fact that they seldom heard from him was well accounted for with the almost daily mention of his name in the shop, when customers would ask after him. Hilda was beside herself when one of the priests or religious came into the shop. They'd ask about Damian and offer to have a quiet word with Norah, if she ever wanted to talk.

Norah's mother hadn't been too pleased when the curate made reference to seeing her with Agnes Foley. Somewhere where they shouldn't have been, her mother had said.

"I don't know what he's talking about, Mam, and if we shouldn't be there – what was he doing there himself then – wherever it was?" Norah had defended her friend.

From that day forward Norah was given more hours in the shop. They couldn't hold her in on a Sunday, when the shop was closed, but they used every excuse to keep her off the street. No more delaying on the way home from school – she had to help her father out in the shop.

But the girls made time to be together whenever they could, and Aggie wasn't shy about calling in to the shop for a chat when Norah was there, knowing by the look on Hilda's face that she wasn't welcome.

The bell on the door would jingle, but on a hot day when the door was left wide open, there was no jingle, and Agnes would be there in the shop laughing and joking with her pal. Until Hilda would appear from the kitchen.

"Come on now, Agnes Foley, Norah can see you tomorrow."

Norah hadn't mentioned to her parents that she wished to look at other options for her life. Aggie had been pestering her to broach the subject. But she couldn't.

Every evening after tea when they recited the rosary, her parents added an extra prayer.

"Holy Mother of God, bless our Damian and Norah. Keep them safe from the perils of evil. Grant that Norah remain pure in her thoughts and keep her free from mortal sin. Amen."

Norah said nothing. Believing that when the time came she would handle it. Norah didn't like upsetting people.

Chapter 15

Best Friends

1964-1968

Aggie Foley's house was little different to the rest of the small houses on the left as you walked up Mill Road. The houses had been built to house the mill workers back in the day. In later years the tenants were given the option to buy out their homes for one pound each. Those that couldn't afford the money were accommodated to borrow the pound. The result was a row of privately owned cottages on either side of the road. Big enough to rear all the children that came out of them, and small enough for people in bigger houses to turn their noses up at. Whitewashed fronts, some stripped back to stone, others not.

One door in, facing the back door out. Long narrow gardens reaching down to the back alley where the dustbins were kept. Same on both sides of the road. Gardens that produced flowers in backyards that reared pigs in harder times.

Two doors up from Stapleton's public house, a three-minute walk down the road and across to Gormans' shop.

Agnes didn't need to duck her head as she walked through her own front door. Neither did any of her family. Norah Gorman had to lower her head or risk banging it off the lintel.

Agnes couldn't wait to leave home when she was older, as she threatened her mother when she was being given out to.

She loved her parents, but was looking forward to living her own life when the time came.

Herself and Norah would move to London, just the two of them. They would get the train to Dublin and take the ferry from there, just like her sisters had done when they'd left. Or they could get the coach the whole way over, like Aggie's parents did, when they were going over on the ferry to visit her sisters. Having family there made all the difference.

And when she left home her parents could just get on with their carry-on in the bedroom, without her having to cover her head with the shame. The embarrassment of it. And at their age. Hearing the grunting and groaning through the bedroom wall. With her father pleading "*Oh Josie . . . Josie . . . Josie . . .*" as if he was in pain. And her mother shushing him to be quiet. It had taken her some time when she was younger to figure out what they were at. She used to think that he was showing her something. Or that her mother had passed out in the bed. It had taken her time to work out exactly what her mother had belonging to her father. With him half shot with the drink, looking for his conjugal rights from her mother, who seemed intent on sleeping. Keeping Aggie awake half the night.

Aggie shouting out at them from her bed. Banging at the wall between them. *"Mammy, will you for God's sake give him back whatever the hell you have belonging to him!"*

And she certainly wouldn't miss listening to her father singing "Danny Boy" from the bed, until four in the morning, and she looking like a wet rag going to school the next day.

And she wouldn't miss the snoring every night of the week. Through the walls and the whole house rattling. Aggie didn't know how her mother managed to sleep for as many hours as she did. Then again, she had a lie-in, most days.

Some nights her mother would move from her own bed during the night, and get in beside Aggie. "Shove over, Aggie. Your father is snoring like a pig in there." But she'd be back in the marital bed the very next night.

Josie Foley loved her man, and wouldn't have anyone say a bad word against him.

Aggie recalled the night she had played the trick on her father. She put a two-foot plaster statue of the Virgin Mary at his side of the bed, under the covers, with the veiled head resting on his pillow. It had belonged to her grandmother who had died the year before. Sniggering as she got back into her own bed beside her mother, who slept soundly. Unable to stay awake, she'd fallen asleep, waking up to hear him calling out for her mother. In an awful state.

"Josie, come here! Josie! Josie! Jaysus, will you come here? 'Tis a miracle. The Virgin Mary has appeared to me. Oh Jesus, Josie!"

Aggie left her bed to witness the spectacle. There was her father in his long johns, kneeling by his bed, hands together, head bowed, praying to the statue in the bed. And her mother giving her a dagger of a look.

"Our Lady, Aggie. It's a miracle. A pure miracle."

The following evening her mother and father were waltzing around the kitchen to Nat King Cole when she walked in the door from school. No dinner ready, and she starving and bleary-eyed from the lack of sleep.

On the way to school that morning Aggie had told Norah what she had done to her father the night before. The two girls had laughed their way up the road.

They were seldom seen without each other. Agnes the petite, sharp-tongued extrovert, who cursed and swore, using every expletive known to her, five-foot-two in height, her black curls bouncing on her shoulders as she walked. Brown eyes and a voice that she wasn't afraid to make good use of. Norah, the opposite. Introverted, quietly spoken and naïve – at her happiest when in the company of her best pal, Aggie Foley.

Norah Gorman wasn't the sort of girl to draw attention to herself. Tall. Strong tall. Big round blue eyes that gave her away before she ever opened her mouth. Her voice in keeping with the look in eyes that welled up at the slightest mention of a sob story. Soft. Norah's eyes were big enough to hold the tears for longer than most. When the tears did fall, they'd be big huge tears, followed by great big sobs. Aggie said that it was best that she didn't get upset too often, as there was no consoling her once she started.

Aggie became well used to hearing about the vocation from Norah, but she wasn't at all convinced that Norah wanted it for herself. She wasn't afraid to call her friend out on her daft notion.

"Are you stark raving mad, Norah Gorman? A nun, if you don't mind! Mass every day. What am I saying? Twice a day. And you'll be sent to convert the pagans, I suppose, in no time, in the missions like."

"Aggie, will you please let it go. Just leave it alone. It's hard enough having it drummed into my head at home, besides you starting."

"OK. No more messing so . . . But can I just say one more thing? You'll be a glorified baker in that order, making Communion bread for the priests for half the day, and praying with the rest of them in between times. And how the hell is your hair going to look, sticking out in the front from that hood or veil thing or whatever they're wearing nowadays? I've seen the old ones, the hair never gets to see the light of day, flattened to the last, and hidden forever more. And when the new shorter uniforms came out, 'twas too late for them. I'd say half of them were well bald by that stage." Aggie made it up as she went along. Anything to deter her friend from entering.

"Agnes Foley, you're a terrible young one. Of course they're not bald. What a horrible thing to say. They just chose to stay in the old habits. So would you, if you were covered up from head to toe for fifty or sixty years."

"But I wouldn't be, would I? Be a nun like. Ever."

"I don't care, Aggie, what you say, about all that material stuff. My love will be for the divine, not of a worldly nature. So it's a small sacrifice to pay. Anyway, I'm following my vocation. You know that."

Aggie lost her patience at times with her friend.

"What I know is that your mother and father have you brainwashed, Norah. They want you to be a nun just to make themselves look good, that's all. Look at you. No offence, like. Down on your knees every evening after your tea, with your elbows resting on the kitchen chair, saying a decade of the rosary to keep you pure. So you'll be trained as a baker or a teacher, if you want. So what? Or a nurse. But you'll never have a husband or a family of your own, Norah. And you'll never know what it's like to have it off."

"I'll have God, won't I? And the sisters in the congregation will be my family."

Aggie couldn't tell half of the time if Norah was getting it up for her or not.

"What did you say the vows were again, Norah? Oh Yeah. Chastity. Well, you'll have no worries there, if you don't mind me saying so. Or with the Obedience for that matter. Now. If 'twas me. I'd have a right problem with them two. Especially the Obedi– I mean the Chastity."

Aggie loved to watch Norah laughing at her jokes. "Well, it wouldn't be for me. That's for sure. I love my curly hair too much. Just imagine what a veil would do to it." She pondered before speaking again. "I wonder do nuns ever put a rinse in their hair, dye their hair, like? Or shave their legs, come to think of it?"

Norah wasn't enjoying the conversation as much as her friend was.

"Aggie, there's no need to be so disrespectful. Anyway, It's a long way off yet. I don't expect to be going anywhere until I'm at least seventeen, and that's ages away. As for my hair, it will sit very nicely under the veil, thank you very much. Now, will you give it a rest or you can walk home on your own."

Aggie and Norah could never fall out for long.

Aggie was pleased when Norah finally admitted that she sometimes had doubts about entering.

"I'm still too afraid to bring it up at home," she said. "But I've two more years. That's ages away."

Aggie would finish school after her Inter Cert the following year. Once she'd finished her three-month secretarial course, she'd get a job around Ballygore to improve her typing speed, and wait for Norah to leave for England with her.

Her sisters sent money home on a regular basis to cover the cost of the ferry for her parents, who regularly travelled over to Birmingham on the night boat. Agnes had gone with them when she was younger, but not so much of late, remaining at home to mind the house and cater for herself. The few times she had gone over as a younger teenager, she ended up babysitting for the growing number of nephews and nieces, while the adults went off to the social clubs around Birmingham.

She liked being at home on her own, where she could do as she pleased. Smoking one of her father's cigarettes had nearly choked her that first time. After trying her first vodka, taken from one of the duty-free bottles in the press, Agnes looked forward to her parents' trips. She added small amounts of water to replace what she'd taken, before realising that her parents didn't notice the difference. They drank what was there. And when it was gone, they bought more duty-free.

Her mother had made an attempt to persuade her to leave school before the Inter Cert and apply for work at the draper's on Spring Street, where she herself had worked from the age of fourteen.

"Aggie, you're going to be fifteen at the end of May. Time to be thinking about getting yourself a job, love. 'Tisn't as if you're all that interested in school. Look at your father and me. Didn't we do all right and we both left school after the primary exam?"

Aggie would bring Norah to her house where she was assured of being made welcome.

The girls found a way of poking fun at most things. Up in Aggie's bedroom – Norah trying on her friend's more up-to-date clothes, the laughter being heard all over the house.

Aggie pleading with Norah, "Norah, Jesus! Stop. Take

it off. I said take it off, or you'll burst out through it. Stop, will you, don't move an inch, and I'll ease it off over your head. Sit on the bed. Jaysus, my new top, it'll be all stretched. No offence, Norah Gorman."

"None taken, Agnes Foley," said Norah, laughing her way out of Aggies crimplene top.

Aggie, trying on Norah's good camel-hair coat, reaching down past her ankles, the sleeves long enough to cover her hands.

"Aggie, with your petite little limbs, a child's coat would fit you. I'm a grown-up size. Here, give it back to me. No offence, Agnes Foley."

"None taken, Norah Gorman."

The girls burst into a fit of giggles.

Aggie thought it a good idea they become blood sisters. She'd read it in a book, she said. Screaming her head off, using a pin to draw blood before pressing her bloodied finger together with Norah's.

"Blood sisters, Norah."

Sincere in their belief they had a bond that could never be broken.

"Let's get one thing clear here right now, Norah Gorman. Just because your blood is making its way through my veins as we speak, I am not related to your parents. No. Thanks all the same, let's get that one straight. And there better be none of that vocation stuff going into my veins either."

"That works both ways, Agnes Foley, though I *am* very fond of your parents. I'd be half afraid in case any of that alcohol in your father's blood has reached yours. Then again, you've enough of the stuff in your blood as it is. No offence, Agnes Foley."

"None taken, Norah Gorman."

The girls burst out laughing, entwining their little fingers, making a vow to have no secrets from each other. Ever.

"Imagine, Norah, think about it, now that you have my blood running through your veins, you'll probably lose the notion of joining the nuns. And I might become pure. Well maybe. *Aah,* think of all the fun we'll have in England when we move in together!"

Norah hadn't replied. Aggie knew her well enough to know that she had a mind of her own – precisely why Aggie liked her so much. She trusted her far more than any of the bitches in school, that'd be all smiles to your face, and then cut you in two the minute your back was turned. Norah Gorman was the best friend in the world and Aggie Foley knew how lucky she was to have her.

Chapter 16

Moving On

The time was coming for Aggie to sit her Inter Cert. A pass was all she wanted. She was having far too much fun to be studying more than she needed to.

At last, waving her cert over her head, she walked up the street. Relieved.

After a night out with Norah to celebrate at the local dance, Aggie stayed away from the shop, knowing that her mother wouldn't be too pleased to hear from a customer that her daughter was out on the floor, stuck to a fella during a slow waltz.

Aggie was of the mind that once Norah got a taste for the fellas, she'd give up the crazy notion of entering the convent. A couple of nights around the back of the dancehall, with a few vodkas in her, might shift her focus. But Aggie had been wrong. Norah was Norah. "Norah, come on – you're making a holy show of yourself, sitting there, refusing to dance with them. Just say yes when they ask. Doesn't matter if they look like fecking eejits, just dance with the feckers!"

The slagging that Norah got from the boys was more than Agnes could bear for her. If they'd spoken to her like that, she'd have told them where to go. To fuck off for themselves. But not Norah, whose big eyes welled up with the biggest tears when the slagging started in the dance hall.

"Where's your knitting? You should have brought it with you."

"Stay where you are, girl, the size of you! Jaysus, there aren't too many here that would see the top of your head, if you stood up."

"What have we here, a giant, is it? Norah Gorman and the Beanstalk."

Norah didn't know where to turn. Mortified. Aggie felt for her friend. Thinking that Norah would loosen up with some vodka, she slipped a drop into her drink. Well ... a lot more than a drop, after which Norah took to the dance floor for a slow waltz, holding on to the poor fella for dear life. Worse still, she then found herself standing with her after the dance, around the corner of the dancehall, holding her up. Norah had vomited up the vodka and orange, along with whatever else had been in her stomach. Aggie had nearly vomited herself when she spotted the carrots. And the stench. It hadn't helped her friend's image when the boys came around the corner to slag her off. But Agnes was well able for them.

"Fuck off with yourself, Marcus Glynn, and take a

good look in the mirror when you get home! If it's not fucking cracked already. You'd be better placed in a field of soft sheep with their arses facing you, than standing there gawking at the two of *us*."

The other boys laughed. Marcus was fuming.

Norah straightened herself up. Aggie linked her friend and started towards the main door, fully intending to go back in to the dance.

But Norah had had enough.

"Aggie, come on, we'll go home. Don't answer them back. Please . . ."

The boys were not giving up.

"Aggie Foley! Who the fuck do you think you are and you after being dragged up? Miss High and Mighty and you living in the Mill Cottages with an auld fella who doesn't know his arse from his elbow half the time, and a mother who spends more time on the night boat to England than staying at home with you."

"I said fuck off, Marcus! Or are your ears stuck up in your arse, like the rest of you?"

"Miss Mighty yourself, and you off behind the hall every Saturday night, dropping your drawers for whoever might fancy a bit of rotten meat."

Agnes was well able for them, but from the look on her friend's face it was definitely time to leave. Norah's face was green, the front of her blouse covered with bright yellow vomit. Once Aggie had seen her safely in the side door of the shop, she ran home. Relieved she hadn't been seen by Norah's mother.

Norah had been mortified the following day.

"Ah, feck them, Norah. They're a right bunch of dopes. They just act like that with the drink on them. Meet them on their own in the cold light of day and they're wimps. They'd piss in their pants if I caught one of them up a laneway, I can tell you."

Norah hadn't been convinced.

As Aggie began her secretarial course, the conversations between the two girls took on a more serious note.

"Jesus, Norah, you better tell your mother you've having second thoughts about joining the convent next year. You'll only have to finish out the year at school, and they'll have you packed off before you know it. It won't come as such a shock to them, if you prepare them now like. If you leave it any longer, they'll drop dead with two heart attacks when they do hear."

"Aggie, I'm so scared I'll disappoint them."

"Seriously though, Mammy said your mother is telling every second person who goes into the shop that you're going to London as a postulant next September. And then off to Alabama for good. Jesus, Norah, even I'm getting nervous now. You can tell your father that Aggie Foley said 'We're heading off to London to get two fellas, with plenty of dough. And we'll be shifting all around us'."

Agnes couldn't control her giggles, but she could sense Norah's discomfort the more she broached the subject.

"I don't want to talk about it, Aggie. It makes my heart

race when I think of it, and if I was going to change my mind I should surely have said something before now. Somedays, I don't know what I want. I never thought to even question it until I met you. And now I'm all confused. But I don't really fit in around here, like you do. Do I? You saw the state of me at the dance. I stood out like a sore thumb, and how embarrassing to get sick all over myself in front of those fellas! And then having to face my mother, covered in vomit."

Aggie knew that Norah had a point. Her mother maintained that Norah would fit right in with the nuns.

"Well, in fairness, Aggie, I can't exactly see Norah being too comfortable sitting on a high stool below in Stapleton's on a Saturday night. Can you? Apart from anything else, the two below in the shop would throw a fit."

But Aggie wasn't going to say that to Norah. Preferring instead to concentrate on her plan for the two of them.

"Anyhow, just think about the two of us together in England. We could leave the month after you finish school. And there'll be loads of places to go. We can stay at my sister's place in Birmingham, 'til we get our own flat. She'll sort us out no problem. But you have to mention something at home, Norah. *Now.*"

Chapter 17

Shop Gossip

1968

Moira Kiely tugged at the belt of her new white knee-length Mac, as she left her house on Mill Road. She liked to show off her figure and, if that meant tightening her belt beyond what was comfortable, so be it! Her soft permed blonde hair sat just above her shoulders. At forty-six, five foot one inch in height, her cork-soled platforms gave her the few extra inches to stand on. Tapping the side of her pocket to make sure she had her cigarettes and lighter, Moira crossed over the street to Gormans' shop.

Moira's house gleamed. Bleached once a week, first thing on a Monday morning before she headed out the door to work. Moira enjoyed scrubbing. She did it for a living.

No boots allowed in her house, especially on a Monday. With herself and Arthur and the five kids, it hadn't been easy. But they had managed with Moira's wages. Arthur hadn't been so lucky with work. She was regarded by many as being the best cleaner in Ballygore. Proud of her profession, she raised her children to appreciate the value of money, keeping a post office book for each of them once they were old enough to earn, taking their wage packets from them on a Friday, leaving them with just enough to keep them going, putting the rest away.

Two of the girls had married well in England, both working. Good jobs. One in the school canteen and the other a dancer on the stage.

Moira had been raging when Hilda Gorman said she'd heard that her Delia was working in one of them queer places. Maura told her to mind her own bloody business, that her daughter was working on the stage in a posh club, and nowhere near the places that anyone from Ballygore might be frequenting. Hilda had shut up when Moira enquired as to her source. She asked had it been her Francis who had said such a thing, half joking that Francis must have been in one of them queer places himself.

Moira was well able to hold her own and defend her family when she saw the need. Especially with Hilda Gorman who was only waiting to dish up the dirt.

Expertly flicking the burning end of her cigarette, before replacing the butt back into her cigarette box, she opened the door to the shop, the bell above the door tinkling to announce her.

"Cold one, Moira," said the voice behind the counter. Hilda Gorman was stacking chocolate bars in the glass stand in front of her.

"A pan loaf there, Hilda, and twenty Carrolls. Jesus, 'tis giving them up I should be, Hilda, with the cough I've on me. Give me out a bottle of bleach there, as well."

Clearing her throat before she spoke again. Breathing in deeply.

"Grand smell, Hilda, were you baking?"

"Oh, that'll be our Norah inside. She's a devil for the baking. Won't the convent be delighted when they get their hands on her?"

"God, yes. She'll be off next year, isn't it? God help us. She's a great young one all the same, knowing what she wants at such a young age. What will she be … sixteen? You were saying that 'twas what she always wanted, Hilda. No fear any of my lot would join the religious! I could hardly get them up out of the bed to go to Mass. And now that they're all off living their own lives, apart from poor Johnny, I'd say they don't darken the door of a church. Was Norah always religious, Hilda? She got that from Francis' side, I'd say."

Moira liked to rise her.

"As I told you before, Moira, she's always been inclined towards the religious life. Francis has two sisters nuns, you know. One is in the convent in London. Did I mention that she's the community's Novice Director? And the older sister, very musical, high up in the missions in Alabama."

"Yeah. You told me that a few times, Hilda. Francis' people are very respectable all the same, aren't they?"

"Our Norah has wanted nothing more since she could

talk. Francis and myself couldn't be prouder."

"I'd say ye are all right, Hilda. And your parents, God rest their souls, would be more than proud, I'd say. The only religious to come out of Martha's Park."

Moira could see Hilda's face redden in annoyance as she continued.

"Different, I suppose, for Francis' family. Country people. They'd be well used to it, wouldn't they?"

Sensing the frustration building up in Hilda, she quickly changed the subject. Moira knew exactly what she was doing. Who did that Hilda think she was, with the tone on her? And she as working-class as Moira herself?

"I don't know what poor Agnes Foley above is going to do when your Norah goes. Sure, they're as thick as thieves, the two of them. I see them up –"

"Oh, Agnes Foley will be just fine!" Hilda snapped. "She'll latch on to some other poor fool, ever before Norah touches down in London. That's of course if she doesn't get herself in trouble in the meantime – one thing we'll never have to worry about with our Norah. We're paying the money for her to fly over to London, you know. Ourselves."

Moira could see that Hilda was flustered.

"Well, any news yourself, Moira?" said Hilda in an attempt to thwart the conversation.

Moira knew well how to get one up on Hilda. The two women had come to live on the road twenty-five years before. Both from Martha's Park. They had history. All

Hilda wanted was gossip, as long as she wasn't seen to be giving away anything herself. Moira knew that she'd go inside that kitchen of hers, relaying everything back to that excuse of a husband of hers.

They ran the shop between them. Hilda looking for information and Francis with the ear cocked, rarely getting involved except when weekly payments on the book had been missed. He'd have a pinched smile on his face, as he brought the customer to the far side of the shop, to advise them that there would be no more tick, if a payment wasn't made by the end of the week. And only essentials allowed on the book for a week afterwards. Everyone on the road knew that once Francis Gorman did his weekly tally on the books, someone was bound to be in for it the following day.

"Oh sure, divil a thing, Hilda. I'm working flat out at the vet's place in Kilnarick these last few weeks, making the place shipshape for the new vet and his American wife. In fairness, the place was in a bit of a mess when they landed but, Jesus, if you heard her, you'd think she was after coming straight from Buckingham Palace. Poor Cox, the old vet, wasn't able to take care of the place with the gangrene. Although, wouldn't you imagine he'd have it spruced up to some degree, him being a vet and all? Educated, like."

"Oh, I heard about that, Moira, the other day. I believe a couple of his toes fell off."

"Jesus, Imagine, Hilda. I heard them say he's not doing well at all. He's well stuck now with the sister above in Monaghan – there'll be no more tearing and dragging for him."

"I wonder will he be able to walk without the toes?"

"Couldn't tell you, Hilda. Poor man. This new lad is a researcher of some kind. Seems like a nice enough man. Julian. And wait 'til I tell you the wife's name. Darlene … Darlene, if you don't mind. She's much younger than him. Chatty. She doesn't hold back I can tell you. Telling me that they're only here for the eighteen months before heading back to America. And you know the place really wasn't half as bad as she was making it out to be. Different, I suppose, to what she came from. 'Twas through Paul Grogan I got the hours, fair play to him."

Moira was enjoying the chat. Relighting her cigarette.

"Isn't it a fine place out there in Black Post Inn, all the same, Hilda? And the Mattie fella, above in Stapleton's with the Johanna one. No shame on either of them all these years. And I used to think that one was a lady up there. Shows how wrong you can be.

But, sure, look at poor Connie, left to fend for herself when he took up with Her Ladyship. Must be what? About fifteen years ago now. Connie doesn't be great, you know, these days. Whatever medication she's on, I suppose. Paul had to have a word with the doctor. There's men for you, Hilda. Mattie wanted the younger flesh and when Connie wasn't giving it to him, he went crawling to Johanna, who I'd say was well up for it after all them years without it. I remember Mattie in the horse and trap, with Paul propped up beside him, and when he got the truck it used to be parked at the back of the pub. And Paul asleep on the bench at the fire. And the town talking about them. I remember it well."

"Jesus, Moira Kiely, you're wicked for the gossip. Do you know that? Just wicked."

"No more than yourself, Hilda. Anyway, I better be off!" Picking up the loaf of bread off the counter, she continued, "Look at Paul now. He's a stickler in the house – he leaves me a list to do, as if Connie wasn't living there at all. He's been out with the vet all the week, giving them a hand. Of course, we all know the only reason he's there is to free up the vet, to tend to them half-dead animals he does be buying all over the country."

"You've more than enough work to keep you going so, Moira. You're a professional at this stage. I wish that our Norah would get herself a little job outside of here for a few months, to keep her away from ... off the streets. If you hear of anything, let me know?"

"I will indeed, Hilda. I'll get back to you if I hear anything. She must be bored all the same, now that Agnes has nearly finished her secretarial course. What month are we in at all? May, isn't it? Anyway, I'm on my way back out to Kilnarick this minute to help the Yank with a bit of wallpapering. Jesus, she has mad taste. 'Tis all big squares and hoops. Orange and yellow. Like something you'd see in one of them kaleidoscopes."

Both women laughed insincerely as the door bell sounded.

"Jesus, look at the time, Hilda. I'm here all day. Put

them on the book for me like a good woman, and you might as well throw me out another packet of fags. I'll see you Friday."

Moira chuckled to herself when she left the shop. There wasn't many who could get a rise out of Hilda Gorman. But she could. She felt bad for talking about the vet's wife like that, but sure what was she saying – only the truth. Commenting on the wallpaper – well, she was entitled to her opinion. She felt sorry for the Yank all the same. There'd be plenty gossip going on around the town once Darlene made herself known. She was certainly different, and that was for sure.

The following evening, as Hilda went out the back to lock up the gate, she was muttering to herself. Francis had said he'd check to see it was closed. No sign of him.

It was a bright night. Hilda opened the gate to hunt the cats who were making a racket outside on the lane. Jumping back as fast as she could with the shock.

Agnes Foley nearly fell in on top of her. And Moira's Kiely's son, Johnny, in after her. She didn't need to ask what they were doing. His pants down around his ankles. And as for the Agnes one, the shock on her face was enough.

"Off with ye now, you dirty articles! Wait 'til I see your mother first thing in the morning, Johnny Kiely. And as for you, Agnes Foley, what else would we expect? You're a common trollop. Off home with the two of you now with your disgusting carry-on. Filthy things, the pair of you!"

Banging the gate shut, hearing the two outside running down the back lane. Giggling.

She turned around. *"Francis! Francis!"* she called. *"Where the hell are you?"* She could see no sign of her husband.

Then Francis seemed to appear out of nowhere.

Agnes was sure there'd be a backlash, after being caught with Johnny Kiely by Hilda Gorman on the back lane. And that Francis fella had a creepy look in his eyes when he'd stuck his head out the gate earlier. Anyone that used the back alley to go for a shift, knew that Francis was probably in behind the wall. Spying. Peeping out his own back gate which everyone knew had been left off the latch by him. The dirty bastard.

Johnny said that Francis was definitely in behind the wall. He said he got a kick, thinking that Francis might be watching them. It had been bright enough with the light from the moon. He said that everyone knew Francis Gorman was a Peeping Tom. Except Hilda.

She'd a hunch Hilda Gorman wouldn't open her mouth to her mother. She'd be half afraid to, in case her father had a go at her for bad-mouthing his Aggie. Drunk or sober, no one could say one bad word about any member of his family to Peter Foley and expect to escape the consequences.

Opening the door of the shop the following morning, Aggie prepared herself for what was to come. Hilda stopped what she was doing, checking behind her to make sure the kitchen door was closed.

"What have you to say for that disgusting carry on last night, Agnes Foley?"

"Two loose Carrolls, Hilda, and a box of matches. Thanks very much." Ignoring the question. Leaving the exact coins on the counter in front of her. The ice was broken.

Hilda Gorman knew better than to refuse Aggie in the shop.

As for Johnny, that was the last time Aggie'd be caught going up the back lane with him. The twat.

'Twasn't worth it. Aggie had learned her lesson. And no sign of Norah all week, and when she rang the hall doorbell no answer. She thought she saw her at the net curtain upstairs. But couldn't be sure. Hilda had probably stopped Norah from seeing her. She'd give her the week to cool off. After that they'd be back to normal.

Aggie had lost her virginity at fifteen. She'd told Norah, who didn't want to hear the details.

"Jesus, Norah, I had it off with a fella. And you haven't even asked me for the details. Or who the fella was even? Well, I'll tell you anyway. I met him at the dance, when you were gone to Cork visiting your relations. He was an English fella, home on holidays. Loaded he was. Very posh. He said he wanted to see me again, to stay in touch like, but I was having none of it. We did it standing up. You do know you can't get pregnant if you're not lying down?"

Norah had covered her ears, not wanting to hear anymore.

Aggie hadn't a notion of telling her that she'd lost her virginity in the back of a van, with the drummer from the band.

Aggie was sure that Norah didn't want to enter. And if Norah were to search deep enough inside herself, she would realise it too. But she wouldn't, because she was always thinking of others. And she would never in a million years let her parents down.

Aggie could see through the two of them. Francis and Hilda. But Norah couldn't, and poor Damian definitely hadn't. He was already done for. And the collection of mission boxes on the shop counter collecting money. Chained to the counter with a loose chain. Full to the brim, all they were doing was grigging the people, teasing those who hadn't a spare penny, rattling the few coins at the bottom of the tins after the priest from the missions called to empty them. When Aggie was younger she'd often been tempted to poke out a few coins, when she saw them sticking out of the slot. She could have easily grabbed a few with the tips of her fingers. She had tried, but Hilda must have known what she was thinking and moved the tin out of her reach. "Conscience money," Aggie's father called it. Aggie's mother said they were selling indulgences.

Aggie had wondered why Norah's parents hadn't joined the religious themselves in the early days. Her mother said it was because they wanted the sex. Francis himself had been earmarked for the priesthood, but had got Hilda in the family way.

Chapter 18

The End of Normal

1969

The doctor in Kilnarick confirmed that Norah Gorman was five months pregnant.

"Twenty weeks near enough," he'd said.

She was sixteen. Her mother had suspected something was wrong when she heard Norah getting sick in the bathroom a number of times. But she had not been prepared for what she was about to hear at the doctor's surgery.

Norah was in shock. Total disbelief. Her mother had cried for two days solid and, for a week after that, every time she looked at her daughter the tears would well up in her eyes. That's when she wasn't roaring at her.

"You're a disgrace, Norah Gorman! A common disgrace! You disgust me! Get out, get out!" she'd roared the minute they landed home. Francis had been busy at the back of the shop. *"Get out of my sight, before I kill you with my bare hands!"*

Then she took to making Norah kneel in front of the holy statue on the landing, trying to force her to confess who the father was. And slapping her when she'd only wail *"I don't know! I don't know! I can't remember!"*

Begging the saints to hear her prayer, Norah felt that Saint Anthony had turned his back on her. She was paying him for nothing, bribing him, putting her money in the tin box chained to the shop counter. She begged the saints. "*Please … please …* stop me being pregnant. *Please, please,* let me wake up and it'll all be a dream. Jesus, please! I'll become a nun in an enclosed order. I'll never speak to another soul again. I'll do whatever you want, just stop me from being pregnant."

At the end of the week Francis had demanded to know what was going on. Being told it was woman stuff by Hilda had not been a satisfactory response for him, given the atmosphere in the house. He waited until he was in bed that night with his wife.

"What in the name of God is going on, Hilda? And don't tell me it's women's business. I can see by you you're upset all the time and our Norah is going around as white as a sheet. You never mentioned what the doctor said. Is she sick?"

Hilda leaned towards him, knowing what she was about to tell him would destroy him. Things could never be the same again, no matter what the outcome. Unable to hold it in any longer she blurted it out.

"Our Norah has only gone and got herself into trouble, Francis. She's expecting. Five months gone."

"What? What?" He sat straight up in the bed. *"What are you saying? What?* You're stark raving mad, Hilda, if you think that. Sit up, will you?" He shook her shoulder.

She didn't move. "I know. I know it's an awful shock to get. I've had the week to think about it. Wasn't I there in Doctor Culhane's surgery with her when he examined her? Right there. There's no mistake. She's expecting all right." She breathed a deep sigh of relief that she had finally told him.

Her husband did not offer to comfort his wife who lay on her side, her eyes wide open.

Francis was not holding back. "Wait 'til I get my hands on her. There's no question of her having it. That's not going to happen – we'd be ruined in the town. Destroyed. And there'll be no bastard child coming in my front door, I'll tell you that much. What about the auld one in Spring Street? What do they call her? The Knitting Needle. Let her take care of it. Every dog in the street knows that she's got rid of many a mistake in the town."

Hilda shot up in the bed.

"No way are we getting mixed up with that one. You know why they call her the knitting needle, don't you?"

"Don't be so stupid, woman. Of course I do."

"No, Francis, she's not a great knitter. She uses the bloody knitting needle on the girls. Put it like this, many a girl was left with a badly damaged bladder after being poked by her. Now do you get me? No convent would accept her then. She could end up with us for life, wearing a nappy."

"Lord Almighty, woman, that's enough. You'd better pull yourself together – now isn't the time for going soft – we need to be practical. She went off and got herself into this mess and there's only one way out of it. And in six months' time, once it's all out of the way, it'll be water under the bridge. I feel like going in there this minute and dragging her out of the bed. She's no better than the Foley bitch up the road."

"You'll do no such thing. She'll get her come-uppance, don't you worry."

Hilda went straight to Norah's room the following morning. Norah was kneeling by the bed dressed in her school uniform, her eyes swollen from crying.

"There'll be no school for you today, miss. And no meeting up with the Agnes one. You're banned from leaving this house. Do you hear me? *Banned.* Your father and myself have been awake all night talking. We've made our sorry decision, and if you even attempt to talk to Agnes Foley, or anyone else for that matter, believe you me, it'll be the end of us all. You might as well have it announced from the pulpit. I'm warning you now in time or there'll be hell to pay."

Norah looked back at her mother, her eyes welling up with fresh tears. "Yes, Mam. I mean, no, Mam."

"Now, get out of that uniform. You're not fit to wear it. You're not to leave this room unless myself or your father say so. Is that clear?"

Hilda stood at the bedroom door, looking down at her daughter who remained on her knees by the bed. Raising her hand, she walked over and struck the back of Norah's head.

"Get that innocent look off your face, and you after having it off with some fella. How could you have done this to us?" More tears.

Her mother had again pleaded with her, wanting to know who she had intercourse with, before slapping her again across the head with the full force of her hand, telling her daughter she'd beat it out of her. Then shouting at Norah to get out of her sight.

Herself and Francis had talked until dawn. Eventually coming up with the best course of action. The only course of action.

There were places for girls like Norah. She would go to the Mother and Baby home down the country. Francis would make the call first thing in the morning. Hilda would stay out of it. Francis would take care of everything.

"Fran, we're in the month of May. Norah was due to go to London over to Celine anyway at the start of September. According to Doctor Culhane, she's due around the end of September, so we can make up some excuse for Celine, for the delay in sending her. And by the time it's born and out of the way, she can go straight to the convent from the Home. Tell Celine she's thinking of doing a three-month bookkeeping course before she goes. That'll cover us. And we'll say here to the customers that she left early for London, that 'twas her own choice.

It'll all work out, as long as the Foley one is kept away from her."

"I hadn't thought of that. I'll write to Celine once she's gone out of Ballygore. It'll be five or six months so, before she's ready to leave for London."

Francis had tried to accuse Hilda, but she wasn't having it.

"And how come you didn't you notice all this before now? And you a woman yourself, looking at her every day. If she's five months gone, surely you should have copped it?"

"Don't start on me now, Francis. How in the name of God was I supposed to cop that? Never in a million years would I have thought this could happen. Never in a million years. I'd say the fact that she's so well padded around the middle, 'twas easy hide it."

"Jesus, what a bloody mess! Can you imagine the talk in the town, if that gets out? History repeating itself, but the difference was that you had me to marry you. Well, it won't get out. Never. Do you hear me, Hilda, *never*. And if I knew the bastard that she opened her legs for, I'd swing for him, kill him stone dead. Are you sure she said nothing to you?"

"Fran, if I knew anything, I'd tell you. I can't for the life of me think who it could be. She was only ever out with that Foley one, and didn't we catch that one with Johnny Kiely from across the road, at it like alley cats at the back gate. She's fit for anything that one. Oh Jesus, Mary and Joseph, unless Johnny Kiely is the father!"

Francis glared at his wife as she continued.

"I asked her if someone attacked her, forced themselves on her, but she denied it. I've tried my damndest to find out. And nothing. She won't budge. She says she has no memory of it at all. Unless the Foley one got her drunk, of course. That's it! No wonder she had no memory of it. Remember the state of her the night she came home from the dance-hall covered in vomit. And we thinking she'd eaten something bad. It must have been drunk she was. And she denied that, as well. She's deceived us badly with her lies and trickery. At least Agnes Foley is open about her carry on, the trollop. It's the lies and deceit that gets me. Every time I look at her now, I feel like beating her around the room."

"You've been doing enough of that already, Hilda, and we all know where you learned that from – your family."

"Yeah, I've shouted and roared at her, Francis. And threatened her. I've even caught her by the scruff of the neck and tried to fire her out the back door. And all I get are great big sobs and sorry tears. Nothing else, but if I find out who she was with he'll be sorry that he ever spent a day on this earth."

"No! You won't mention a word of this to your brothers. Or anyone else, is that clear? We're decent people, we don't resort to that sort of violence, in my family at least. We just need to be clear about the road we're taking and stick to it, otherwise we might as well go out and inform the street. Bad enough we're in the public eye here in the shop every day. Remember our livelihood depends on our good name – we wouldn't be able to show our faces outside the door."

Hilda knew when to keep her mouth shut.

"And no school for her, you hear me? Your job now is to keep her inside. Lock the doors and put the keys in your pocket, and she's not to go near the shop. And when Miss Foley comes calling at the hall door, which she will, tell her that Norah is sick in bed with the flu. Lie through your teeth. You'll be good at that."

Sensing his anger rise, Hilda let him finish.

"Once she's gone off to the Home, we'll tell them all 'tis off to London she's gone to join the order, earlier than expected. The important thing here is that once our minds are made up, we stay on course. Tell the same story to everyone without exception. It's the only way."

Hilda was quietened by the digs that Francis had thrown in about her family.

Chapter 19

Banished

1969

The black Morris Minor headed out on the main road towards the railway station. Francis Gorman was driving his wife and daughter in plenty of time to catch the eight-forty-five train. He'd left a note on the shop door saying *"Back in twenty minutes"*.

The weather was bad for the month of May, but no-one in the car commented. Weather was the very least of the Gorman family troubles. Everything had been organised by Francis, leaving Hilda to get her daughter ready. Two weeks had passed since she had left Doctor Culhane's surgery with her mother, her life in ruins.

Warned by her mother that if she left the house there would be hell to pay, in any case she had been far too traumatised to call up to Aggie, now that she had found out the cause of her mystery illness. She'd been told by her father that if she were to tell her best friend about her condition, he would discontinue the Foleys' book and bar the entire Foley family from the shop, by putting a notice for all to see in the shop window. Norah knew she could never have that on her conscience. She would tell Aggie in time, when things were sorted. She would write to her. But for now she had no choice but do as she was told.

The breeze on the platform cut through them.

Hilda kept an eye out to see if she knew anyone. Watching people rush along the busy platform, disembarking from the train on platform one, she was nervous but determined. Peeping through the dusty window of the waiting room. Looking around. Anxious. Anxious to lie. To get it over with. Wanting to try out the story that she and Francis had rehearsed, over and over again.

Two women sat at opposite sides of the waiting room. Strangers to her and each other. Had she been able to practise her story on the platform or in the waiting room before they got on the train, it might have grounded her. Made her less nervous. The invented story that Norah was leaving in a few days for London to enter the convent. It would have got around Ballygore well before she got back to the shop to add to it, and keep adding to it, until the sorry nightmare was over and they could get on with their lives. Without Norah.

Moira Kiely would no doubt see it in her face straight away. But she had met no-one to tell her tale to. People were rushing past each other, pulling their jackets around them, tying scarves and rushing to leave the station, as the breeze on the platform helped them along. Leaving

Nora's suitcase down at her feet, she removed her purse from her pocket.

The ticket master held his hand out.

"One adult same day return. And one child single to Kent station in Cork."

She thought the man looked at her oddly, over his glasses. And then at Norah. Did he know something? No. She was relieved when he asked what age the girl was. Norah looked a lot older than her years. It was the innocent look in her big blue eyes that gave away her age.

Handing the two tickets to Norah.

Hilda briefly faced her daughter. "We better start bringing your birth certificate with us in future, if you keep growing at this rate. We're off to Cork. My daughter here is off to join the religious next week. She's going down to Cork to say goodbye to her father's side of family, before she leaves. Last-minute plan, it was." There, she'd said it.

The ticket master didn't respond to her offering.

Feeling the heat breaking out from her neck up, Hilda loosened the knot in her headscarf, opening the first button at the neck of her coat. Fanning her chest to leave in the now welcome cold air, she swore under her breath at the unwelcome intrusion of the hot flush.

The change of life was on the way and there was nothing she could do about it.

Just as the two women boarded the train, Hilda heard a voice behind her.

"Hilda, I thought 'twas you all right. Hello. Is this your Norah that I hear all about?"

Hilda's face grew red as another flush of warmth made its way up her chest. The sweat at the back of her neck made her want to throw her coat off as well as her cardigan inside it. But she couldn't. Not now. The sweat dripped down her face.

Of all the people to bump into! The new curate in Ballygore was standing behind her, waiting to board the same train to Cork. Waiting for her to speak. The last person she wanted to know their business. Francis had been adamant that he wanted no attention from the priests and Hilda knew from the customers that this new man hadn't the same way at all as poor Father Mac. The new man made it his business to get over involved in family affairs. Too involved. Father Mac was at least more tactful.

"Oh Father Ryan, yes, indeed, we're off to Cork. Can you believe the weather for the month of May?" She handed the suitcase to Norah, giving her a nudge in the back. "Walk along down the corridor there, Norah, and find us a good seat. Off to Cork, Father, to stay with the relations. Sending her down for a few days before she heads off to the order. It's all happened so quickly, Father – she's leaving us sooner than we expected. But Celine, that'd be Francis' sister, the nun, said she could come earlier, to settle in. If she stayed around Ballygore much longer, I'm afraid that Francis would keep her in the shop altogether. Now that wouldn't fit in with God's plan for her. Would it now, Father?"

"Well, God bless you, Hilda, and your daughter. I'll call in to you in the shop next week to enquire after her."

Lies, all lies. And to a priest.

Norah had walked far down the smoke-filled carriage, finding a seat for them both.

Hilda nodded to the young priest. "I'll let you go so, Father. Look! There's a seat behind you there, just inside the door. I'll have a few Mass cards all ready for you to sign when you call in to the shop the next day." And she hurried away.

The train was full. Hilda didn't recognise any of the faces. Bad enough they'd bumped straight into the new curate. But she'd have had time enough to calm down, should she bump into him again at Kent Station.

Mother and daughter didn't speak to each other during the journey, until Norah leant towards her mother, who was so caught up in her thoughts that it didn't register with her for a moment what her daughter was saying to her.

"I'm going to be sick, Mammy. The smell. I'm going to be sick."

Hilda saw that Norah was struggling to hold it in. It almost made her feel sorry for her. But it didn't. Pulling a brown bag and a white cotton hanky from her handbag she handed them to Norah, whose eyes were pleading with her.

"She's a bad traveller," she said to the man in the black business suit, sitting opposite. The well-dressed woman beside him was asleep. Dribbling out the side of her mouth. "It's just travel nerves." She clenched her teeth and nudged Norah in the side with her fist. "Quickly.

Pass me out here and go off to the toilet, down there to the left of the door. That's all the cigarette smoke making you sick. *Go on.*"

The girl with the white face did as she was told and walked away from her mother, holding the paper bag in one hand, the hanky in the other. Hilda suddenly felt cold, reaching beside her to put her coat back on. This change of life thing couldn't be happening at a worse time.

When Norah returned Hilda had no words of comfort for her and there was no further conversation between the Gorman women as they travelled their final journey together – Hilda too consumed with shame to consider that this might be the very last time she would set eyes on her daughter. She had hoped that Norah would make them proud but she had done the very opposite.

From now until this business was finished, there could be no going back. No regrets. No going soft, if she wanted to keep the peace at home. Once Francis had his mind made up, there was no backing down. Hilda could scarcely believe how fast he had turned on Norah. The apple of his eye for all these years, and look where that had got him. From the minute she had told him what the doctor had said, he had changed in a way that she would never have thought possible. Blaming *her*. Hinting at her family history. Her breeding.

But, in the stillness of night, she had heard him sobbing in his sleep. Cries of terror. She had tried consoling him, but to no avail. Francis Gorman wasn't one to show emotion. He said he couldn't believe that the daughter whom he had such hopes for had spread her legs. She had been that easy. The names he had called her. Names he usually reserved for loose women who had no respect for themselves or anyone else. Slappers and whores.

The hackney would be waiting at Kent Station to take Norah out to the Mother and Baby Home. Francis would meet Hilda's train at ten minutes past one, on her return from Cork. They had it planned out to the last. Hilda would be back behind the counter in the shop by two o'clock sharp. And they'd put all this behind them.

Chapter 20

The Home

1969

Norah Gorman put her brown leather suitcase on the grass verge while she pushed open the heavy black iron gate. She turned around, half expecting the hackney driver to get out of the car to help her. He didn't. Staring ahead, his face gave nothing away.

It wasn't his first time at the gate, watching a girl walk down the path of shame.

The very fact that her mother hadn't come as far as this place had said it all.

Hilda had said her goodbyes on the platform at Kent Station, before returning to Ballygore on the train. She had given Norah a cold look. A memory to hold.

Her parents were too ashamed, and the less they saw of her now, the better. Minds made up, intent on keeping to the story they had concocted. Their Norah had left for London to start her training in the novitiate, after which she would fly to Alabama, to join her other aunt, before taking her final vows when the time came.

Hearing the car pull away behind her, she headed up the long driveway. A lone magpie landed on the path in front of her. "*One for sorrow*," she said quietly. But no looking back.

They would be expecting her. Her mother had said so. She was going to be here until sometime after her baby was born, and they'd see what happened after that.

It had crossed her mind in the dead of night that God must be punishing her for having had doubts about becoming a nun. It had always been her parent's plan. Never hers alone. She had accepted their word that she had a vocation, until she started to doubt it herself. The day she had met Aggie, cycling down the main street with her bloomers on parade.

Her parents would tell Aggie the story they had concocted. That she had left for London. Saying goodbye to her blood sister would have been too painful. Norah had meant what she said, when she had agreed not to contact Aggie, who would have without a thought headed straight down to the shop, demanding justice for Norah. If she found out what had happened, there would be no stopping her.

Norah herself couldn't make it out. How could she be pregnant when she had never had sex? Real sex. Well, at least she didn't think she had. But she must have. Somehow. She had drunk alcohol a few times. More than a few times. Must have happened then. But surely she'd remember or have felt it afterwards? Unless something had happened the night she had vomited at the back of the dancehall. Except she couldn't remember much about the night.

She pressed the bell on the black door and two nuns were standing there within seconds. One smiling. Showing small even teeth. The other severe-looking. Thin lips. Identical in every other way. The smile remained on one of their faces. The other, nothing.

"Hello, Norah. Come on in now. Straight into the front room and we'll sort you out. Bring your suitcase with you.

Norah didn't know quite what to expect. No expectations. She did as she was told.

Opening her suitcase, the nuns began to remove the contents, putting aside the items they said were too personal. Her mother had packed the case, telling her that her name would be changed once inside the home. That her identity would be concealed, just in case anyone traced her back to Ballygore. Back to Gormans' shop on Mill Road.

One of the nuns removed the one item that she had wanted to keep. Snapping it quickly out of Norah's hand as she tried to retrieve it. The nun with the smile painted on her face.

A photo of herself and Aggie taken at the carnival the summer before. The blood sisters. Swinging their schoolbags, the photo had been in the local paper the following week captioned, "**Two friends from Mill Road, without a care in the world**."

Agnes had made it her business to meet the photographer afterwards, ordering two copies which she had framed, giving one to Norah for her sixteenth birthday in June.

The girls had to duck on the street every time they met the photographer after that. Agnes never paid the man.

Now Norah most certainly had a care in the world. A care that was growing inside her and she was confused as to how it got there.

The doctor had prodded and poked her that day and her mother became concerned that he would damage her hymen.

"Doctor Culhane, I hope you're not giving Norah an internal. What about her hymen?"

"I'm afraid, Mrs Gorman, your daughter's hymen is well torn. If it's her virginity you're concerned about, I'm afraid we're well past that stage. Unless this baby that I'm feeling here got in there by some way other than anything I'd know about." Turning to Norah. "Is there a young man involved, Norah?"

The two women answered in unison.

"No."

Norah didn't believe what she was hearing. It was all a mistake. A terrible mistake.

Her mother had fallen back into the chair. Her eyes staring ahead. Shaking her head. "What are you saying, Doctor Culhane? That Norah here is in the family way?

You're mistaken. It's ridiculous."

She got up and stood beside her daughter whose legs were held wide apart in stirrups. Tapping her arm. "Will you speak up and tell him, Norah? Will you tell him he's wrong?" Shaking her, frightening her.

The doctor beckoned her mother to put her ear to the tin bugle-like instrument which he had pressed against her abdomen. Hurting her.

"There it is. The heartbeat, loud and strong."

Too afraid to open her mouth, Norah looked to her mother for comfort.

The slap came out of nowhere, across Norah's face. She had never seen a look such as what she was witnessing on her mother's face.

"You . . . you . . . tramp!"

Hilda was sobbing at what she had heard. Wailing.

The doctor spoke firmly to her.

"You'd be well served, Mrs Gorman, to take your daughter home and discuss it there. The waiting room outside is full – if you keep up with that racket, they'll hear you down the main street.

Hilda wiped her face clean and stormed out of the room.

The doctor hurried after her and caught up with her in the hall.

He spoke to her quietly but urgently. "You've a lot to discuss with your husband. You've three choices here as far as I can see as there's no young man involved to put a ring on her finger. Keep her at home and rear the child.

Send her to a Mother and Baby Home where she'll be cared for, and the child sent to a decent home. Number three, I strongly advice against. Don't even consider using the unsanitary services of a certain woman on Spring Street. I've seen more than enough of her handiwork here at the surgery. Once you've had time to calm down, your husband and yourself will be better equipped to deal with this. She's not the first and she certainly won't be the last."

Nora appeared within minutes, fully dressed.

Mother and daughter walked home in silence. In shock.

The more serious of the two nuns placed a grey uniform on top of Norah's belongings in the open suitcase.

"Come with me now and I'll show you where you'll be sleeping while you're here. You'll be in the dorm with other girls just like yourself. We're here to take care of you during your confinement, so it's not a hotel service we're running. Or a babysitting service. You'll work for your keep until your confinement ends, and we'll find a good home for the baby."

Norah was scarcely listening to the cross-looking nun as she continued.

"Everyone here is the same – all ending up in trouble. Your name while you're here will be Carmel. No second names to be spoken. And no talking about home. No newspapers in or out. Are we clear?"

Walking alongside the stern-faced nun, Norah looked across the hallway. Staring back at her were a group of girls, most with big rounded bellies. Looking into their eyes as she passed eased her anxiety. Some of them nodded at her. It was enough for now.

All wearing the same uniform. Same grey shoes. They looked like normal schoolgirls. Pregnant schoolgirls.

Kathleen befriended Norah from that first day. "You'll be fine, Carmel. Just forget about the outside and remember we're all in the same boat. We stay here until the babies come. They put them in the nursery and if we're lucky we get to mind them until the day they …" She couldn't finish. "Some of the girls are still here with their babies and the children are two years old. Imagine that. We each have our own jobs. Seems like they give the worst of the jobs to the girls they think don't know any better, and if they have any sense that you come from a snobby background they'll go easier on you. Money talks. If they think you're a bit soft like Melda over there, they'll give you the shite jobs. But outside on the grounds is the worst. The nursery is the best place to be – there's the infant room and the toddler room. They'll probably send you there. And here's a tip I got when I came here. If they think your baby is in any way too sick to go to a family, they'll leave it with you for longer. So it's up to you to make what you like of that one. One of the girls even got to take her baby home a month ago, when her parents changed their minds.

Another girl ran straight out the front gate with four weeks to go, and she wasn't brought back either, like they used to do before. But some of the nuns here are right weapons."

Norah liked Kathleen who reminded her a bit of Agnes. She couldn't stop talking.

"But they say it's not as bad here as some of the other places. And it was much worse years ago. One or two of the nuns are fine, but they're too fecking weak to stand up for themselves against the bullies. Tyrants with smiles plastered across their faces, so don't be fooled, girl. There'll always be the cruel bitter bitches. The ones with no hearts. So, let's hope we all go into labour when the good ones are on."

Norah didn't comment. She didn't want to know. All she wanted to know was that they'd take hers away, the minute it was born. She didn't want to set eyes on it. Whoever it looked like. Maybe she'd recognise the father in it. But, if she did see it, she mightn't be able to let it go. And she had to. The baby had to be adopted.

Norah wished she could talk to Aggie. She'd know what to say. She'd understand. Or would she? Norah began to doubt herself. Doubt Aggie. She couldn't talk to anyone from Ballygore. How could she? Who'd believe that the good living Norah Gorman had a baby growing inside her, without a bull's notion of how it got there?

Who'd believe that Norah Gorman had been such an eejit to let a man's penis inside her? Answering her own question in her head: everyone probably. Because that's what she was. A big eejit. Unworthy of the support of her parents.

But she didn't have time to be dwelling on all that now. She had to be practical as Kathleen had said. Forget home. Forget Aggie. Just concentrate on getting through one day and the next would follow, and before you know it, it'll all be over.

Norah was assigned to the nursery that very first evening. Her duties for the week would be taking care of the older babies, alongside those who knew what they were doing.

Awakened from her sleep the following morning by the sound of a bell in the distance, Norah sat up quickly. Confused. Laying down again, closing her eyes shut.

She'd been having the dream. The same dream. The one about the china doll. In bits on the floor. Blood everywhere. Coming out of the doll's eyes. Its mouth. A china doll that called her name.

She lay where she was, staring up at the ceiling, wishing she could close her eyes and be back at home, leaving this awful nightmare behind her. The picture in her head of her cosy bedroom at home in Ballygore was a far cry from the reality of her surroundings. She thought about her pink-and-green wallpaper, the paper that she and Aggie had chosen together. Well, Aggie had picked it out. She'd said it was all the go.

Aggie, whom she had not been allowed say goodbye

to. Aggie, whom she knew in her heart would have ruined it for all of them. Without meaning to.

Hearing the familiar sound of the tinny rattle of the shop-door bell, she blocked her ears. Coming nearer. Louder. Stop.

Looking around the dorm seeing the stressed faces of her roommates, roused from their slumber, brought her back to the present. Two of the girls were kneeling by their bedsides, heads bent, hands joined in prayer.

Four beds facing four. Eight single beds. White iron beds sitting on shiny wooden floors, polished to the last by the stocking feet of the fallen. High ceiling. White walls bare except for the plinth, on which sat the four-foot-tall statue of the Virgin Mary. A reminder to all that this lady had never succumbed to the weakness of a man's loins. No. She had been pure and clean. The Immaculate. Her baby a blessing from God the Father. He was God the Son.

The nuns had told the girls to pray to Our Lady, to beg the mother of all mothers for forgiveness. They were the sinners. Offenders. Tempting men who were weak-willed and begotten by desires. They were all Eves. Adam and Eve. Eve the temptress. Poor Adam.

Norah placed her hand on her abdomen before opening her eyes. Those around her had little to say, each caught up in their own world of thought. There were no 'Good Mornings' here. No-one asking "Did you sleep well?" or "Was your bed comfortable?" or "Were you warm enough?"

The dorm without laughter. Without hope. The dorm

of the fallen. Whispers and sounds of those, empty retching into buckets, trying to avoid being seen or heard, in case they'd have to change dorms.

The nun wearing the long white apron, relentless in her bell-ringing. Punishing. No understanding. Without empathy. Judging. Wanting only to get the day started. Keeping to the rota. Keep it moving.

Norah had been forewarned the evening before about the morning bell, which would be rung along the corridor before entering the dorm, stopping at each of the beds, until there was movement.

The bell would be rung in accordance with the mood of the bell-ringer. Never a good morning when it was Sister Joseph holding the bell. The girls could tell who was on duty by the way they rang it, ever before the nun appeared at the door.

Sister Gregory gentle in her way, gentle in waking the girls, not gentle enough to stand up to those she feared herself. Weak.

This morning it was Sister Joseph. Unrelenting. She wasn't in a good mood.

Norah had only ever spent a night in the same room as Aggie. No room here for embarrassment.

The nun stopped at the foot of Norah's bed. "Carmel, you're to go straight to the office after prayers. Sister Gregory has forms for you to sign. Come on now. Up you get. No rest for the wicked, girls."

The girls made their way down the polished stairs in their stockinged feet, to avoid scratching the wooden stairs with their shoes. No time for conversations, each caught up with their own thoughts, about to start the day ahead.

Each of the girls had their job list to be completed by evening, when they retired to their dorms. Exhausted. Grabbing whatever time they got together, the girls were cautious at first in protecting their identities. As they began to trust one another, they relaxed. They even shared a laugh.

Kathleen said that she came from Galway. Martha was from the Midlands. All from places far enough away for them to talk freely without fear of future ramifications.

Kathleen told Norah that she had been sexually assaulted by an old uncle. For years. Leaving her in the family way. It started with him asking her to sit on his lap. She didn't like it when he touched her that way. Then he'd laugh, and feel her breast. "They'll soon sprout, pet, and I'll be here waiting for them when they do. Just checking them for you, girl." Then later on, as she began to feel stupid, too big to be sitting on his lap, he'd sent for her to come to his cottage, to run an errand. And he'd feel her budding breasts and get her to hold it. He said that it was all part of growing up. How he himself had learned the facts of life. It hurt. She ran home. But he gave her a ten-bob note and told her to put it in her pocket and tell no-one. He'd warned her if she'd open her mouth, no-one would believe her lies – he'd make sure she was sent off to the nuthouse. Their secret.

Norah believed every word. Confiding in Kathleen

that when the doctor told her she was pregnant, she'd no idea how it happened – she'd never gone that far. Kathleen just looked at her.

The following Saturday morning, Martha went into labour. She was fifteen. "Keep walking, Martha. Come on. Up and down." Sister Joseph was on duty.

The girls knew what to expect after weeks of watching those who went before them. Doing their best to comfort her as she walked up and down the corridor. Stopping at times as the pain became too much for her. Worn, tired and in pain, she walked all day.

Martha did as she was told, the crippling pain showing on her face every time she stopped on a contraction.

Biddy from Cavan walked alongside her. The nun turned on Biddy.

"Leave her walk on. The more she walks, the quicker the labour. Go on in and help Mary in the sluice room. Carmel, go with her. Now!"

Each day was much the same as the one before. Norah familiarised herself with the routine.

Kathleen had told Norah that if a girl's parents had money, a hundred pounds was paid to the Home and the girl could leave ten days after her baby was born. A sum of fifty pounds meant that the girl could leave the home after three months. Those who had no money to offer had to stay on to work for their keep. For others there was little hope. Norah had no idea what would happen in her own case. She didn't know if Kathleen was telling the truth or not. She didn't care.

Watching the new mothers bond with their babies made Norah anxious. Bonds which were about to be broken. Cut off. Every week without warning, babies were send off to their new homes, often within minutes of leaving their mother's breast.

The tears welled up in Norah's eyes as she watched girls dress their babies in their going-away outfits. Clothes that had been chosen so carefully, clothes they had knitted, crocheted, or bought, knowing there was no other way. Being told by those who held the power that it was "all for the best in the name of Our Lady of the Blessed Virgin". Watching girls crying, weeping for their little babies, upset Norah. Screaming. Feral sounds. Eyes bloodshot and swollen, with the pain of having their babies taken from them. Norah found it unbearable.

Hearing Sister Joseph, with her sharp unforgiving voice. Punishing. "Stop your crying now. Your baby is one of the lucky ones. It'll want for nothing. You knew all this when you walked through that door. You can't change your mind now."

Kathleen had told her that some of the girls were not of the mind to understand. Unable to speak up for themselves. Following every order they were given.

"Come on. Keep walking up and down. You can do it. The baby is coming whether you like it or not. You accepted the seed, didn't you? The next time you might give a bit of thought before you offer yourself."

The pains started two weeks after Norah arrived at the home. Thinking it was as Kathleen had mentioned. Dummy pains. Saying nothing, she continued cleaning the nursery.

Hearing Martha's voice. "Carmel, are you OK? You're sweating and your face is as white as a sheet. Will I call the nun?"

"No, look, it's fine. it's just a cramp in my back from all the stretching. Kathleen told me I might get Braxton Hicks. Fake pains."

Norah was admitted to the maternity hospital the following morning, the first of June. Kathleen had found her sitting on the toilet bowl earlier that morning, covered in blood, a tiny infant in her arms. Kathleen had picked the baby up, wrapping the loose end of Nora's nightie around him, before handing him back to his mother, who responded by kissing her baby on the head. Rocking. Not heeding the presence of two nuns when they arrived. She thought her heart would break.

They laid her on a bed, saying "The baby was not for this world." Norah holding the still infant closer, as one of the nuns tried to take it away from her.

"Come on, Carmel, give the baby to me, he might still be alive. The ambulance is on its way."

"Let me hold him for one more minute. Just one minute, sister, please. I beg you."

The nun reached out, taking the tiny baby out of her arms.

A week later she was brought back to the Home from the hospital. "Three days to recover," she was told, "then back to the nursery." They told her she'd had a miscarriage. Her father had been in touch, arrangements were being made by him to have her moved from the Home in three weeks. Her father seemed like such a gentleman, they said, who didn't deserve all this trouble at his door. He had offered to cover the cost of his daughter's six-week stay immediately.

Norah was asked to pray for the couple who had been looking forward to collecting their beautiful baby. "They were beyond consoling," according to the nun.

No longer pregnant. Her baby had been stillborn. No hope. A boy. She would have told them his name was James. If they'd asked. Nobody did. Small enough to fit in her two hands. He had been gone for some time.

Where had they taken him? Where?

No time for pity. No time to grieve. She would have the rest of her life to love the baby that was never hers to have. The baby they didn't get to hand over to the loving family. The baby who for evermore would belong to her, in her, by her. Only to her. A child whose love she would never know. A child who need never wonder who his birth mother was.

James. He would live for evermore in his mother's

heart for as long as she breathed, never to be forgotten or forsaken, as he might have been had he spent his life outside of her. Confused as to her emotions. Feeling guilty. Relieved at the same time. No longer having to wonder where her baby would end up. Where she herself would end up.

His name was James. "*James!*" she screamed.

Whose eyes had never seen the love on his mother's face.

Owning him. Claiming him as her own. No one else would ever lay claim on him now. Not even for a second. He was her son and she was his mother, and no-one could take that from her. With her baby tucked away safely in her heart, Norah Gorman would enter the convent in London. Goodbye, Ireland.

That day at the doctor's seemed like such a long time ago. It had changed her life forever. Twenty weeks or thereabouts they had said. No dates to go by. Listen to the heart. She hadn't been in bed with a man. She had messed around with the fella at the fairground and once in the back lane, but she hadn't done anything she could regret. And even if she had, hadn't Aggie said that a girl couldn't get pregnant standing up? Aggie had told her it was OK to fool around. Aggie had been wrong.

The nuns had, in fact, declined Francis Gorman's request to keep Norah for longer than three weeks. Norah was holding up a bed, which would be filled by another poor misfortunate girl the day after she left.

"Mr Gorman, your daughter will be best served by moving on with her life. We would normally expect a girl in this situation to be gone by the end of the week."

Francis wanted to hear no mention of a baby, or any detail of her short time in the Home. Plain and simple. Norah had let them all down. Hilda had told every customer coming into the shop that Norah had already gone to London to join her aunt in the convent. There was no way out of it now but to ask Celine to take her niece in three weeks' time, telling her that Norah had decided not to embark on the secretarial course after all. Only then could life get back to normal.

Her father collected her from the Home on the day of her seventeenth birthday. He had said the shop was too busy to come for her at the weekend. Saying goodbye to the girls she hardly had time to get to know, the nameless girls whose secrets she had shared. She could see it in their eyes, some sad for her that she had lost her baby, others happy that she got to leave the Home. Francis, her father, handed over the money, thanking the nuns for their great kindness. He'd pray for them.

Norah didn't speak to her father, who advised her of the plan for her future as if he were talking to a stranger. Destination – the airport. He hadn't even mentioned her birthday.

Ballygore was no longer an option in Norah Gorman's life. Her father asked her to send a card at Christmas to her mother. She wouldn't. Whatever they threw at her now, she would go along with it, until such time as she was ready to make her mind up. Her own mind. Norah Gorman's mind. Not the mind of her mother or father who were so worried about what the neighbours might say. They didn't care if they never saw her again.

Her life had turned upside-down. If the past six weeks had taught her anything, it was that Norah Gorman would never be the same again.

Chapter 21

The American

1968

Darlene Fletcher was born on the May 2nd, 1946, on the west side of New York city, overlooking Central Park. A silver spoon placed in her mouth to remind all present that Judge Fletcher's youngest child would want for nothing. Her parents, well in their forties when she arrived, ensured that they had enough help to look after her.

From the moment Darlene Fletcher was delivered, she screamed. And screamed. Letting everyone know that Darlene Mai Fletcher would not be shy about making her presence felt.

Her parents made sure the child wanted for nothing, apart from their constant attention, which she sought in abundance. Trying their utmost to shower her with the hugs and affection which she craved, she was raised by young Irish nannies, who despaired in their efforts to contain the child.

Darlene did not make it easy for those looking after her. She refused to take no for an answer. A child who was just as likely to leave her teeth marks on an arm attempting to grab her as she was to kicking the shins of whoever tried to restrain her.

Darlene had become quite a handful by the time she was twelve. By which time both of her brothers had long since left home to live their own lives. Her parents, unable to control their wild child, left it to the staff to manage the rebellious youngster.

Many a wage packet had to be subsidised at the end of the month, to prevent another nanny from walking out on her charge. Letters of complaint from middle school had become a constant, a sizeable yearly cheque ensured that the school would hold off on expelling the child who refused to be disciplined.

Turning sixteen, Darlene's parents could scarcely believe that their young maverick had finally calmed down. She had found God. Changed overnight. Offering to assist elderly people on the street, sometimes causing them distress when she refused to take no for an answer, cheekily telling the non-believers amongst them a few home truths.

Volunteering in the local church, praying for forgiveness. Her bedroom in a state of constant disarray, adorned with small statues of various saints, holy beads draped over her mirror to help her reflect on her vanity. Modesty had become important to the chaste teenager.

Long skirts showing no part of her body that might

entice pleasure in a man. Keeping a small bible on her nightstand, reading from it every night before she went to sleep. Finding it difficult to concentrate, reading the same paragraph over and over.

But it didn't take long for Darlene to question her new-found religion. The more she read, the less she was convinced.

Looking for consolation from the priests in the parish, to support her wavering beliefs, had made her worse. Asking questions to which she sought answers served only to disillusion her.

Enquiring from the ageing Irish cleric in the diocese as to the apparent lack of women in important roles in the church. Curious to know why there were no women present in the painting of the Last Supper. The jovial cleric had tried his best to hide his mirth as he answered.

"The women were probably back in the kitchen cleaning the delph, having cooked the meal and served it up."

Darlene was less than impressed.

"You've got to be kidding me, Father. Right? So you're saying that God allowed Mary Magdalene to wash his feet, to show her that he forgave her. So ... she was a prostitute then, was she? And you know this for a fact, Father? Do you? He allowed her to wash his feet. Did he just? *Allowed*. Well, I wouldn't wash anyone's stinking feet. I'd throw the pitcher of water at them first. It would have been better if he had made the men who were paying her to wash her very own feet. That'd be more like it."

Darlene had stormed out the sacristy, banging the door hard behind her.

She was incensed enough to dump her black mantilla in the first trash can she came across on the sidewalk outside the sacristy. Hiding her bible behind her father's books in the library at home. Back far enough that it wouldn't be found unless someone was to look for it, and it certainly would not be Darlene Fletcher, who knew without a doubt that religion was not for her. She decided she'd be better served as an atheist.

Getting her a start with an interior design company on 56th Street at the age of eighteen, her parents hoped it would be a turning point for her. Her first full-time job. She had refused to go to college. She got the job as a favour owed to her father.

After a year with the company, Darlene was bored.

Walking through Penn Station on 34th Street, she stopped in her tracks on seeing a small group of women and men dressed in colourful robes, chanting and playing drums. Smiling. Darlene approached them, eager to find out more, asking them questions, reading their leaflets. A new awakening, she was told.

Within weeks, she was standing on the same corner on her days off, ringing bells, chanting, wearing her leather sandals and an orange maxi dress which she picked up in Macy's. Collecting stray dollars from passers-by, who couldn't but feel happy at the sight of the happy colourful group.

Losing her job didn't bother her. It hadn't been for her.

The creative director had told her father that he couldn't pay her another dime. Darlene hadn't shown up for days at a time. Her parents had become so exasperated they expected the worst for their daughter. The only comfort they had was that she was living at home where, they said, they could keep an eye on her.

Until she began to disappear without warning, for days at a time, staying away, leaving her parents anxious and stressed as to her whereabouts. Her days were spend attending rallies, championing great causes. Following other like-minded people across the states to venues where they would wave their banners. In protest.

Travelling to the latest rally in Houston by bus had taken forever. Everyone who embarked on the journey had a cause of some sort, some losing sight of their passion, getting caught up in the haze of whatever they'd taken along the way.

Being more disposed to breaking the rules than accepting them. Darlene Fletcher was proud to be her own person. Too much of a free spirit to follow order.

But Darlene felt lost. There was still a hole in her life.

Resigned to the fact that their daughter was heading for a fall, believing that it was only a matter of time before she left New York to join some commune or other, her parents were constantly worried about their daughter.

But Darlene had a change of heart just when they least expected. She had grown tired of reciting mantras, banging bongo drums, selling flowers on the sidewalk. Tired of making banners. She'd smoked the marijuana and felt the magic. Taken much of what was offered. She'd had the free sex. Tired of searching, she was craving a new direction, except she wasn't sure what it was yet.

Meeting Julian Taylor, on the pavement outside a restaurant on 4th Avenue, gave her just what she had been searching for.

Chapter 22

The Newly Weds

Darlene listened attentively to her new husband on the plane journey from New York to Shannon Airport. He had been telling her how welcoming the Irish people were, how green the grass was, how people tended to say what they felt. He warned her that it might take time for her to adjust to life in rural Ireland.

"Ballygore is going to be a far cry from New York city, although it's years since I've been down there myself, but be prepared. Kilnarick, where we're headed, is a tiny village just outside the town."

He told her about the Irish cities. Dublin, and Cork further down the country. Galway to the west and Limerick just below it on the map. He mentioned the hardships the people had endured, in times past. He mentioned Belfast, his home.

"Darlene, people at home haven't forgotten about the

harsh realities of the past. So be mindful when you're in conversation. Ireland is a republic, nothing to do with England. Well, the northern counties are still under British rule, but that's another story. People often get that wrong. Put it like this, I wouldn't be parading the triumph of the Brits around Ballygore. And definitely not up around where I come from – so be careful."

"But didn't you tell me all about the Irish who emigrated for better lives in England? Why do they still go there, if they hate it so much?"

"Little choice, love. Remember they didn't leave in their droves to take up the best jobs in England. Many were unskilled labourers. They left to work on the building sites, breaking their backs, the women working as maids in the better-off houses. Yes, ma'am, no, ma'am. And there were those who took the Queen's Shilling, to be recruited into the British army."

"Jeez, darling, do I detect a rebel here? Have I just gone and married a true Irish republican? What else are you not telling me? What the hell, Julian? At least the Irish had jobs, sending money home to feed their families. And look at you, graduating in veterinary medicine in America, because your father couldn't pay the college fees in Dublin."

She could see by her husband's face that she had said enough. But she didn't get it. If all those people went to England to work, and to America, well, they were lucky to get the jobs that they did and get better educated. Weren't they?

Time for some shut eye before she contributed any more to what was becoming their first awkward conversation.

The plane bumped to a halt as it hit the ground. They had arrived at Shannon Airport.

The first thing that hit Darlene as she walked across the tarmac, to begin her married life in Ireland, was the dampness. And the cold. Leaving behind the clean, snow-covered Central Park, and the clear blue skies high above them.

The clouds above her head loomed low and heavy.

Julian had reminded her to consider her wardrobe carefully. She assured him that she had. He had advised her to wear warm clothes, but Darlene had never been the best at taking advice, especially when it came to taking fashion advice from a man. In this instance, she wished she had heeded him. Most of the clothes in her suitcase were one-off pieces, more suited to the streets of New York City or the Grand Hotel in Hyannisport, Cape Cod, than here in Ireland where the wind would surely rip through them.

The heavy rain lashed across their legs as they walked towards the terminal to collect their suitcases. Darlene's coat had been a gift from her aunt. The latest in New York fashion, bought at Bloomingdales on Lexington Ave. Winter-white, soft merino wool falling just above the knee. Six black buttons, three on either side, which Julian said looked like flying saucers. She wore a black beret, and on her feet white-patent knee-length boots.

Mrs Darlene Taylor from New York City was far from impressed on feeling the rain seep through her new coat.

The cab was waiting for them outside the airport to take them to their new lives in Kilnarick, three miles outside the town of Ballygore.

She couldn't understand much of what the hackney driver was saying. Even Julian's accent seemed to have changed while in conversation with the man. Deciding they must be speaking in Gaelic, she didn't involve herself much in the conversation. Every now and then, she caught the driver looking at her through the rear-view mirror, his eyebrows heavy and wild. She wanted to stick her tongue out at him. Or ask him what the heck he was looking at.

Instead, she stared right back at him. Feeling his wife's knee press against the back of his seat, Julian checked up on her.

"Are you all right, Darlene? You OK there?" to which she nodded.

She was not OK. Keeping her knee pressed against the back of his seat for the remainder of the journey, jolting him every now and then to show her discontent.

Julian was mostly ignoring her, seemingly caught up in a full-blown conversation with the driver, while she sat in the back seat of the smelly cab, which had definitely seen better days. Taking her perfumed handkerchief from the pocket of her coat, she waved it in front of her nose, in an exaggerated attempt to ward off the fumes of stale cigarette smoke and whatever else was causing her to almost gag.

The windows were closed. Both handles on the back windows swung loose when she tried to open them. The ashtray on her side was overflowing with cigarette ends and ashes. She began to feel nauseous. Sticking her feet under the passenger seat in front of her, she rooted out a pair of dirty wellington boots, covered in wet muck. She had found the source of the smell.

Leaning forward, she said, "Darling, would you mind awfully opening your window and ask the driver to do likewise. His boots, here under the seat, are making me feel nauseous!"

"What did she say, boss? Open the window, is it? Does she not realise 'tis February we're in? We'd get our deaths and we wouldn't want that now, would we?"

Julian looked back at her. She could see from the look on his face that he was less than pleased at her last comment.

She wanted to scream. She needed air. Kicking the dirty boots back in under Julian's seat, hoping that the smell would fill the front of the car, she removed a bottle of spray perfume from her bag, spraying it around her, until the scent filled the air.

The driver started coughing, quickly winding down the window. Julian said nothing. The two men in the front seat were not impressed.

"How long does it take to get to Kilnarick, if you don't mind telling me?"

"What did she say, boss? How long is it?" Answering her as if he were speaking to a child. "Not too long now at all. Seeing as the road isn't bad, we'll be there in no time."

The tears built up behind her eyes as she settled herself back in the seat – she would say no more until the journey was over. Then she would let Julian have it.

The car pulled into the mucky driveway at Kilnarick. Their new home for the next eighteen months. A bloody lifetime, thought Darlene.

The key was under the flowerpot to the left of the front door, just as the letter had stated. The empty flowerpot.

Watching the two men take the heavy suitcases from the trunk of the car, Darlene waited for her husband to open the door to their new home. When he did, she thought her heart would stop. They'd got it wrong. This wasn't the house. Some mistake here.

The driver got back into the cab, having gratefully accepting the crisp new notes from Julian.

"Well, boss. I hope yourself and the missus will be very happy in your new home and don't be strangers now. Give the wife a shout if we can help you in any way."

Darlene couldn't speak. Looking around her trying to make sense of it all. This hadn't been anything like the romantic picture that Julian had painted for her, after making love in the warm bedroom they'd left behind in New York.

It wasn't supposed to be like this.

She was speechless, raging with Julian who had filled her with such excitement and expectations about Ireland.

Taking in her surroundings, her dreams were bashed. This was not the bright new beginning she had expected.

The house was shabby, surrounded by fields. A large barn with a rusty red roof stood beside the house. The front door was certainly not what she had pictured – it was brown and dull, with an opaque yellowish glass panel in the centre.

Having opened the door, Julian lifted his new wife to carry her over the threshold. Darlene, winding her arms around her husband's neck, began sniffing the air.

"What's that smell, Julian?"

"What smell, Darlene? I don't get any smell. Steady there, I don't want to drop you. Ah, that's just the smell of a house that has had no fire lit for a couple of weeks. No air getting in. That's all."

"Don't you dare drop me! Don't put me down! Take me out of here right now! *Right now, I said. I'm not staying here.*"

"Darlene, you're overreacting. There's nothing wrong here that a few hours of cleaning won't fix. You know that Harold Cox had to leave in the ambulance at the last minute."

"A few hours. Forget it."

Remaining in his arms until they were back outside the threshold and he put her down, she quickly walked angrily away towards a wide aluminum gate at the far side of the yard. She hadn't noticed the cow pie, until she felt it under her foot. *Squelch*. The heel of her white patent boot had cracked through the caked surface, splashing what was underneath up along the leg of her boot.

Hearing Julian laugh behind her, shaking with merriment, angered her, as she stood there lamenting the state of her new boot. She started to scream at him. The more she screamed, the more he laughed, unable to control himself.

"Look at my boots, that'll never come out! It's turning them green! Get me water, quickly!"

"There's a tap there on the wall, love. Sure, all they are is a bit of plastic. It'll wash off and, if it doesn't, we'll get you a new pair in town. You can wear those ones around the yard."

Darlene screamed at him. No words. Just a long scream.

"Oh Darlene, they'll think I'm killing you – they'll hear you in town. That's good luck, you know – stepping into a lump of cow shit. That's all."

She ran around the back of the house. There was nowhere else to run to get away from this dump that he had brought her to.

Julian followed her, holding her in his arms until she calmed down.

The couple returned to have a better look at their first home together.

There was no entrance hall. Straight into the living area. A faded red towel was hanging over the stove. A green plastic basin full of murky water had been left sitting on the kitchen table, a bar of dry cracked soap beside it. Newpapers were strewn on the table. The floor looked as if it hadn't seen water in years. Old armchairs, covered in grubby overstretched covers, showing the original fabric underneath. An ashtray sitting on the armrest, full to the brim with cigarette ashes.

She shoved Julian away when he tried to console her.

"Darlene, just give it time. I know it's a bit of a shock for you, but it's just this way for now. It's different to what you're used to, that's all. It's a lived-in country house, nothing at all wrong with it. We'll soon have it sorted and made into a home."

She was paying no heed to him.

"Julian, I can't stay here. I *won't* stay here. The photos you showed me were nothing like this dump. Is there a phone here? *I said is there a phone?*" she screamed at him, before sitting down.

"Yes, there should be a phone here, somewhere, under something."

She watched her husband scatter the newspapers aside, lifting boxes out of his way, eventually finding the phone which had been plugged out. Taking her mirror compact from her handbag, she saw she looked a mess. Her cheeks were black from the mascara running down her face. And now the elbows of her damp wool coat were marked from the dust on the table.

Julian tried to console her.

"Let me have a look upstairs. I'll take up the suitcases and you can sit right here. I'll light the stove later, and look, there's plenty of dry wood there in the basket. It's really not as bad as you're making it out to be, love. It's cold and in a bit of a mess but you must remember Harold Cox is a bachelor. We'll soon have it lovely, I promise you. Come on, chin up. I'll go into town first thing in the morning and get it all sorted."

"So Harold Cox didn't possess a wife to clean up after him? Is that what you mean?"

"Let's just get the bedroom sorted, and I'll light the fire. You'll feel much better in the morning."

Darlene had travelled all over America and stayed in some rough places. But she'd never experienced the damp cold that she now felt seeping through her bones. If Julian thought that this was OK, he was mistaken.

The following morning, Darlene tucked both arms back in underneath the plump eiderdown. She had put one hand out to touch the quilt which had initially felt wet to her touch, until she realised that it wasn't wet. It was freezing cold.

Scanning the low beams above her head, she could see the misty cloud of her own breath.

She wanted to go home. *Now.*

Julian should have warned her instead of filling her head with nonsense about the green grass of home and the good-natured people. And the rain. He hadn't mentioned the rain. No wonder Ireland was so green. And where were all those lovely people?

All she'd seen in the twenty-four hours since she had left New York was a rude ignorant cab driver, who had spoken directly to Julian throughout the journey, looking at her as if she was speaking a foreign language and half of the time she couldn't understand a word coming out of his mouth.

At least she had her quilt. Having lugged the bulky eiderdown all the way from New York. Her mother had said the gold brocade would look great in her new master bedroom. "Some master bedroom!" she said aloud.

The quilt had cost a fortune, a wedding present from her uncle. She lay back on the white cotton pillow, enjoying the warmth. Checking that the bedclothes were nowhere near touching the floor, she tugged the quilt in around her body. Just to be sure. If there was anything lurking around under the bed, they wouldn't have an easy climb. Unless they could jump. *Yuck.*

Yellowed newspapers were visible where they had been stuffed up the chimney of the small black fireplace. For a second, she thought about getting out of the bed to strike a match to the paper. Best not, she supposed. A bible sat on the chair by the bed. She began to cry. She was done with bibles. Thinking of her home, the beautiful spacious apartment in New York – the apartment that she had wanted to leave so badly.

Finally admitting to herself that she was just being selfish. And childish. She had the most wonderful man by her side. She began to wonder where he'd got to. If he had gone down to make her a coffee and a blueberry muffin, he was certainly taking his time. Her stomach began to rumble.

Jumping out of the bed, Darlene felt the sudden urge to go to find Julian, and bring him back under the warm eiderdown.

The brass knobs on the end of the bedposts were cute, she thought, as she grabbed the Aran wool sweater that Julian had left at end of the bed. Pulling it on over her nightgown, she was glad she had her socks on, avoiding contact with dead bugs or whatever else she might step on.

Surprised to feel a blast of heat as she opened the door of the bedroom, she stepped straight onto the landing at the top of the stairs. Two men in overalls were standing in the kitchen below, looking straight back up at her. One was her husband.

"Oh, you're awake, Darlene. Come on down and meet Paul. Paul Grogan. We have a kettle here and mugs. And bread, butter, and eggs, and tea – what more could we ask for? And before you say anything, I've scalded the pot. No coffee, I'm afraid. I met Paul here in the shop in town earlier. He knows this place like the back of his hand, he's a friend of Harold Cox's."

Darlene suddenly felt hopeful as she descended the stairs. Smiling at the tall man in the tan-leather boots who struggled with her name.

"And your name is Dar…"

"Darlene is my name."

She could see the smirk on his face.

"Darlene … so it's not Darling?"

"Yes, right in one. And now you know my name."

"Pleased to meet you, Dar … lin … Darlene. I'm nearly afraid to chance it, in case it comes out wrong."

The two men laughed.

"It's D–a–r–l–e–n–e, Paul," said Julian. "An American name. Not widely heard in these parts, I'd say. And I am the only man besides her father lucky enough to get to call her *darling*. And there wouldn't be many brave enough to do so."

Both men laughed. Darlene failed to get the joke.

Paul, she thought, was handsome in a rugged sort of way. About thirty, she thought. Dark, wiry hair. Odd stare. Hard to say whether his eyes were brown or green. Huge ears. Rough hands.

Julian had softer, more refined features. Soft enough for her to wonder at his decision to move to Ireland, to work all hours with large smelly farm animals, when he could have chosen to work with small cute, domestic pets, nine to five, in New York city.

As Darlene sipped her tea, Paul explained that he lived at Black Post Inn with his mother Connie at the far side of Ballygore. He said he was a livestock dealer, mainly cattle, but sometimes horses. He said he travelled all over the country, buying up weak and under-nourished livestock off poor land, to fatten up back on his own land, before selling them on. "Quick turnaround," he said. "The quicker the better."

He said that having a vet in the locality was key to his

trade. Since Cox had to leave due to ill-health, it had slowed him down. He said that Cox hadn't been great with the leg for a long time. He had promised him that he'd help Julian out, to get him up and running. He had also promised to move the cattle from the near field to graze out on his land at Black Post.

Darlene had asked if he was married. He'd paused before he answered.

"No. Not for me, I'm afraid. My experience of marriage wouldn't have been too healthy, if you get my drift. But, having said that, I've never met the right girl either. But 'twould be hard enough for me to find someone who'd be willing to put up with the mother in the home place. She's not the easiest."

Darlene wasn't convinced – it was the look in his eyes.

"Have you no other family?"

"Well, seeing as you asked, I have an aunt living in town, my mother's sister Johanna. She runs Stapleton's pub on Mill Road. My father lives there too. It's an odd situation, but she's like a mother to me, always has been since I was knee-high, but that's enough about that. It all in the past."

It hadn't been difficult to read between the lines. His father must have married the wrong sister. And by the look on his face she knew not to continue.

The two men seemed to hit it off. Engrossed in conversation relating to the practice, Paul proved to be a great help to Julian, who took notes as Paul filled him with information pertaining to the locality. Handing him the key to the cabinet where Julian would find more information. Cox had left clear written instructions in the drawer in his desk. And Julian could phone him if he needed to.

The surgery at the side of the house had held the greatest surprise. It was spotless. Black stone floor, the room bare, apart from the heavy block table in the centre. A smaller room held two glass cases full of labelled empty bottles, with plenty of storage. A small office to the front. And a restroom with toilet and wash-hand basin.

Darlene felt giddy, childlike, noticing that once she acted like the young innocent from New York, Paul Grogan seemed to relax in her company.

Once the stove had warmed the place sufficiently, Darlene headed back upstairs to get dressed. There was little point in her wearing the street clothes she had brought with her.

Tying her blonde hair back in a tight ponytail, wearing a pair of dungarees belonging to Julian, she was ready to start cleaning, but remained upstairs until she heard her husband call to her.

"I'm away into town again with Paul, love! I'll be back as soon as I can!"

Darlene was glad they had gone. There was something about Paul that unsettled her. Dismissing her thoughts, she looked around the house for a closer inspection. The place was grubby in her eyes, even if Julian insisted on telling her otherwise. One thing was for sure, she wouldn't be staying another night in it until she was satisfied that it had been cleaned to her satisfaction. Paul Grogan had mentioned he'd ask the woman who cleaned for him at Black Post Inn to call to Darlene, to help her out. Moira Kiely was her name, he'd said.

Returning to New York, with her tail between her legs was not an option. For now. She would not have it said that her new home was a dump, after the trouble she had gone to, convincing her parents that it was the right decision for her.

The brown-painted light switches covered in sticky old cobwebs which refused to become unstuck from her hands, had cleaned up nicely.

The stone floor, when washed for a second time, surprised her, revealing pretty coloured tiles underneath. The place was taking shape.

Home-made shelves covered one entire wall. Painted in bright green shiny paint. A man's suit as well as other items hung from wire hangers off the shelves. One holding an array of men's ties. Darlene put the lot in the trash.

Spending the morning cleaning, while Julian attended to matters in town, had calmed her. Darlene was filled with pride for her hard work, by the time Julian arrived back. They would soon have the place in order.

Chapter 23

Stranger in Town

1968

Darlene needed no introduction as she walked down the main street of Ballygore. Everyone knew who she was, and if they didn't, they made it their business to find out. Confidently striding down the street, head held high. Never shy in excusing herself to interrupt a conversation if she had a question.

Darlene Taylor, the Yank, certainly had the attention of the locals in Ballygore. There weren't too many brave enough to dismiss her, or walk away from her. Some said she was a brazen hussy. Loud and uncouth. She certainly had the admiration of men in the town as they gathered in their usual spot on the main street, waiting until she had passed to eye her up and down. Wearing short colourful summer dresses. Always short. Slim-legged bell-bottoms in luminous colors. Smoking tipped cigarettes from a long slim holder. Bright red lips. Gaining attention, whether driving her red Mini Minor into town, windows wide open when the weather allowed, wearing long flowing scarves in the loudest of colours, floating out the open window as the car passed by. No announcements needed to say that she had arrived in town. Wearing her winged sunglasses, often perched on her head, brazenly tooting the horn as she passed by the local women. "Dreadful driver," they said. "She'll cause a crash one of these days if she doesn't stay on her own side of the road."

The Yank became the talk of the town. Walking into shops paying upfront for her purchases. There was no book behind the counter in Gormans' shop with Darlene Taylor's name in it. Or in any other shop in Ballygore. No taking out clothes on approval before bringing them back the day after. Worn.

The shopkeepers loved to see her coming, laughing and chatting away, always in good humour, and she never had to ask the price before she bought something.

As the days passed, Darlene made an attempt to become involved in the community, on Julian's recommendation. Feeling like an alien at times no matter what she did, she felt that people were looking at her in an odd manner. It didn't bother her as much as intrigue her as to why. Let them look, she thought. In the street she felt their eyes boring through her back as she passed. She could see their images in the shop window as they nudged each other.

Julian tried his best to encourage her, but most of the time he was either out attending to sick animals, which he insisted needed him far more than she did, or he was engrossed in his research project in the back room of the surgery.

Darlene longed for friendship, for fun. She had Moira the cleaner to talk to in the early days, but they had little in common.

The first person Darlene had met in town who hadn't looked at her as if she had two heads had been Agnes Foley. She'd met her in Gormans' shop a few weeks after her arrival.

"What can I get you, dear?" Hilda had asked Darlene, just as Agnes arrived.

"Hello! Darlene, isn't it?" Agnes butted in regardless. "I heard all about you – you're new in Kilnarick. I'm Agnes – they call me Aggie. I live across the road and up a bit."

Darlene liked the girl's openness.

"Pleased to meet you, Agnes. Yes, it's a big change, not to mention the weather."

"Well, Agnes, what can I get you?" asked Hilda. "I'm sure you're in a hurry."

"Not at all, Hilda, I'll be with you in a minute."

Darlene could see that the woman behind the counter was far from pleased. She had turned her back on them to tidy the cigarettes on the back shelf.

But Agnes hadn't quite finished with her. "Any sign of Norah around, Hilda? Will you give her a shout for me, while I'm chatting to Darlene here? I haven't seen her in days?"

Without turning, Hilda answered in a sharp tone. "Her head is stuck in her books upstairs."

Darlene picked up on the atmosphere between the two.

The following day as she walked up the main street towards the car, she heard her name being called.

"Darlene, wait up! Darlene!"

Surprised that someone was actually calling her name in Ballygore, she turned around to see the high-spirited girl she had met in the shop the day before, running towards her.

"Well, Darlene, I was calling you there. Come on. I'll walk up along the road with you."

An hour later they were still chatting.

Darlene enjoyed the company of the girl who couldn't have been more than seventeen, at least five years younger than herself. She felt a connection with this petite sparky girl with the big personality. There was something fresh and honest about Agnes Foley.

In the shop a week later Hilda tried to warn Darlene off Agnes.

"I saw you with Agnes Foley in town last week passing the window. Just to be warning you, that young one wouldn't be the best company – she's a tongue in her head the likes of what you wouldn't hear in a barrack square. Sure, how are you supposed to know who's who in Ballygore, unless you're told. You'll give that one a wide berth if you've any sense."

Hilda looked pleased with herself as Darlene took a step closer.

"Well, it's like this. Hilda, isn't it? I've been here for

two months now – not easy to blend in, I must say. I like Agnes. She doesn't me ask what I had for my breakfast. She doesn't look at me as if I've two heads." Darlene felt like bursting out with laughter when she saw the look on Hilda's face. "But thanks all the same, Hilda, it's nice to know that I can count on you."

Darlene told Julian later that Hilda had tried to warn her off Agnes.

"She *is* a good bit younger than you, love, at seventeen."

"She might be younger, Julian, but I really like her. When I'm with Agnes I don't feel like a stranger. Like I've broken the social mores by wearing my yellow flares into town. Or by ordering a vodka martini in Mansons' hotel. And we have such a giggle when we meet."

Darlene and Agnes stopped for a chat when they bumped into each other in town over the coming weeks, enjoying each other's company, having a laugh. When Agnes happened to mention that she would be starting her secretarial course after the summer, after which she needed to find a three-month placement, Darlene promised to put a good word in for her with Julian when the time came.

Darlene hadn't connected with many apart from Agnes. She felt odd at times when she tried to engage with people. Like she was butting in. She felt like an outsider. She didn't know what else to do apart from keep herself busy at the surgery, answering the phone.

And Julian worked longer hours than anyone she had ever known.

When he did take an evening off Darlene liked nothing more than to lie in his arms, talking about the future ahead of them. A bright future, full of promise. A future in America when they would buy their own place, or build even. A future where laughter and fun and happy times would soon erase this awkward start. Things hadn't been easy of late. Julian had become more frustrated with her for constantly demanding his attention. She had perked up immediately when he suggested she go home on vacation for a few weeks, even if she wasn't sure he had offered out of compassion.

"You know, there's nothing at all stopping you from going home for a holiday any time you feel like it. We don't have much to spend our money on here if you think about it, and the rent we're paying to Cox is a joke compared to the rents back in the States. He's only charging us in case we claim rights on the place. I have the research projects to work on as well as the practice, so what's stopping you from going back home for a couple of weeks? And for a few weeks again at Christmas if you feel like it."

Darlene hugged her husband who had just made her life a whole lot better.

"But won't it be just so expensive, Julian? Are you sure you don't mind?" But she had her mind already made up. The money her father had given them as a wedding gift would more than cover a return ticket. "Imagine, we'll be here in Kilnarick four months in June. It feels like a darn lifetime."

"Yes, Darlene, four months gone and fourteen more to go after that."

Darlene was quick to take him up on his proposal before he had a chance to change his mind.

"I suppose I could go back and stay for just a few weeks. And you could get on with your research here, without me pestering you all the time. Agnes Foley would be more than delighted to give a hand in the office if you need her, and you've Paul Grogan to take care of you in the evenings." Julian didn't seem to notice the sarcasm in her voice. "And by the time I get back, we'll be just like we were before. That's it, Julian!" She kissed him repeatedly. "I'm off to the travel agent's to organise my ticket first thing in the morning."

Julian was relieved, if a little surprised at how quickly Darlene had jumped at his proposal. He needed to give more time to his research, to stay ahead of the game. Being on the research team was a job in itself. He had never expected Cox's practice to be so busy. Working from early morning to night, he had set aside weekends when not on call, to concentrate on his project. Having to spend most nights being attentive to his wife, who couldn't see beyond the fun and freedom she yearned for, had not helped him stay on track with his research. Having Darlene back in the States would certainly relieve the stress and allow him the time to get on with it, without being reminded constantly that he wasn't spending enough time with her.

Darlene's parents changed their minds about coming to Ireland when Darlene told them that she would be soon home on vacation, and she would be home again at Christmas. They said they wouldn't tempt fate. Darlene hadn't been quite sure what they meant.

Landing back in New York that first summer was the happiest day that Darlene had known since she'd left home four months before. It had felt like forever.

The warm air that caressed her face was what she had longed for. Her parents, delighted to see her, wanted to know all about Ireland.

"Jeez, Mother, I've only just left the place to come home. I don't want to be reminded of it just yet."

Darlene felt better now that she was back in the city that she loved. Spending her days shopping, catching up, calling Julian briefly every evening, telling him what a wonderful time she was having, Darlene was happy to be home.

Julian seemed to be spending every spare moment while she was gone in the company of Paul Grogan. The two had become good friends. Paul gave her the creeps, but she wouldn't be sharing that around Ballygore. He was showing great interest in Julian's research project on veterinary anaesthesia and Julian seemed to have no issue sharing his findings with him. She had been surprised when Julian had remarked to her on the phone that Paul seemed to have a greater knowledge of veterinary medicine than some of the students he had met over the years.

There was so much to miss about America. She missed

the noise. The busy streets where no-one knew your name. But she missed the smells most of all. The smell of chestnuts wafting from the makeshift rusty barrels on every street corner in New York City. The smell of cigarette smoke wafting in the air. The mouth-watering aromas drifting from the ethnic eateries all over the city.

Joining local women's groups around Ballygore had been a disaster. The women were years older than her. She was just a blow-in, according to Agnes, who insisted that her own mother was still considered a blow-in after living in the town for nearly thirty years. Darlene didn't mind. She was a proud New Yorker. That pride would never leave her. This she knew. Looking at her skin which had paled with the Irish weather, Darlene thought about her city. People passing each other on the street, without as much as a glance. Anonymity. Nobody standing at street corners, heads close together, waiting for people to pass by. To pass judgement. No net curtains twitching. People going about their business, owning their own day, their own lives, without being morally policed by the good and the holy. Sitting in Central Park with a hot coffee and a doughnut. Reading a book in a coffee shop.

The memories of her childhood vacations, spent in Dennisport, Cape Cod, would stay with her forever. The Nantucket ocean warm and inviting, like bathwater. Sailboats on the bay. Birds on long matchstick legs, racing along the water's edge, with their long pointed beaks, feeding. Soft-serve ice cream from the ice-cream parlour on Holiday Hill. Running home afterwards for clam chowder. The memories of time spent roaming the streets, on the bicycle trail, meeting long lost summer friends who returned each year to their vacation cottages. Meeting vacation renters who came and went. A million miles away from her life in Kilnarick.

From that first day back in Kilnarick when she'd walked into the cow dung, as everyone seemed to call it, things went downhill. As for the smells, they were far removed from anything she had ever experienced at home.

Agnes had laughed at Darlene, when she told her she had stepped straight into a cow pie. Agnes had called it what it was. Cow-shit. "Call it cow-dung or cow patties, it all smells the same. Shite. You're a city girl, Darlene. That's all."

Agnes had explained to her that the smell on the roads was the smell of slurry leaking out from the pump attached to the slurry tank at the back of the tractors.

"Yeah. Shite and more shite," Darlene had said, the two of them breaking into peals of laughter.

Chapter 24

The Cleaner

1968

Moira Kiely prided herself in keeping tight-lipped about the houses she worked in. Knowing that if word got out that she was anyway involved in spreading rumours, her livelihood would be at stake. At the same time she loved to chat, standing at her front door of an evening, arms folded, looking up and down, enjoying the few words with the passers-by.

When the Yank was mentioned, Moira couldn't help herself. She was secretly envious of the flamboyant young woman, who was gaining quite a reputation for herself in the style stakes. Moira hated to admit it so she didn't admit it, but Darlene looked damn good.

Reporting back to her husband Arthur, at tea time.

"Jesus, what do you think of the way *your one* dresses? You'd think 'twas on a film set she was, or going to meet the queen herself. She'd be well-placed plonked above in

Clery's window in Dublin, with a price tag on her lapel, rather than parading around Ballygore like she owned the place."

Moira couldn't hold back when the subject came up, adding a few words just to keep the conversation going.

"He has his hands full, and I wouldn't mind but he seems like such a nice chap."

Moira was careful not to commit herself to detail. She had her image to protect. She cleaned for the vet once a week on a Thursday whether Darlene was away or not.

Julian was rarely at home these days and, when he was, he seemed to be spending most of his time in that surgery of his.

Moira had a key, but wasn't allowed in the back office for whatever reason. But it didn't stop her from having a peek to see what all the secrecy was about when the coast was clear. The place was spotless, everything in its place. The cabinet where he kept the drugs for his experiments as neat as the rest. Rows of small bottles of powder, some containing liquid, all with the same mark on them. CI-581.

His precious journals were kept locked in the cabinet, the one that her Johnny had been asked to build. She knew where he kept the key. All in alphabetical order, ten or so of them. Julian was ever so particular about keeping his books in order.

She was good enough to clean the animal shit and blood from the surgery, and everything else that came with it. But when it came to tidying the back office, he insisted on looking after that himself. Outside of mopping the floor, she wasn't to touch a thing.

Well, she had. No harm at all in taking a peek.

He had journals in that cabinet dating back to 1958. She couldn't make head nor tail of what was written in them, apart from recognising the same numbers that were on the bottles. Weights and doses administered. Batch numbers. Details of which she couldn't make head nor tail.

Pity he couldn't give the same attention to his child bride, who seemed to be spending more time in town parading around the streets, dressed up to the nines, than she did at home in Kilnarick.

Moira would have loved to find out from where Darlene was buying her clothes. She'd seen her in a white faux-fur coat the week before and that certainly wasn't bought from any of the drapers in town, or in either of the two boutiques. Moira had always prided herself on knowing when the new stock would be coming in, and she'd seen nothing like the outfits Darlene wore. Dublin, she guessed. Must be Dublin. Or else she's buying them in the fancy department stores in New York.

"Arthur, what kind of a man leaves his wife off gallivanting back to America? He has a good fifteen years on her, you know. Sure, didn't she tell me herself she was mistaken for his daughter a few weeks ago? And she's off again for Christmas, so Aggie told me. Of course, Aggie has all the news – and did I tell you she's working out there in the office? I suppose 'twas Darlene that got her in there. And himself holed up in the surgery with Paul

Grogan, every spare chance he gets. Oh! Before I forget it – Paul wants me to stay over with Connie the odd night while he's away over the next month. She's in a cast for the last few weeks and not doing great. What do you think?"

"It's up to yourself, love, as long as you're not going to be out there the big night of the cards in Stapleton's. As for Paul Grogan, he's nothing but a fucking whoremaster. From what I hear from the lads down the pub, he's responsible for many a young one's troubles around the country."

"I'll tell him so I'll do it and, sure, I can get Aggie and young Norah across the road to fill in for me, if I have to. I'm definitely not missing the raffle above at Stapleton's over the Christmas."

Moira put on her coat and went straight across the road to Hilda.

"I've only a minute or two, Hilda. You know I do a couple of hours cleaning at Black Post Inn for Connie Stapleton, Paul's Grogan's mother. You heard, I suppose, she fell and broke her wrist some time ago. Well, he asked me would I stay over if he was away for a couple of overnights coming up to the Christmas. She doesn't be great with the nerves and that. I was going to ask young Aggie Foley if she'd like to earn a few bob over the Christmas, I'd say she's not on much out at the vets, and she'd know Connie. Arthur likes me to sit in with him on the poker above at Stapleton's. Could Norah go with her, Hilda? And he'd pay the two of them. 'Twould keep them out of harm's way over the Christmas."

"Oh, thanks for thinking of her, Moira. I'll get back to you on it as I'd have to run it by Francis. Our Norah has never stayed in a strange house."

"Well, maybe 'tis time she did then, to get her used to it. She'll be away from home for the rest of her life once she joins the religious next September, won't she? And 'tis only out the road in Black Post Inn she'll be. Not a million miles away, Hilda, and she may as well be out there than up to mischief in town."

Moira had wanted to get the ball rolling before she got back to Paul. No point in trying to organise the girls at the last minute, only to be disappointed. Moira liked to know where she stood.

Putting it to Aggie the following evening.

Aggie had refused at first, saying that she wouldn't be caught dead staying with Connie Grogan on her own. And she definitely wouldn't be emptying any chamber pots or commode yokes after anyone.

Moira was annoyed with her tone.

"For God's sake Aggie, Connie's in her fifties, a bit shaky with the balance is all. And her nerves mightn't be too good, but that's more so when Paul is around. I've already mentioned it to Hilda for Norah to go with you."

Paul was paying twenty pounds for the overnight, and the girls could be well gone by morning, when either herself or Paul would be there to relieve them.

"It isn't as if you'll have to wipe her backside, Aggie. All you'll be doing is sleeping in the bedroom in the next room. Have a bit of tea and toast in the morning and off you go. There's no way you'll earn that much cash anywhere else in town."

"No way, Moira. Forget it. Jesus, what if she landed in the bed in top of us. Connie is built like a tank. She'd make mincemeat of us."

"Oh Jesus, Aggie, will you stop that nonsense! Just lock the bloody door. The commode is beside her and she'll get up to use it if needs be. It's only for two or three nights in December, until she gets the cast off, while Paul takes a few nights away. Since she broke the wrist, he wants someone there at night. He'll be back the following morning." Moira had been fast losing patience. "Oh forget it, Aggie. I'll put a note up in the shop. Paul has to OK it anyway, and he mightn't even want ye out there at all."

"No, no, I'll do it, Moira. Of course I'd be delighted with the few extra bob. As long as Norah can come with me. You said we'd have the double bed – sure that's fine. Just OK it so with Hilda and play it down, I don't need the third degree from her. Just wondering though. Why the hell doesn't he get a nurse in to look after his mother, Moira? He can well afford it."

"Paul Grogan doesn't want strangers snooping around the place. He's odd in that way and suspicious as hell. He trusts me, he knows I'm straight up." Moira was well pleased with herself.

She had her own suspicions about Paul dosing Connie with the sleeping pills, but no point in saying as much to young Aggie, who she knew who couldn't hold her own water. There hadn't been a sound coming from Connie's room over the two nights she herself had stayed out in Black Post.

Connie hadn't appeared down the stairs until well after eleven the following morning, which was nearly the middle of the day for Moira, who had been ready to leave at that stage, having finished the cleaning.

Connie had confided in Moira that Paul had threatened to have her committed several times, or have her carted off to the County Home.

"Sure, how can he do that to you, Connie? Apart from anything else that place is only for ordinary people, who wouldn't have the finances to pay for private care, like you would have. Anyway, you can't be near that age yet?"

"And what makes you think that I've a penny in my own name? What I get for the eggs is a pittance. And I've little to show for keeping the fowl over the years, and the rest. I've nothing in my name here, and I'd rather die than end up in the County Home."

"*Ah*, it's all changed now, Connie, it's a grand place from what I hear. All done up, and the staff are lovely now that the local women are working there. It's not at all like the old days."

"Well, *you* go there yourself so, Moira. I paid dearly for my place here in Black Post Inn. I sold my soul for the place. I'm not leaving it until they take me out of here in a wooden box."

Relaying the conversation to Arthur, he agreed that Paul Grogan showed nothing but contempt for his mother. Arthur said that Paul Grogan was well capable of keeping his mother controlled. And he said that Paul was in the golf club every other night, when he wasn't gallivanting, chasing skirt around the country.

But Moira wouldn't be saying as much. He was good to pay and she wasn't going to be accused of spreading rumours about the man who wouldn't be slow about taking her to court for slander. It was the likes of that crowd who got away with things, because people would be afraid to take them on.

Chapter 25

Meeting Connie

1968

Darlene stood at the door of Connie Grogan's farmhouse in Ballygore. She didn't much like the look of the woman who opened the door, her right arm in a sling. Small woman, wearing a navy patterned housecoat, with a look in her eyes that she didn't much care for. Difficult to tell her age. When the woman spoke, Darlene took an instant dislike to her.

"Come in, come in, girl. 'Tis cold enough out there besides you leaving it in on top of us. State your business."

"*Em* … pleased to meet you too, ma'am. I'm Darlene Taylor. Julian Taylor the vet's wife, from Kilnarick. Julian asked me to drop this over for Paul as I was passing through town. What happened to your arm?"

"Don't mind my arm at all! That's my own affair. That must be the stuff he was waiting on for the cattle. Put it down there on the table. Is there money owed on it? If there is, he'll have to settle up with you himself. I don't hold the purse-strings here."

Connie was eyeing her up, from head to toe.

Darlene felt uncomfortable. She had guessed from Paul that his mother could be awkward, but, Jeez, this lady was just plain rude. The look in the older woman's eyes was less than receptive.

"So you're the new vet's wife, are you? What age are you, girl? You don't look old enough to be anyone's wife."

"Well, if you call being in town for ten months out of an eighteen-month stay new. Well, that's up to you, and it's not as if it's any of your business. And I'm old enough to know when I meet a rude person. What age are you yourself then?'

Darlene had the latch lifted and was gone out the door as quick as she could.

"*You old bat*!" The words were out before she could stop them.

She thought she'd heard the older woman laughing, but surely she had imagined it? There was certainly no gaiety in the person she had just encountered.

She bumped straight into Agnes, who was parking her bicycle against the wall of the house.

"Hi, Darlene! Jesus, 'tis freezing. I'm everywhere you go, aren't I? Paul asked me if I'd call out to his mother, to check on her. He's away up the country this evening, afraid of his shite she'll burn the house down with the fags."

Darlene squinted at her. "The fags?"

"Oh! The cigarettes ... we call them the fags here in Ireland. Paul said that when he came home one of the mornings last week, he found a fag-burn on the armchair. Connie must have taken off to bed and left the lit fag on the ashtray. He said he knew by the length of the ash on it. Imagine. But then again we all know men what are like with the measurements." Agnes made a two-inch gesture with her thumb and forefinger. "He's afraid he'll come back some morning and she'll have the place gone up in smoke and herself along with it. Not that that would bother him too much, I'd say."

Darlene pulled a face. "Well, if that's how she behaves on a daily basis, I can't say that I blame Paul," she said, opening the door of the car.

"I can tell by you that you're not impressed with the welcome you got, Darlene. Ah ... don't mind Connie, she's tough out though maybe a bit doddery – but it's whatever she's taking for the nerves, I reckon. Paul treats her like a piece of shit on his shoe, and she stuck out here in Black Post with her family barely talking to her. Moira Kiely says she's tormented from taking shite from them all."

"Agnes, I got a shock, that's all. It wasn't quite what I was expecting. Where I come from, we tend to be pleasant to other people when we meet them for the first time. The next time Julian wants me to drop off one of his cocktails to Paul, he can give it to you. Or damn well bring it here himself. She's one grumpy lady in there."

The women giggled, enjoying the banter between them.

"Sit into the car for a minute. Come on, it's too cold to be standing here."

Aggie sat in.

"I hope Julian isn't too hard on you these days, Agnes. He's singing your praises, you know. You're only there a short time and already you've made such a difference. I've a feeling he'll keep you on. Anyone that can keep track of his precious journals, as well as the day-to-day stuff in the office, deserves an accolade in my book. I did my best, but Julian didn't want me stressing, so I got laid off. I feel like the delivery boy of late – he sends me off to town with the post and such – to get rid of me I'd say. But I'm off home in two weeks for Christmas and Julian will just have to manage without me. *Yippee!*"

Agnes laughed, thinking about what Julian had said about his wife's office skills.

"Am I glad to have you, Agnes!" he said. "Darlene tried her hand at manning the phones. I'm afraid she mixed up the diary so badly I was lucky I wasn't sued. I was turning up to treat animals on the wrong farms. And, worse still, not showing up for emergencies. No. Darlene is definitely not cut out for the surgery. But don't tell her I said that. 'Tis worth every penny to send her home every now and again."

Darlene continued. "So, Agnes, I have all this free time on my hands when I get back. Any suggestions apart from the golf club? Not! At least I have you to call on me. You must tell me more about Paul's mom. Gosh, she's so rude and bad-tempered. But I'm feeling guilty now after meeting you. Perhaps I was a bit too hasty in judging her."

"Between you and me, Darlene, Connie's bark is much worse than her bite. I like her. Myself and Norah are coming out to stay with her the odd night while Paul's away over the Christmas. The poor devil fell down the stairs and broke her wrist in three places. She was lying there for ages on the floor before he found her. Look around you at the garden. She does all that, but now that she'd laid up she probably can't. Moira said she suffers from some type of balance thing on top of the nerves. That's why she sometimes looks half-drunk. I remember her in her heyday, flying down Mill Road on a motorbike. And look at her now."

"Jeez, now I feel guilty. No wonder she's as irritable as she is. Has she any friends at all?"

"Nah. My mother maintains she's a ... you know what." Agnes leaned towards Darlene, whispering into her ear. "A lesbian."

"Gosh, I thought you were going to tell me she's a serial killer. Or a mass murderer. So what if she's a ..." she whispered close to Agnes's ear, "*lesbian?* Jeez, Agnes, I'm surprised at you. I thought of all the people you'd be more broad-minded than that. I thought 'twas Moira Kiely I was talking to there for a second. So frigging what?"

The two of them laughed but Darlene had seen the colour rise on Agnes's normally pale face.

"Oh, hear me out," said Agnes. "I'm as broadminded as they come – just that Mam said that when she was very young she went off to America with her *friend,* if you know what I mean. Yonks ago. They were going to stay there, only she was called home when her mother got sick. She had every intention of going back to the States, but her mother died and she was stuck here to look after her sister. Mam says there were two brothers who went off to Canada and haven't been seen since, leaving poor Connie to take care of the place. And Miss prissy Johanna, the younger sister, who couldn't give a fuck about her. Excuse my language, Darlene."

"Oh gosh, Agnes. How sad."

"And that Johanna one, according to Mam, isn't as sweet as she makes out to be either. All smiles when she's raking in the cash. Sweet as pie and lethal behind it all. You know that Connie's husband, Mattie, Paul's father, has been shacked up above in the pub with her, for years. And there was you thinking that nothing ever happened in a small town like Ballygore."

"Oh, Agnes, I've just been so mean. I just banged the door shut in her face and called her an old bat. I guess I just took Paul's word for it, that she's difficult. To be honest, I'm not entirely sure I trust him. There's just something in his eyes."

"I'd say she well used to having the door banged in her face. Don't mind that Paul Grogan, you should know him well enough by now. He's snooping around the surgery looking for your Julian every chance he gets.

He'd sell his mother for the price of a cow, if he could. All he wants is for both his parents to kick the bucket and he'll get the lot. If he had his way, he'd shift her into the gate lodge, out of his sight. But he can't as long as his father Mattie is alive. Mattie wants to keep the peace – he wouldn't be seen to be cruel to her. It's a minefield out here in Black Post Inn. There's bad blood between them all, but my heart goes out to poor Connie."

Seeing Connie lift the half-net at the window ended their conversation.

"I'd better go in quick or she'll think we're talking about her," said Aggie, getting out of the car. "See you on Monday, Darlene."

Darlene couldn't focus on the road. She couldn't get what Agnes had told her out of her head. The woman obviously had good cause to be suspicious and lacking in trust. Darlene felt sorry for the grumpy lady, who had given up on her dreams for the benefit of others, only to find herself a prisoner in someone else's life. Making her mind up to visit Connie again on her return from America after Christmas.

She certainly had the time now that she was no longer needed at the surgery, and there was something about Paul Grogan that she couldn't quite figure out.

She would order a cake from the bakery after Christmas and return to Black Post Inn to apologise to Connie.

Chapter 26

Babysitting Connie

1968

Norah overslept that first morning at Black Post Inn. She was anxious on waking, finding the space empty in the bed beside her.

"Where are you, Aggie?" she called quietly.

Hearing noises coming from downstairs, she dressed herself quickly, scolding herself for staying awake so late the night before. She ventured down the stairs, slowly. The door to the kitchen was wide open.

Aggie and Paul were standing by the Jubilee stove, drinking tea. Aggie, who was still in her nightclothes, turned around quickly to face Norah, an unpleasant look on her face. Paul was the first to speak.

"Well, '*the dead arose and appeared to many*'."

Norah felt shy and awkward, speaking directly to Aggie.

"Why didn't you wake me, Aggie?"

"You were fast asleep, and we up chatting half the night. I just came down to make tea. No big deal is it, Norah?

It was clear Aggie was annoyed. Norah felt like an intruder.

"No, Aggie, it's just that ..."

Aggie was abrupt in answering. "It's just that what, Norah? What?"

"Now, now, girls, come on, time ye were getting ready for the road anyway, or I'll have Francis Gorman outside in the yard. I've left the makings of breakfast there on the table, so ye won't have to be rooting around in the presses."

Agnes blushed.

"We'll see you next week so – Friday night? OK. I wouldn't normally be away so much around December, but you know what they say. Strike while the iron is hot."

Once he had left the room, Agnes wasn't long about telling her friend that she'd ruined the moment for her.

"Jesus, Norah, I was just chatting him up when you marched down the stairs like a bloody madam. I had just put the fecking bottle of booze back in the press, and in he walked. He started to set the table, if you don't mind."

Paul had already left when they'd got there the following Friday night. He was meeting people up the country.

Connie was sitting in her armchair by the fire. They'd chatted for a while, until Connie went off to bed, announcing she was tired. The following morning both girls arrived down to the kitchen at eight thirty, to find tea and bread for toast laid out for them on the table, as it had been the case the week before. Paul had appeared through the scullery door at the back of the house and given them twenty pounds each. A fortune. Asking if they were available for the following Friday night. The last of the dinner dances before the Christmas, he'd said.

Norah had insisted on the way back into town that she wasn't going to be trying out anymore of Aggie's mixtures the next night.

"And that mattress has to be the worst I've ever slept on, I've a right pain in my back after it. It's completely sunken in the middle."

"Probably Paul and his latest fancy pants, whoever she might be, lepping and jumping all over it. Jesus, Norah, will you give over. My bed at home is no different, and I bet most of the beds on Mill Road are the same. Soft and comfy. I couldn't sleep on a flat mattress, if you paid me. That's just you, Norah, and the big long legs on you, and you not knowing where to put them. Look at the money he's paying us! One more night of Connie-sitting and that's it, so stop bloody complaining ... will you?"

The two girls got into the double bed on the following Friday night, confident that Connie had settled down. They giggled. No matter how they tried to keep to their own sides of the bed, they rolled in towards one another. The room was chilly enough, with no heat apart from the hot-water bottle, that Moira had warned them to bring with them. Huddling together, the two friends chatted until after two, when an exhausted Norah told her pal to keep on talking – she might not answer, but she'd be listening all the same. Aggie had continued.

"Norah, just think. If we had a flat in London together, this is what it would be like every night. We'd have our own beds of course, but we'd have some laugh. So, forget about that convent business and stand on your own two feet. You're not going to go? Sure you're not?"

Norah didn't reply.

"Norah, come on, talk to me. I'm wide awake here. Norah, will you stay awake? Will you? Oh Jesus, never mind!"

Norah had pretended to be asleep. Aggie had been too wound up to sleep, even if Julian was collecting her at her house to be at work for eight in Kilnarick. She wouldn't normally be working on a Saturday, but when he'd asked she'd told Norah she couldn't refuse.

"Norah ... my fecking head is spinning here, every time I close my eyes." The rain was pelting against the window outside.

"That *poitín* is dangerous stuff – how's *your* head?"

Norah opened her eyes.

"Well, I hope it's better than yours will be in the morning, Aggie. Goodnight."

Norah had been so excited to be away with Aggie. She had to cycle back in to town on her own in the morning, once Paul arrived home. No point in telling her parents that Aggie had left for work earlier, or there'd be hell to pay. It had been difficult enough to persuade them in the first place to let her go, but once Moira Kiely had guaranteed them that Paul wouldn't be there until morning, they had agreed.

"You're just the nervous type, Norah. Just as well you're marrying your intended. You won't have to look at him, never mind sleep with him. Well, you might sleep with him, but he won't take up any room in the bed. And you'll never get pregnant unless it's the Immaculate Conception."

They had talked often enough about Aggie's idea of a good catch. Paul Grogan's name had come up more than once.

"How could you fancy him, Aggie? He must be at least thirty, and you're not even eighteen."

"Thirty, Norah? Far from it. He's twenty-eight if you must know. And he's loaded, with a farm of land under his arse. It'll be all his one day – it's only waiting for me to put my stamp on it. Imagine, Norah ... Mrs Agnes Grogan."

"You mean Mrs Paul Grogan, Aggie."

"Norah, I'll be keeping my own name. I've no intention of taking anyone else's name. Taking on their dirty washing will be enough. Agnes Foley-Grogan, how does that sound? Did you ever wonder, Norah, where the women come in, like? Oh yeah, I forgot, they disappear down the man's line. Stop laughing, I said line, not loin. I'm deadly serious. Where the women's line? Even our names aren't our own, they're from our father's side. So at least, Norah, when you're married to God, you won't be taking on his surname. You don't even know what it is. Mrs Norah God."

Norah loved Aggie.

There was something about Paul Grogan that scared her. Not that she had much experience of men, apart from her father.

It wasn't that he was rude to them, or rough or mean. He couldn't have been nicer to them – he just made her feel uneasy. It was his eyes.

Waking up on the couch in his front room, to find him towering over her, had been mortifying. So embarrassing. She didn't know where she was at first, she was all confused. Agitated.

Shaking her. Roughly. With his huge hands.

"Come on, Norah. Get up. 'Tis ten o'clock, what's up with you? Time to go."

It had taken her a while to straighten herself up back in the bedroom, too embarrassed to face down the stairs. But she had. She'd cycled into town and gone straight home to bed, telling her mother on the way up the stairs that she'd just got her monthly and needed to lie down with a hot-water bottle. She had an ache in her groin. She didn't want her mother knowing that she was in such a state from the drink the night before.

Aggie had joked with her mam that same evening, telling her that Norah had been giving out about the bed in Black Post Inn.

"Don't mind her, Aggie. They probably have one of them divans down at her place. No headboards on them, so there's nothing to lean against when you sit up. All they are is one mattress down on top of the other, on the ground. Cheap stuff in them, although I'd say the old springs are well worn out at this stage, with Francis and Hilda."

Josie changed the subject. "How'd you get on outside there anyway? I hope you got your money. You were lucky the boss collected you himself this morning, or you'd have been well late. Easy known he isn't paying you a whole pile, he's getting great value out of you, expecting you out there on a Saturday morning. And very short notice too, Aggie."

"Ah, he's just busy, Mam. He had to go to test a herd first thing this morning, an emergency, and from what he said he was up all night with the research stuff."

"It was fine last night. Connie was in her room when we got there. She knew we were coming, and she'd met Norah the last night, so there wasn't a peep out of her. She knows me well enough by now. She's not half as bad as they make her out to be, she couldn't be nicer really. Although I thought she was dead at one stage, when the snoring stopped for ages. I was going to knock at the door to check up on her, but Norah pulled me back – she said not to. We were laughing and gabbing half the night and Paul gave Norah twenty quid each for us again this morning. I called in to the shop earlier but she was still in the bed. She suffers awful with her monthlies."

"Pity you won't get a few more nights out of it all the same."

"Well, Moira said she'll call us if he ever wants us again

but I doubt it. Connie gets the cast off her arm soon and Darlene has an appointment made for her about the balance thing, with some specialist. At least myself and Norah got to spend a few nights together, that was the best crack, and now we've enough money to go off buying Christmas presents. You should have seen the huge wad of cash Paul Grogan carries around, all rolled up. He's loaded."

Her mother didn't hold back.

"That Hilda one was always as mean as dyke water, so don't be too surprised if she takes the money straight out of Norah's hand. I'd say you well earned it, Aggie. Moira was saying that Connie hasn't a moment's peace with that son of hers, since she broke her wrist."

"Paul's all right, Mam. Did I tell you he calls her by her Christian name? Connie. And he calls his father Mattie. Weird."

"Aggie, he's a bully boy, that's all he is. He won't leave her on her own out there, for fear she'll burn the place down. And, according to Moira, he locks her in her room to control her. She smokes like a trouper apparently. With no say at all in her own home. Does there be much talk out of her?"

"Not much. She's a bit shaky when she walks though, I thought 'twas drunk she was at first. So, we didn't see her at all last night, and Norah said she still hadn't appeared when she left there this morning. She was slagging us the last time, that 'tis she should be babysitting us, and not the other way around. They've a fancy toaster out there as well. We'll have to get one for here once I start earning proper money. Why don't you get one from the weekly man and pay in on it?"

"Give over, Agnes. Your father would have a fit if I get any more on tick and the Christmas nearly in on top of us. I bet Hilda Gorman below has one. I can see Francis right now, bringing her up her tea and toast in bed on a tray, and she lying there on the divan waiting for him, in her black-and-red lingerie. I'd say that's as much as she gets from him. The tea and toast, like."

"Jesus, Mam, give over, will you? That's my best friend's parents you're slagging off."

"Ah, they make me sick, Aggie, that shower. Thinking they're better than the rest of us, just because he has two sisters in the nuns. And their eldest lad off in the missions. And if you ask me, they're forcing Norah into the convent. Anyway, I don't know for the life of me know what you were thinking, bringing that young one out to Black Post. She'll be off to the convent next year and, if you take my advice, you'll do more on your own while she's around so that you'll miss her less when she's gone."

Moira was at her front door the following day when Agnes passed by.

"Just looking at the decorations across the road in the shop, love. Hilda has the window covered in tinsel. Isn't the crib lovely? Look at the size of the figurines, they're nearly as big as the ones above in the church. I suppose she'll have Francis out there next!"

"Moira, you're gas."

"Jesus, 'tis perishing altogether! Look at the ice on the window! I just came out for a bit of fresh air. I've the plum pudding on the cooker and four fruit cakes made this morning alone. You've been a great help out in Black Post over the past few weeks, so you have. I don't know for the life of me why she insists on staying upstairs – she's spoilt for choice out there, but she nearly took the head clean off me when I suggested she move to the bedroom downstairs."

Moira looked up and down the street, arms folded across her chest. "I better go back in and put on a bit of grub for our Johnny. Anyway, tell me, did he sort you out with a decent few bob?"

"He did, Moira, and thanks." Aggie wasn't about to tell her just how much they got. "We were delighted. Paul paid us well and not a peep out of Connie last night, apart from the snoring."

"OK, pet, I better go back inside, Johnny does be starving when he comes in for his tea."

Chapter 27

Making Amends

1969

Darlene couldn't take her eyes off Connie who had a smirk on her face when she saw the cream cake and the jar of instant coffee.

"I've a distinct feeling 'tis myself should have baked that cake for you." Connie smiled at her guest.

"I'd better remember my manners today, I suppose. Good to see you, I hope you had a good Christmas. We got off to a bad start – my fault, I suppose, as usual."

Connie sat with Darlene drinking coffee, eating the cream sponge cake.

Darlene watched as the older woman let her guard down. Slightly.

"I'm having the cast off next week, they tell me, it'll be such a relief. My son won't have to be asking half the town to check up on me."

Darlene didn't reply.

"The cast, girl, the cast here on my arm," said Connie, raising her right arm.

The two were soon laughing. Connie praised Darlene for arriving back at the door after the reception she had got on her last visit.

"Call me Connie. My full name is Cornelia. But it's been a long time since anyone called me that. I'd say I'm called a few other names as well behind my back."

"Well, I will call you Connie, if I may. I've a feeling we have much in common, you and I. Both well able to speak our minds for a start."

Darlene could see the suspicious look creep up on Connie face, her eyes squinting every now and then. Until she felt relaxed enough to let her guard down with her American visitor, who had just returned from New York. Telling Connie that it had been her second trip home since she had arrived over ten months ago.

"I went back home for the first time three months after we came here last year. It was summer, so I spent most of the vacation time down the Cape – Cape Cod. My recent trip at Christmas was really to visit my parents in Manhattan."

"How lucky you are to be able to travel at the drop of a hat. In my day, travel had to be planned months in advance. And there were no planes just the steamships then … Ah, New York, I remember it well, many moons ago. And Cape Cod …"

Darlene could see the sadness creep across the older woman's face.

"Tell me," Connie said then, her face brightening up. "Tell me all about New York."

Darlene told her as much as she could.

Connie asked about Broadway. Had she seen a show there? Which theatre? What about Harlem? Had she been there? And Greenwich Village, had she been there?

Connie said that she had spent many a great night there. Her face changed when she mentioned Cape Cod again. Telling her visitor that after a brief stay in Provincetown, she had fallen in love with the place, intending to settle there. She talked about the sea water on the elbow of the Cape. Herring Cove beach. Street names she remembered. Blueberry Road. Snail Road. Smuggler's Beach. "Oh, and the round shells scattered all over. Pink ones. Every shade of purply-pink you could think of. And the huge bell crabs. I've never seen them anywhere else since."

Darlene could scarcely believe that this was the same dour lady who looked as if she'd never left the town of Ballygore, yet here she was, interested in the very places that Darlene loved to talk about. Reminiscing about the past, Connie talked about the happy times in New York in '29, just before the Wall Street Crash. She talked about prohibition and the homemade alcohol that she and her friends had concocted, leaving her fuzzy-headed for days. The conversation allowed each to escape in different ways, to form a bond, leaving behind all suspicions or judgements.

The following week, as Darlene prepared to visit Connie, she was told by Julian in advance of her visit that Paul had said there was no need for her to be putting herself out by calling to Black Post any longer. That Agnes and her friend from town had been calling in on Connie over the Christmas, while Darlene was away. And Moira Kiely would be there herself on a regular basis.

But Darlene wasn't one to be fobbed off.

She wouldn't be told who she could or couldn't visit. And certainly not by Paul Grogan. Unless it came from Connie's own mouth, and it hadn't. Paul obviously didn't want her to be sticking her nose in his family business. Either way she decided to dismiss what Julian had said.

"What are you on about, Julian? I'm my own woman and you've known that since the day you met me. And I'll have you know that Connie is also her own woman. At what point does one decide that decisions can be made about them? That their choices don't matter any more? It's obvious that Paul has issues with his mother and I don't want to intrude, but something must have happened in his life to turn him against her. What the hell is he trying to hide? It's probably just because she's lesbian."

Seeing the exasperated look on Julian's face wasn't enough for her to hold her tongue.

"It seems to me he's been resentful of her since he was a child. He despises her, plain and simple. So he makes her suffer by ignoring her most of the time, keeping her in her box. But that doesn't mean I have to join his club and I sure as hell won't. I'm surprised you're entertaining him at all ... he's a big boy now."

Julian's face was as red as she had ever seen it. He was furious with her. "Now you're telling me that Paul's mother is a lesbian. I'd be careful where I'm talking, if I were you, Darlene." He walked away from her in a huff.

Darlene called to Connie the following day, making sure first that Paul's cattle truck wasn't parked in the yard.

Connie smiled at her visitor, saying that she hadn't expected her to come back so soon. The two friends sat facing each other at the table. Understanding.

Darlene enjoyed her time with Connie who listened intently as Darlene refreshed her memories of her time spent in America and she continued to visit Connie every week. The older lady opened up more as she became more familiar with her visitor.

"I told you, I lived in New York for six months as a young woman. On Broadway, with my Italian friend Lucrezia. We had a plan that I could never speak about back then. But what odds. I'm in my sixties now but herself is that bit younger. We've held on over the years, living in hope, Darlene, that myself and herself will one day be together but somehow I doubt it'll be above ground at this stage. My son is another matter altogether. As long as I live and breathe, he won't have her name mentioned. It's a long story. It's probably best if we leave it there."

Darlene couldn't get Connie out of her mind as she relayed some of her conversation back to Julian later that night. Careful not to say too much. Saying that she was going to make it her business to visit her more. To bring her out of herself.

He suggested she leave well enough alone.

"Darlene, I know you like to have a cause. And you do like picking up strays. But, for Jesus' sake, don't be taking on Paul's mother as your latest cause. From listening to Paul, she has her own problems. Don't be butting in where you're not wanted. That's all I'm saying."

On her next visit to Connie, Darlene sensed that Connie wasn't as bright as she had been the previous week. Sullen and guarded, she seemed to have retreated back into herself. She said she'd been sleeping a lot. They'd changed her tablets. She told Darlene that Paul had warned her against entertaining visitors. She was not to be encouraging Darlene at Black Post Inn.

Darlene was returning to the States at the beginning of May to spend two weeks on the Cape. Their time in Ireland would soon be coming to an end. They were due to return to America permanently in July. Julian had booked the trip for her as a birthday surprise.

Connie's eyes had opened wide when Darlene told her she was off home again. Darlene sensed the deep longing in her friend. There was more to Paul Grogan's mother than a grumpy old woman. A lot more.

"What? You're away again? Haven't you only a few months left in Kilnarick? He must have more money than sense, that husband of yours."

"Oh, Connie, believe me, Julian will be relieved to see the

back of me for a few weeks. He tells me I'm a distraction, if you don't mind, just while he's winding up the research. Now what would you like me to bring you back, Connie?"

Connie smiled. "If you'd bring me a small container of sand from one of the beaches on Nantucket Sound, I'd be delighted. Just to feel it falling through my fingers. And maybe a couple of those pink rounded shells that we mentioned. If you can find them."

Darlene recognised the look Connie's face.

"And if you happen to be near Provincetown ..." Connie voice trailed off, leaving Darlene anxious to know what she was going to say.

"What were you going to say, Connie? If I happen to be in Provincetown – what?"

"No, girl. It was nothing. Best leave well enough alone. *Em* ... I was going to ask for a piece of salt-water taffy. I'm looking for too much now, aren't I?" She was grinning but her eyes told another story.

"Connie, tell me, please? Just finish what you were really going to say."

"No. She's happy now. And all I'd be doing is upsetting her. Not after all these years. Paul wouldn't be too happy and my life here wouldn't be worth living."

Darlene had no choice but accept that the conversation was over.

Driving her father's car from New York up to the Cape the following weekend gave Darlene the headspace she needed. Her parents' vacation cottage on the Cape was hers to enjoy. The weather was warm enough for the month of May, and she'd soon be back in the States for good. Her parents wouldn't be travelling up to the Cape until after Labour Day, when they would swop their air-conditioned apartment for the late-summer ocean breezes on the Cape. She had the place to herself.

Taking the old route, over Bourne Bridge onto the Cape, always excited her. She would be at the cottage in Dennisport in thirty minutes. The atmosphere changed once over the bridge. The lazy days ahead were in focus.

Turning up the radio, Darlene couldn't help but smile at the joy she felt in her heart. Stopping along Route 28 for clam chowder, a favourite of hers. Buying supplies at the first convenience store, very different from shopping at Grogans' back in Ballygore. Laughing at herself as she recalled her reaction setting foot in Ireland fifteen months before. The green fields and the friendly inquisitive nature of the people had certainly not enchanted her from the beginning. Trying her best to fit in amongst the small community. Over-eager. Too pushy, she now realised.

At least Julian could spend his evenings winding up his project while she was on this vacation. He wouldn't have to feel like he was neglecting her. And no doubt Paul Grogan would be there 'til the small hours, looking over his shoulder.

Sharing her new husband with Paul hadn't been at all easy for Darlene. The unlikely pair had become close, the idea of which was beyond Darlene.

The cottage was a three-minute walk from the ocean. Compared to the sea water in Ireland, the ocean water was warm and inviting. Darlene sat out on the deck for the evening on her father's old Adirondack chair, sipping a glass of wine, cooking her food on the stone barbecue, the bright ornamental grass swaying back and forth against the painted wooden fence. The lace hydrangea, just inside the gate, awaiting the arrival of its dainty pinkish-white flowers which would bounce in the breeze once they came into bloom. The stars and stripes flag, once again proudly in place, to the left of the front door, a sign that the *Captain's Cottage* was now occupied.

The enclosed outdoor shower, warm and inviting. Looking up at the clear blue sky, washing away the remnants of sand from the beach, before stepping out in the sunshine caressed by the softness and warmth of her towel, Darlene was grateful to be back.

The air-conditioning box was fixed to the window in the bedroom, if she needed it. Settling herself underneath the cotton handstitched quilt that had belonged to her grandmother, Kilnarick, and Ballygore faded from her mind. Connie and her sad life might as well be a million miles away. Darlene was delighted to have the cottage to herself. Filling the fridge with the foods she herself chose to eat. Shrimp with fresh corn husks bought from the market. Baby octopus fried with garlic and oil, served with linguine. Darlene Taylor couldn't wait to return home for good.

Searching for shells along the beach on Old Wharf Road. Letting the soft, dry sand sift through her toes, Darlene couldn't help thinking how much Connie's face would light up if she could swap places with her just for an instant. Returning from her trip, she was full of excitement, telling Julian that it had been exactly what she had needed.

Anticipation creeping through her as she realised that in two months' time, they would be packing up and preparing to return home for good. The realtor in New York was on the lookout for a place for them to live. Julian had finally signed off on his research and submitted it.

Having felt every bit the stranger in Ballygore since she had first arrived, Darlene found herself sad to be leaving. She had warmed to the place. But she had reserved the badges of friendship for Connie Grogan and Agnes Foley. She would be keeping in touch with the two of them.

Agnes, with her wild rebellious streak. There was a warmth about her which had impressed Darlene. Never afraid to speak the truth as she saw it, even if she did use expletives in almost every sentence. And she was so funny. Admirable qualities as far as Darlene was concerned.

Connie Grogan likewise. Honest to a fault. Sincere. No interest in pretence. Out it came. With Connie Grogan, you knew where you stood. A friend for life – even if she was more or less the same age as her own mother.

Chapter 28

The Pink Sea Shells

Connie's excitement on receiving the mementos from America had been heart-wrenching for Darlene. Connie was smiling widely, showing off a set of even dentures which Darlene hadn't noticed on previous visits. Putting the small glass bottle of sand into the pocket of her housecoat, she smelled the round pinkish shells, before holding one close to her ear. How easy it had been to put a smile on her face.

"Don't tell him, mind. Paul. Say nothing at all. They think I'm soft enough as it is and some days I probably am. You know … I'm better in myself lately, when I don't take half of the medication. Look at it all there in the press. Sure, I didn't know what I was taking."

"You must know surely. What does the doctor say?"

"Ah, I only see that man every now and then, and Paul collects the stuff for me at the chemist in the meantime. I ended up with a bad bout of depression at one stage and they put me on the tablets. But thank God I haven't had that terrible foreboding that I had after Paul was born, this long time."

"Oh, I'm sorry, Connie."

"You've done me a power of good, Darlene, having someone to laugh with after all this time. Mattie passes in and out the lane – we haven't spoken for years. Would you credit that? He wouldn't come through that door if he thought I was sitting here. Imagine that. Husband and wife and not a word to say between us. Mattie was always like that – he'd ignore a person rather than have to talk to them."

Darlene felt uncomfortable for Connie, reaching over to hold her hand.

"You've really helped me, Darlene. You've no idea how much. And I'm going to take your advice and straighten myself out – I've started with the teeth. Look!" Connie smiled, showing her white set of dentures. "And I want you to stay in touch with me when you go back. Promise me. You've a light heart – you remind me of my Lucrezia, you know."

Squeezing Darlene's hand, she whispered, "Thank you, Darlene. Thank you."

Darlene understood.

"And right until the day I leave, Connie, we can travel any time you wish, and never have to leave Black Post Inn. We can bring America right here to your kitchen. And we can go to town for a coffee. Yes, that's what we'll do."

The older woman sat smiling at her, pleased to be in her company.

"So where shall we go today?" Darlene asked. "We can travel out to Provincetown and go whale-watching, or we can go to Boston and I'll show you where the famous Boston Tea Party happened. Or we can go back to New York. "

Connie smiled contentedly as she joined her friend in revisiting old haunts. Familiar places. Familiar smells.

"You've a lovely way about you, Darlene. You really do remind me of Lucrezia as a young woman. Not in looks, mind. She was dark. Brown eyes. Latin-looking. But in your spirit, as Lucrezia herself would say. In your soul. She was always talking about the soul and the spirit. And the senses. I didn't really understand at the time. But I do now, because that's as much as we have of each other."

Darlene felt sad for her friend as Connie returned to her thoughts.

Julian scolded his wife once again for continuing to entertain Connie, saying Paul wasn't too pleased with her for sticking her nose in. That his mother wasn't the same as she had been.

"Julian, Paul Grogan can go and take a jump for himself. Connie is nothing like Paul would have us believe. In fact, I'm of the view that it suits him for us to think she's unstable. In more ways than one. You know she had vertigo pretty bad, she's been putting up with it for years. So I made an appointment with a specialist for her. It's what Dad had, until he got the treatment. She told me Paul had a tonic made up for her at the chemist. He told her it would keep her steady. Whatever that means."

Julian suddenly turned around. "Jesus Almighty! What are you trying to infer now, Darlene? Keep out of it."

"Are you for real, Julian? Connie is a human being, for Christ's sake, and her son has no right whatsoever to be dictating what medical care she should or should not have. She's been on way too many meds and doesn't know what half of them are for. They're making her sleepy. Not good."

"Huh! A lot you'd know about medication," he answered, dismissing her.

"Well, for your information. I had a peek in her medicine cabinet. I found a brown glass bottle of liquid in there, with no name on it. Smells bad. Like one that you'd have in the Controlled Drugs cabinet. I've a feeling he's medicating her to keep her controlled."

"Jesus, am I hearing you right? Your mind is definitely running away with you. I'd be careful who you're saying that to or you'll end up in jail. Don't be ridiculous. She's his mother, for God's sake. *His mother.* Whatever she's on would have been prescribed for her by her doctor."

"Well, I took the brown bottle to have it checked. Just in case."

"What! Jesus Christ! Give it to me. Right now. I can't believe you're so stupid. Accusing Paul of bullying his mother. And drugging her. Jesus Christ, Darlene, hand it over and I'll find a way of returning it and there'll be no more about it."

"It can happen, you know, Julian. I'm not saying it's common, but it happens. People just hide it under the carpet. And tell me, why would you be so worried about Paul? You choose to believe that oddball against your own wife? You two are as thick as thieves."

Julian stood in front of her with his hand out, requesting the bottle.

"*Ah,* for God's sake, Julian! Calm down. I'm kidding. Just kidding. Of course I didn't touch anything. But I had you worried there, didn't I?"

Darlene couldn't control her laughter.

As the colour returned to her husband's face, Darlene couldn't help but wonder at the level of his reaction.

Darlene had every intention of helping her friend Connie. She would not forsake her.

"Myself and Lucrezia were going to open a shop there, you know. In Provincetown. Right there on the busy street, beside the harbour. Lucrezia was going to sell her paintings and I was going to have a little tea shop at the front. In those days it was easy. Rather, it could have been easy, if it weren't for circumstances beyond our control. But I should have tried harder to keep her."

Darlene watched Connie's face soften, her blue eyes sparkling as she reminisced about the good days. Telling Darlene how lucky she had been to get out of America at the time.

How Lucrezia had been ordered back to Naples. How

she had persuaded her to go back home to protect her.

"That's enough now, love. Put on the kettle like a good lass. Where's that jar of coffee?"

She had never in her life met anyone like Connie, but she would soon be leaving Ireland for good. There had been a huge change in her friend over the time she had known her. She had become much more alert and confident. The older lady in front of her had lived such a life, and it certainly wasn't over yet. Travelling from Ireland to England as a young girl to earn a living to support her family. Being forced to return to take care of her sister who had no time for her. Connie had lived a selfless life.

"But why did you two conform to the rules, Connie? I refuse to conform to anyone else's rules. Surely Lucrezia could have refused to return to Italy?"

"No, love. 'Twas very different in those days. And when the big Crash happened, we were left penniless in New York. Where would we have lived? On the street? She had been used to the best, coming from wealthy people. I couldn't bear to have her suffer, which she would have done – no doubt about it. We had mighty plans to settle in America. Great plans. All up in the air. All pipe dreams now."

Darlene didn't interrupt.

"Lucrezia had no option, you see, but to marry. Women didn't have the same freedom as they have now. The fascists were in control there and women were seen to be the breeders of the fascists of the future. I was busy keeping the place going in town. And after my mother died … I couldn't leave."

Darlene felt that Paul Grogan's mother deserved a lot more from life than she had been getting.

"You know, Lucrezia was here with me in Black Post Inn. Twice. 'Twas easier back then when I had the place open for guests. I love to hear you say her name. I haven't heard it spoken aloud for years, and you pronounce it properly."

Connie laughed, her cheeks lifting as she held her smile.

"The first time Mattie brought her here, I nearly died with the shock. He hadn't a notion who she was, except to know that she was my travelling companion from years before. I think she came first in '37 and didn't come again until the 50s when she could travel again. And each time we met it was as if we had never been apart, if you understand me? Her husband Marco got hit in the eyes with shrapnel. He'd been involved in shady dealings with the Mafia during the war. She looked after him all those years, even though in my mind he didn't deserve her. He was as good as blind till the day he died. She stayed here three nights and four days the first time she came and the same the time after, after Marco had passed on. We were happy out here in Black Post snatching whatever precious moments we could when the coast was clear. Until Paul burst in the front door from school. Unannounced. I'd say he was eleven. He caught us red-handed. But I never mentioned it to him after. Mattie couldn't have cared less. He was well ensconced in my sister's bed by that stage. I often thought that he didn't have an iota of the full extent of my relationship with Lucrezia. He was always innocent enough in that line. Kind of simple. So I lost both my husband and my son's love as a result. And that was the end of myself and Lucrezia. They never understood. No-one ever did. And now ..."

Darlene leant forward to hold Connie's hand as she continued.

"I had to stop writing to her with everything that happened. It nearly finished me. A card at Christmas is OK nowadays, and the odd phone call, when he hasn't the lock put on the bloody thing. If Paul found all the old letters, he'd burn them. And me with them. They're all I have of her now, all I have in the world. She loved to quote Shakespeare, you know. What's this she used to say? '*With great love comes great pain.*' And how true is that?"

Darlene felt saddened by her friend's disclosure, Connie's face showing a lifetime of regret. Giving her word to Connie that she would not discuss her business with another soul. Asking herself who would she be discussing it with anyway? Agnes, with the best of intentions, wouldn't be able to keep it to herself. And she couldn't trust Julian not to let it slip to Paul, who would no doubt rubbish his mother's version of her own life.

As Darlene said her goodbyes to Connie, she promised to stay in touch.

"I'm not one to give up easily, Connie, that's all I'll say. I'll be in touch. Gosh ... I so hate goodbyes!"

The unlikely pair hugged as tight as two friends could.

"Darlene, I'll never forget your kindness. You've given me the push I needed to smarten myself up and there'll be no stopping me from now on. There'll be no goodbyes between us. Safe journey home and we'll speak soon."

PART THREE

Chapter 29

The Registered Letter

1977

Flat 12b
36 Crowford lane,
London
21/3/77

Dearest Aggie,

Don't get too much of a shock now, it's Norah. Remember me, your blood sister? I'm sorry I couldn't get in touch with you before now, and for leaving in such a hurry without saying goodbye. I sent you the holy picture few years ago just to let you know I hadn't vanished off the face of the earth. Too much of a coward at the time to write. I just couldn't talk to you before I left, Aggie, then as time passed it became more difficult. You see I was pregnant, and had to get out of Ballygore. I refused to believe it myself and still can't get my head around it. They sent me to a Mother and Baby Home within two weeks of finding out. The baby was stillborn at five months. James I named him. James.

My parents locked me in the back bedroom for ten days before I went. I was too traumatised to go against them. I was in shock and still am in many ways. But now is not the time to go into all that. Aggie, you have to believe me that I've no idea how I got pregnant or by whom. I've gone through every possibility and I still can't find the answer. I've had three rounds of counselling and they all told me that I must have blocked it out with the shock. When I think back on it, you were working at the vets and I was still at school and we hadn't seen much of each other over the few weeks previously.

The longer I put it all out of my mind, Aggie, the easier it became to forget Ballygore and that meant forgetting everything about it. The memory of my father's face, warning me to keep quiet, haunted me.

But you've been on my mind lately, and I couldn't forget my blood sister, could I? My birthday last June brought it all back for some reason. We were having a little party at the flat here, nothing grand just a few drinks and cake. The sisters in the convent send me cards and I had one from Damian (he's left the order too) and for some reason you kept popping into my mind.

There's so much to tell you, Aggie. First I thought you'd never speak to me again and who could have blamed you? Anyway, here I am after eight years, begging you to forgive me. I hope we can rekindle our friendship. I'll say no more for now as I expect it'll take you some time to let it all sink in.

I remain,

Your blood sister,

Norah Gorman

P.S. Not a word to anyone that you've heard from me, apart from your mam of course cos I know you'll tell her anyway.

Love Norah xx

Agnes couldn't believe her eyes. She couldn't believe what she was seeing. Reading it over and over again, to make sure. Checking the envelope which she had signed for, wondering if it was a cruel trick someone was playing on her. But as she read on, she knew it was from Norah. The two red biro dots at the end of the letter, a symbol of their bond. Blood sisters. Warm thoughts for her best friend flooded through her.

As she finished the letter for the third time, her worries and fears faded to the background. It all fell into place.

Norah Gorman had sex! Norah Gorman had sex! She repeated over and over until it sank in. With whom? When? Surely she would have remembered. Of course she would have known. But here she was, saying she didn't.

"Never in a million years. Never."

Speaking aloud.

"Well, you're a dark horse, Norah Gorman, and there was I thinking 'twas an angel I was hanging around with. And you riding away on the quiet."

The shock of reading Norah's letter made her want to go straight down to Hilda Gorman and have it out with her. But she knew well enough not to bother. No point.

She had asked numerous times for an address for Norah, but they had sidetracked her every time – she'd had a feeling they were lying all the time.

For a week before Norah left, Aggie had a sense that she was at home, but every time she called for her she was told that Norah was busy. She had wondered why Norah hadn't contacted her, and why her parents wouldn't give her the address of the convent. It was as if she had vanished off the face of the earth. And the big smug face on Hilda when she finally admitted that Norah had been gone for two days.

Aggie had been hurt – more than hurt. Gutted. Her best friend gone without even a goodbye.

It had taken her a long time to come to terms with it and, once she did, she let go of any hope of hearing from Norah again. She had busied herself working in Kilnarick and Darlene Taylor had been just what she had needed. A friend.

Asking after Norah in the shop had proved pointless, the answer was always the same. "Yes, she's doing just fine."

It didn't matter whether 'twas Norah's mother or father, same answer every time. She finally decided she was wasting her time. Norah was gone and no one seemed to want to talk about her, or even mention her name. All very strange.

And now eight years later, a letter.

So, they packed poor Norah off to the Mother and Baby Home to get rid of the problem, and when they could have brought her back home to Ballygore they punished her further by packing her off to the convent. Her parents had made her disappear and that was the bones of it.

Agnes was in shock but happy and relieved to have heard from Norah – there had been times when she'd doubted that they'd ever been as close as they had. Times when she'd blamed herself for being too bossy with Norah. Overpowering her. No. Now that she knew the truth, the real truth, it had nothing at all to do with her. Norah had only gone and got herself pregnant with some fella, and been banished from Ballygore. But how had she, her best friend, not known?

Thinking about the day she had banged the door of the shop in a temper. "*Bitch!*" she had called Hilda. "Bloody bitch!"

Hilda hadn't as much as acknowledged her. Standing behind the counter with her arms folded, with a face on her.

"Hilda, it's been over three months now since Norah left and I've heard nothing from her. What's Norah's address in England?" Repeating her request. "Norah's address in England." Before adding, "Please."

Hilda's arms tightened across her chest.

"Leave her to get on with it, now she's settled. That was always the plan. You'll only unsettle her. So no, there'll be no address given out."

"Well, I'll write to every order of nuns in London then. I'll find out myself where she is."

"Oh, off you go then! And by the time they get the letter, she'll be well on her way to America. She doesn't need you, Agnes Foley, she said it herself. You're too much of a liability. She's in an enclosed order, so you can write all you like and create whatever stink with it, but you'll be told nothing. 'Twas Norah's wish to join the nuns and her wish to go to an order where she'd be segregated from the outside world. So you can write away, but you'll be wasting your stamps, I can tell you. Norah is gone, that's the end of the matter. And if she chose not to call up to you before she left, well, she must have had good reason. Get on with your life now and leave our Norah get on with hers. Now ... leave the door open on your way out."

Aggie couldn't believe what the bitch had told her. Surely Norah would have mentioned that 'twas to an enclosed order she was going to? Aggie had heard the nuns in school talk about enclosed orders. Working and praying all day in silence, and up at cockcrow every morning.

Three years had passed before she heard a word, and when she did hear from Norah, it was nothing worth talking about. The red Christmas envelope had arrived with others through the letterbox, addressed to Agnes, with a London postmark. All was in it was a holy picture with Norah's handwriting on the back.

'To Agnes, wishing you a very happy Christmas.' That was it. And the two red biro dots at the bottom.

Putting on her coat she had run straight down to the

shop, raising her voice at Francis. She had pointed to the postmark.

"So Norah is in America? Interesting that, don't you think? So how come so I got this from her this morning? From London."

Francis had glared at her.

"You're talking nonsense. That could have come from anyone. How could you have heard from Norah? Didn't Hilda tell you she's in an enclosed order in America, allowed no correspondence with the outside world? We don't hear from her, and we respect that. Leave well enough alone, girl. Now off with you! If you're not careful I'll report you to the guards for harassment."

Aggie had banged the door so hard on the way out that the tin bell had fallen on the floor.

Now it had been eight years since Norah left Ballygore. Aggie had so many questions. Pieces were still missing. Pieces that could be discussed over the phone now that they were back in contact. Aggie didn't delay in writing back to reassure Norah that she was thrilled to hear from her, but so sorry to hear the truth. Asking Norah to call her at six o'clock at the telephone box across the street. She gave her the number.

"I can tap the phone, Norah, so call me and I can call you right back, and it'll cost us nothing. Yes, you heard me correctly. Nothing."

In between the phone calls, letters passed regularly

between Ballygore and London.

Agnes told Norah how she had remained on in Ballygore, working at the vets in Kilnarick. She hadn't planned it that way. Telling Norah that after she had disappeared, one month led into the next. "I just got settled, Norah. Julian was such a maniac when it came to file-keeping and all that. So I was well equipped to set up the admin side of things when the new practice took off. I was offered the position of office manager, so I stayed. And here I am, over nine years later, still there. Can you believe it? It's definitely time for a change, like, wouldn't you say?"

The girls spoke on the phone every Friday evening from then on. Between the tears and the laughter, it was as if they had never been parted. There were no awkward silences between them. Aggie taking the lead, talking so fast at times. Norah with traces of an English accent.

"Aggie, slow down, will you? I don't want to miss a word."

"I was saying, you do remember Darlene, don't you? Julian's wife?"

"Of course I remember Julian and his gorgeous American wife. I have to say I did feel jealous at the time – you couldn't shut up about her. Gosh, I wonder where they are now. Back in America. I guess, with a ton of kids, I suppose. "

"I stayed in touch with Darlene, Norah. We became friends. Now, not as good as the two of us were, but good enough. She's still as mad as a March hare, but in a nice way. She calls me all the time at work, she stayed in touch with myself and Connie Grogan. They've no kids, you know. Don't know what happened there, but I've a feeling 'twas him. She asked about you, she remembers you well. They're living in a place called Sandwich. I know! Imagine. Jesus, when I heard it first, I thought she was taking the piss. Honestly. Norah, are you still there?"

"I'm listening, Aggie. Just enjoying the sound of your voice."

"Anyway, by all accounts it's beautiful where she's living. She sends me postcards all the time. She keeps asking me over, but 'twouldnt be my scene at all. All wooden houses, sun, sea and whatever else goes with it."

The girls laughed, just like old times. Trying their best to fill in the gaps of the time they had lost.

"Imagine. Darlene's in touch with Connie Grogan all these years too. Remember Connie? And us two babysitting her when she fell and broke her wrist. Well, she's been living in the gate lodge now for about five years, I'd say. With her Italian friend, if you don't mind. It was Darlene who got in contact with the Italian in the States, when she saw how lonely poor Connie was. Especially when she was no longer around to drop in on her herself, like. Darlene always loved a good cause, fair play to her."

"Whatever happened to Paul? Did he ever settle down?"

"Paul, the bollocks, passes up and down the lane and barely bids either of the women the time of day. But I think it's better than what it was, since he met this new one he's with. In love by all accounts. And the gas thing is that she's the *double* of Connie back in the day. This new one is well able for him. Old Mattie is still above with Johanna, Connie's sister."

"I remember him well from the shop," said Norah.

"I haven't been out in Black Post in years, but I heard that Mattie planted bushes all around the gate lodge, so as to keep the women out of sight. And the Italian drives her little car into town, with Connie cocked up in the front seat beside her. And a huge dog perched in the back. From the look of him. I'd say he'd ate you. I've a sore throat now from all the talking!"

Norah had missed Aggie so much. They discussed everything over the phone, taking their time to get to what was on both of their minds.

"Jaysus, with the pinched face on the Italian I wouldn't like to cross her. I heard she had a right go at Johanna at the way she treated Connie. There was always something about dark about Black Post Inn. Remember us fecking the drink from the bottle, Norah, and topping it up with water."

"No, Aggie. I remember, you fecking the drink from the bottle and topping it up with water. No offence, Agnes Foley."

"None taken, Norah Gorman."

"I remember you rooting through the presses, Aggie, and the look on your face when you found the bottle of rum, and you pouring half of it into my 7Up bottle. Then doing the same with another bottle you found, pouring it into your own 7Up bottle. It smelt awful. And then you topped them up with water before putting them back in the press. We were as sick as two dogs the following morning."

The friends laughed their way through the happier memories, having made up their minds to leave the more serious conversation for when they would meet face to face. It was too upsetting, especially for Norah.

Chapter 30

Return 1979

The tall girl in the pea-green swing coat boarded the bus at Shannon Airport. Placing her blue weekend case in the space provided overhead, she took a cigarette box from her coat pocket.

She didn't have time to reach for her lighter, seeing the flame from the corner of her eye. She had seen him looking at her as she walked along the aisle to her seat.

"Where are you off to, miss? Any harm to ask?"

Smiling, she didn't answer. She didn't feel the need. Norah Gorman had long since given up polite just for the sake of it.

Turning back towards him for a moment, she thanked the stranger for the light. He nodded back at her, accepting that his attempt to spark a conversation with her had been in vain.

Norah had no intention of getting caught up in

conversation with a stranger on a bus. Returning to Ireland was difficult enough, besides making small talk with strangers. It had been ten years since she had last set foot in Ballygore.

But Aggie had pestered her to return for a visit, when she had visited Norah in London the year before. She'd said it was her turn. She assured her that Ballygore had changed a lot in ten years. New people had moved in and others had moved out, away from the town. Life was not the same as Norah would have remembered. People were getting on with their lives. It was certainly time to let go of the past.

But Norah Gorman could never reclaim the lost years. She was never going to be the same girl who had lived over the shop on Mill Road. The sensible Norah Gorman in the camel-hair coat. The pride of Ballygore.

Being called a whore and a slut by parents who were full of their own importance had been a grave lesson. Parents who had previously held their heads high, boasting to whoever cared to listen that their daughter would be embarking on a most highly regarded profession.

Turning towards the window, Norah settled herself in the seat, glad the seat beside her was vacant. It had been a long time since she had set foot in Ballygore.

She had been sent to the Home without warning, answering to those who showed no respect. A home where girls were punished for accepting the seed of a man, whether they agreed to it or not. Girls like herself, whose parents had rejected their own flesh and blood to save face.

And in the end Norah had nothing to show for it, apart from the memories. Sad and lonely memories. And pain, which she pushed so far back, deep inside, only for it to resurrect on any ordinary day. Hitting her when her inhibitions were down.

The nuns had been so cruel. And they supposed to be women themselves. Women who could never know the pain of maternal loss. Or know what it would feel like to be degraded. Cast aside. Used. Treated like a non-person. Nuns who spoke to their fellow women during labour, using doggish tones. The good ones scarcely remembered, drowned out by the words and wills of the tormentors.

"Not mature enough to live outside of the womb," they had told her.

The brazen womb, which had silently accommodated the baby without her knowledge. Somehow. Humiliated and ashamed, with no idea as to how she had become pregnant in the first place.

It had taken Aggie and herself a long time to figure it all out. But they had … well, Aggie had, two weeks before her trip. After months of going over it again and again she had finally come up with a reasonable explanation. And the time had come to finally put an end to the confusion, to the madness of it all, to get to the bottom of it. To discuss every angle and not stop until there was no doubt. No more buts and what ifs.

The man who had violated her, stripped her bare, of all she held sacred. The man who had left her feeling degraded beyond belief, disgusted with herself. Tainted, like dirt. Her dignity, her self-worth robbed. Gone. Removing her from the comfort of not knowing what it was like to be scared. Suspicious. Of everything. Of everyone. Trusting no-one. One man.

That man was Paul Grogan.

Norah had no memory of it. None at all. Which Aggie in her wisdom surmised was a blessing of sorts.

No such blessing.

It was worse.

She didn't have a picture in her head. She had been abused. Touched in the most intimate way. Destroyed.

But she'd had years to think back through those weeks which had altered the course of her life. Aggie had suggested taking the matter into their own hands. But it was far too late to do anything about it. Useless. It had been ten years ago. And what proof was there? None.

One thing was for sure, she was not the Virgin Mother, as her mother had so cruelly reminded her.

"No such thing as not remembering your first time!" her mother had screamed at her. *"Everyone remembers their first time! Everyone!"*

And she wasn't supposed to have a first time. Any time ever.

She was supposed to be a virgin most pure. Without sin.

Norah had suffered the consequences. On her own.

Returning to Ballygore for the weekend had not been an easy decision to make.

The taxi driver collected Norah from the bus station, taking her directly to the front door of her destination. Foleys' house at number 38 Mill Road, just across the road from the telephone kiosk.

Agnes pulled her friend in the front door. The two friends embraced. They had a lot to talk about.

"Did anyone see you, Norah? Jesus, we wouldn't want your mother breaking down the front door to get at you. They wouldn't have a clue anyway, even if they did see you passing. Your hair is much longer than it used to be. Jesus. No way would anyone believe it's you. *Ah,* you know what I mean, girl. You're not the young one you once were, and neither am I for that matter. Even I had a hard time recognising you on my visit over last year. Look at you. You look even better then when I saw you last. And the highlights in your hair and the make-up. Your accent is nearly like you were born and bred over there."

Settling themselves in, the two friends discussed much of what had happened since they'd last chatted. One thing was for certain: the past was long gone and they had the future to look forward to.

"And you, Aggie, haven't changed one bit. God, who'd have thought that I'd ever set foot again in Ballygore. I wouldn't have come at all, only that you forced me. And if your parents had been home, I wouldn't be here at all. You understand. It's easier this way."

"I get it, Norah. Worked out well with Mam and Dad over in Birmingham this week."

"As for my own parents down the road … I'm well

over the grief. But I'd rather they never heard that I was back in town. Too much water under the bridge. I was on the floor for a long time, struggling to understand. So upset and blaming myself. Trying everything in my power to get them to forgive me. Took me years but it's amazing what the passage of time can do. The counselling was great, Aggie, it helped me deal with so much."

"I told you the shop closed last year when your father took the bad turn. And your mother comes out the side door every morning to pound the pavement up to the church. She goes around with her head down and the prayer book under her arm. It fell on the street one day and Moira Kiely said she was picking up the holy pictures for ages. And a picture of you and Damian fell out. She must be in that church all day praying for her own sins. Very sad all the same. No offence, Norah Gorman."

"None taken, Agnes Foley."

The two girls smiled.

"Aggie, I couldn't care less what you say about them. I pleaded with her and begged her that day I left the house. Down on my two knees. I thought at first that it was all to do with my father, like I told you, but she was every bit as much to blame. She hit me so many times."

"Oh, Jesus, Norah! Had I known!"

"You said in one of the letters that you almost feel sorry for my parents. Well, I don't. They send me away, at sixteen – a total innocent, who had never been away from home. They sacrificed me to save themselves, so that the neighbours wouldn't find out. The gas part about it was, had I been one of the neighbour's children I'd have been better off. Well, you know, Aggie, hard times pass and I'm living proof of it. Only for my Aunt Celine helped me, I might still be there. But I'll tell you all about that later. It wasn't that the convent was bad, it just wasn't for me – at least they never knew about the baby. About James." Norah became quiet.

"Imagine, Norah. I never ever suspected a thing. Sounds mad, but I hadn't a clue. I believed that you just upped and left because I was tormenting you so much about the nuns."

"What could you have done, Aggie? Nineteen sixty-nine, Ballygore. You were a year ahead of me, working in your new job in Kilnarick. All my parents had ever wanted was for me to make them proud by becoming a nun. Because my father had let his own family down by getting my mother pregnant. So they were glory-hunting, using me to redeem themselves. They paid the price, but so did I. I've been happy, Aggie, really happy. It's taken its toll but I've learned that life is too short. These past ten years have gone so fast, and all we have is time. But it passes."

"Ah Norah, Jesus." Aggie couldn't speak.

"And now they have all the time in the world to regret what they've done. But I don't think they will. Celine wrote to them at the time, to say I'd left the convent, and I myself sent them a few home truths on an open postcard, just to rattle their cage. I was kicking myself afterwards, but what the hell – they'd sooner live a lie than face the truth. I'm damaged goods as far as they are concerned. The old Norah is well gone, Aggie. The Norah that thought the world was a wonderful place, full of kind, decent people. The stupid innocent Norah who wanted nothing from life other than to fulfil her parents' expectations of her. My mother, whom I couldn't have loved more, put me out for fear she'd lose face in Ballygore. My father was always headstrong, his way or the highway. Hearing him use language that I would never in a million years expect to hear coming out of his mouth – as long as I live I will never forget the way he spoke to me. It sickened me to the core."

Norah explained how she had got used to the Mother and Baby Home.

"In some ways the last days at home were the absolute worst of the whole time. They had me locked up like a prisoner. They barely spoke to me, unless it was to call me names or shout at me. I had to do as they said, Aggie. I saw no other way out. They threatened to cut your mother off the book and to bar you all from the shop if I said anything. And they said they would put your names on the noticeboard on the window."

"Jesus, Norah, as if my mother would give a shite what they did. My old fella would have beaten the head of your old fella for what they did to you. Fuck them, Norah. Fuck them. Whatever I felt before about you making up with them. Forget about it now. Look at my sister Joanie – she had the two eldest before she was married. And my mother stood by her the whole way through. That's why the self-appointed knobs in the town look down their noses at the likes of us who look after our own, through thick and thin. And if that makes us less than admirable, well, then so be it. I'd rather be a decent human being any day than a fucking hypocrite."

Norah smiled at her friend's outburst.

"But their plan backfired on them when James arrived too early. Much too early." The tears built up in Norah's eyes as she continued. "They had told you, and half the town, that I was in the convent at that stage. But I wasn't, Aggie. And three weeks later they told more lies to Celine, so that she'd take me earlier than September. I left the Mother and Baby Home on the first of June. On my seventeenth birthday. Nobody told me where my baby was. Nobody thought to ask me how I was feeling. They didn't need to. It was time for me to pack up my bags and move on."

Aggie responded in the only way she knew how.

"Well, they got their comeuppance in the end. Your auld lad can hardly move off the chair. He's … shall I say … compromised. *Come, leg, or I'll drag you* kind of thing. I don't want to be mean, Norah, but for fuck sake, they've been so cruel. Your mother doesn't even look at me. I couldn't care less, to be honest."

"It's all the one now, Aggie. I'll never set foot in that house again."

As the night wore on the girls made up for lost time.

"No need to water down the booze tonight, Aggie," Norah said, taking a bottle of vodka from her weekend bag. "I'd say we might need it, before the night is out."

"Norah Gorman! You, drinking? I couldn't believe it when you told me, and all the times I had to lace your orange juice." Agnes went quiet, before quickly changing the subject. "Now, you're not to eat me. But I was on the phone to Darlene yesterday, filling her in about you coming back for the weekend."

Seeing the way Norah looked at her, Aggie grimaced.

"No harm in that is there, surely?" She could tell that Norah annoyed. "I just mentioned our suspicions about Paul Grogan, that's all."

Norah's eyes opened wide. "You what?"

"She'll say nothing to anyone. Jesus, who'll she tell, Norah? She's hardly going to ring Connie and tell her that we said her son is a rapist, now is she?"

"Aggie, can you not keep anything to yourself? Why can't you get it that I don't want my business discussed with anyone? I can't believe that you've told her that much. Some blood sister you've turned out to be! And I suppose you've your mother told as well. Nobody knows the truth about me leaving Ballygore, never mind the fact that we believe that Paul Grogan raped me? That's serious shit, Aggie. Really serious shit."

Aggie could tell that Norah was raging with her. She hoped that by changing the tempo, it would pass.

"Julian Taylor was brilliant to work for though. I couldn't believe my luck when he took me on full-time. Jesus, I didn't give a toss back then. All dolled up, skirt up to my arse and hair up in the beehive. And the bastard Paul Grogan, all eyes. He was considered a fine catch in those days, a stud to someone like me who hadn't the sense to see 'twasn't my intelligence or my family pedigree he was after."

Norah rolled her eyes.

"You don't know this, Norah, and I hate admitting it … but, seeing as we're being all honest here … this is what I didn't want to be saying over the phone. I was with Paul Grogan myself a few times after you left. We never fully shagged, well, not exactly, but that wasn't my fault. I got kind of friendly with him after you went, and he did put in a good word for me with Julian. Then when I started drinking in Stapleton's pub – he'd send a drink across the bar, giving me a wink when I looked over to thank him. I suppose Paul Grogan seemed the best of a bad lot."

Norah sighed heavily. She couldn't be cross with Aggie for long.

"Well, Paul and Julian were, like, the best of mates. And then he asked me out. Out my arse. More like a quick shag he was looking for, in the front of the car. And the handbrake cutting the hole off me."

Norah listened, shifting uncomfortably at certain moments during Aggie's story.

"But he couldn't get it up – if you know what I mean? Or keep it up, when he had it up. So I was thinking about it all lately and something was niggling at the back of my head. Until it finally dawned on me. Paul Grogan didn't want me looking at him when we were doing it, because he couldn't do it if a girl was looking at him. He made me shut my eyes – kept asking me if they were shut. And I looking straight back at him."

"Aggie, I'm not sure I want to hear this."

Agnes continued, though seeing the pained look on her friend's face.

"In the dark, like. I never really thought about it at the time. Anyway, it was all over before it really started, I was fed up with the antics of him. He gave me the creeps after that. It all adds up, Norah. The fucker drugged you, excuse my language. He must have drugged you and had his way with you. That way he wouldn't have had you watching him. And I'm living proof that he couldn't do it with me when I was looking at him. And I certainly wasn't taking my eyes off the fucker. Then he made out I was laughing at him. So there! What other proof do we need? And when I thought about it some more, I realised that he was out there in the surgery all those evenings, showing a wicked interest in Julian's work on the research project he was working on. And then it dawned on me. *Ketamine!* He gave you the fucking Ketamine. The CSI-581. Remember the morning I had to leave Black Post to go to work early at the surgery, and you stayed behind to wait for that bastard to come home in the lorry. Well, that must have been when he did it."

"You mean when he raped me, Aggie?" Norah began to tremble.

"Yes, Norah. Sorry. Raped. When he raped you. Remember you said you woke up on the couch in the kitchen and couldn't remember falling asleep, with him shaking the shite out of you. Well, that must have been it."

"But how could it have been him, Aggie, if I didn't see him that morning? I came down to make tea and toast like we had done the time before. You had left everything ready for me on the table. But Paul wasn't there, because I would never have come down in my nightdress if he was, and if he had walked in on me I'd have run straight back up the stairs."

"So what's your first memory of seeing him that morning?"

"When he was shaking me awake. And I do remember hearing the engine of the truck on outside. He said it had cut out on him on the way back and he had to leave it running. That's why he'd been late coming back."

"Exactly, Norah! Because he was fucking there all the time, knowing that you would come down. I had grabbed the milk jug and cup and sugar and left it out for you on the table before I left. I even put the toast in the toaster for you, and left the tea bag in the cup. He could have been waiting up the road for all we know. It was pitch dark, remember. Or he was there the whole time in the house. He had to have been."

"Aggie, it's such a long time ago, some parts are clear and others are just a haze. I remember feeling stupefied, as if I was coming out of a deep sleep. But I couldn't have been so out of it, if I only fell asleep on the couch. And how or why would a young one of sixteen come down to make tea and toast, only to sit down and fall into a deep sleep?"

"Exactly, Norah!"

"I put it down to the fact that we were awake talking half the night. And we drank more of that awful stuff you took from the press. *Poitín*. I genuinely didn't give it another thought. And I remember when I was getting dressed, I had a small bit of blood on me. But I thought it was the start of my monthlies, because I felt so lousy, and you know how bad I used to be with them. I went straight home to bed. Never gave it a second thought afterwards. But you know, it fits. It all fits. You left to go to work, I went down to make tea and next thing I'm being woken up by Paul Grogan."

Aggie spoke as Norah took a gulp from her glass.

"I remember that morning really well, because I was supposed to be at work in the surgery for eight o'clock, as Julian had a busy day ahead. But we'd slept it out, so I hopped on the bike in the pissing rain and headed for home like a mad thing. I was as sick as a dog from what we drank and nearly puked out over the handlebars a couple of times. Julian was waiting for me outside my front door and my mother shouting at him through the top window. We spent the whole time laughing on the way out in the car – he was saying that he should have left me cycle the three miles altogether, given that I was like a drowned rat in his car by that stage. I set the alarm for you before I left for half past eight, like you had made me promise. Which gave Paul Grogan every chance to be alone with you in Black Post Inn for that time. It would take ten to twenty minutes for the stuff to work orally and he could have been anywhere watching you, biding his time. I'm around the stuff long enough to know how it works, Norah. He could have put the Ketamine in the bloody milk. Connie would have been well out of it upstairs. She never appeared downstairs until well after eleven and what was stopping him from turning the key in the door leading to the stairs? And I'll tell you this much … Moira Kiely always maintained that the Paul fella was dosing poor Connie, locking the doors when he was away."

"Aggie, I don't know … it all sounds too far-fetched. Please tell me right now that you've not mentioned a word of this to Moira Kiely. Tell me!"

"Jesus, you must take me for a right big-mouth. Of course I haven't said a word to her. With Moira all you have to do is plant a word or two, she fills in the gaps in between. She loves to gossip."

"I'd be seriously upset if I thought you told her my story, Aggie. Anyway, go on. What did *she* have to say?"

"Only that Paul Grogan can't stand his mother. Imagine hating your own mother. Everyone knows he resented her for tricking Mattie into a marriage he never wanted. Johanna told my mam that Connie married him just to get Black Post Inn. Apparently, Connie seduced old Mattie and then pretended she was pregnant … *yeuch* … picture that! Everyone says that there was more to it … a lot more. But Paul has kept his mouth shut all these years, making her suffer. Mam said that Johanna only wanted a skivvy and the Mattie fella fitted the bill. Our Connie had pulled him right out from under Johanna's nose."

Aggie punched the air. "Good woman, Connie!"

Norah couldn't suppress the giggle. "Oh, Aggie, you're a tonic. Go on, will you."

"So … sly Johanna got her revenge in the end. Mattie has been all but married to her all these years, knowing full well that Paul will inherit Black Post Inn as soon as Connie is six feet under. He even gave Johanna a wedding ring to wear, an emerald Claddagh, a big thick one. And she wears it with the heart facing inwards, like her heart is taken. That's if she has any fecking heart in the first place. Poor Connie. As far as I know she's happy at last, living in the gate lodge with her companion. And as I told you the fecking dog is enough to keep unwanted visitors at bay."

Norah let Aggie talk. Having had the previous ten years to rack her brains, imagining all sorts, it was almost a relief to hear someone besides herself work their way through it. And what Aggie was saying made sense.

"Well, I'll be damned if I know exactly how he did it. But I'm convinced that he did. As I said, you could have drunk the stuff out of a cup. It would have been a few drops. It mixes easily with any liquid so it can be given any number of ways. Only Paul Grogan knows the answer to that one. It could have been in the orange juice, in anything. And he could have been hiding anywhere, biding his time – there's that many nooks and crannies out in Black Post Inn. Think about it. First, I thought it was meant for me but, as I said already, he knew I had left for work early. You'd made me promise not to tell him that you'd be there on your own after I left for work – in case your mother found out. But I told him the evening before in the surgery. It just slipped out, Norah. So he knew you'd be there on your own."

Norah shook her head.

"And Connie wouldn't dare come out of that room until he called her down in any case. She told me that herself, she was half afraid of him after he threatened to put her into the County Home."

"Oh! It doesn't bear thinking about. My head is wrecked from it all. But, Aggie, you're right. It never even dawned on me that I could have been drugged and raped. And you know I would never in a million years have chanced that he'd see me in my nightgown – I would have made sure I was fully dressed – but I wasn't, was I? It's like it happened to someone else. That's what the therapist said. 'Projection' she called it. She said I projected the trauma of all that happened onto 'the younger me', as a separate entity almost ... if you get what I mean? All the therapy has led me to believe there's no advantage for me in knowing who did this to me, after ten years. Where's it going to get me? What can I do about it? Nothing. The likes of Paul Grogan, with all that money behind him, and plenty to vouch for his respectability. I'd be fighting a lost battle, Aggie. And you know it well."

"But what about Moira and myself? We'd go to the Garda station with you. And Darlene would vouch for all the times he spent with Julian, back when he was researching the effects of the stuff. I'm sure Moira would go with us. Well, maybe she would ... but I'd definitely go and tell the cops my side of the story."

"Aggie, don't imagine for one moment that they'd listen to Moira Kiely, or you, for that matter. And do you think for a moment that Darlene would go against her husband ... to say what? That he was a researcher and just because Paul was friendly with him? No. They'd sue us for character assassination or something. I have spent years dwelling on the damage this has done to my life. And now this. Opening up a can of worms."

"But surely you want to know, Norah?"

"No, Aggie. I don't. At this stage, I actually don't. If I thought I had one chance of nailing the bastard that did this to me of course I would. But I haven't a hope! I know this might sound odd, but I'm finally happy in London. I'm not saying in a million years that I'm dismissing or accepting what has happened to me. Or that I haven't been tormented by all sorts, since you came up with this. But it's my choice to make, Aggie. It has to be at this stage, and the only control I have over this is to take it into my own hands and make a decision. For me. My decision. My power, Aggie. For me and for no one else. Just me."

Norah began banging her fist against her chest. Aggie handed her a box of tissues.

"No need for tissues, I'm all cried out. Once and for all, Norah Gorman gets to choose. It's over, Aggie, and I want to get on with my life, otherwise the bastard wins, and it will destroy me all over again. I won't let the man who did this to me contaminate me for another second.

And I want you to respect my decision. As for my parents down there, I have no interest in them – I'm done with all that family bullshit."

Aggie nodded slowly at her friend.

"I wrote home every single week for the first few months, humiliating myself. After that, what was the point? I called them in the end, but they changed the number or took the phone out – I know because Damian told me. He stayed on in the Philippines, with his partner. We've both walked away from the past. Away from them."

As the weekend came to a close, the taxi pulled up outside the house to collect Norah, to take her to the bus stop at the far side of town. She didn't want to be seen on the street.

"I'm having a ball in London, Aggie – you'll just love it when you move over to me. I know you will."

"I'll be all ready to leave in six weeks' time. I've handed in my notice. Ten years working for the vets is enough for me. I've seen enough cow shit and scour to last me a lifetime. I want to hear no more about milk disease, or distemper or anal cysts. Or tagging animals. Or feckin' TB. I never want to see a pair of shitty Wellington boots again as long as I live. I'm so looking forward to starting a new life in London."

"The flat is all set up, Aggie, and my flatmate will be gone in a fortnight."

"We've certainly waited long enough, Norah, and

that's for sure. And your parents can't do a thing about it. Karma, Norah. Karma. That's what Darlene would say. She's a bit of a hippy, you know. It's Karma all right. Comes back to bite you in the butt, so it does. I always knew that father of yours was a bastard, but I was surprised at your mother for going along with it. Her own daughter, for God's sake."

Aggie, arms outstretched, drew her friend towards her. "From this day forward, it's a new leaf and a new life, Norah Gorman."

The blood sisters hugged tightly.

With Norah gone, Aggie used the time to mull things over. She had been blaming herself all these weeks for having dragged Norah out to Black Post Inn.

She remembered having doubts about spending the night there when Moira had asked her. She'd been half afraid after what her mother had said about Connie. But the money was good. More than good. She had agreed in the end, expecting Norah and herself to have a right laugh. So off they went. It was before Christmas and the dates matched up. Norah said she'd been five months pregnant the following May.

It had to have happened in Black Post Inn and it had to have been Paul Grogan. He had been there at the surgery many times, watching, taking it all in. Asking questions, over interested in what Julian was doing. Aggie also remembered Paul's fascination at the time with Angel Dust, the animal growth enhancer. He was all about using drugs to make a quick turnaround. Bulking up the animals before selling them on. Yes, Paul Grogan was the man all right.

Chapter 31

The Convent

1969

Norah Gorman had felt like a criminal sitting in the back seat of her father's car. He had fiddled with the radio button on the way to the airport, tuning in to listen to the match. His cue that there would be no conversation in the car. He had the journey well timed. So much that could have been said.

Norah had been hopeful that he'd offer her some comfort. Even small talk. Anything would have been better than this. Silence. Awkwardness. No questions asked. No reassurances given. No reason given for her mother not being there to say goodbye.

Handing her the documentation, pointing her in the direction of the entrance to the terminal.

At first she thought it was a birthday card.

"Here. Take your envelope. Everything is in there, I checked it myself, so don't lose it and keep it together.

Your suitcase is packed in the boot. Your Aunt Celine will be at the other side once you land in Heathrow. Your mother might write as soon as she feels up to it, and leave Damian alone for now."

There was no hug offered. No utterance of regret. No sense that he might never see her again. No nothing.

Norah took her suitcase from the boot, putting it on the ground. She turned, her two arms outstretched towards her father. Silently pleading.

He stepped back from her as if he was burned by her nearness. Turning his back to walk away, he just raised his right arm in salute.

Nothing would ever be the same again for Norah Gorman.

Her father would have the rest of his days to ponder over the last time he set eyes on his daughter.

Once inside the building it was easy enough to find her way. She followed the crowd who had gathered under the sign saying '**Heathrow**'. Setting her suitcase down, she opened the envelope to find her ticket. One way. Tears blinded her eyes. Ballygore and its people would get on without her. She was a disgrace. Would she even be missed? Full of regret that she couldn't tell Aggie, but there'd be plenty of time to write letters.

Aggie had always maintained that nuns wrote great letters.

A young couple approached Norah at the airport, the wife putting her arm on Norah's.

"Love, are you on your own? I've been watching you

there. Myself and Danny are on our way over to Kilburn. We'll keep an eye on you if you like. Is it your first time away from home? Come on, pet – Danny will see to your suitcase."

Norah was in no mood to talk. Never one to offer conversation, still she wanted to have someone to stand beside. Someone to ask a question if one needed to be asked. Someone to understand what it was like to be leaving home to travel across the Irish Sea. In tears. The kind stranger with the soft brown eyes smiled up at her. "It's Greta, love. Greta and Danny Hall – and you are?"

"Norah. Norah Gorman from the shop in Ballygore."

"Danny, will you pick up the case for Norah here, for God's sake, and don't stand there looking at it. Or do you want your poor wife to lift it for you?"

Greta's husband smiled as he lifted the suitcase. Norah didn't know what was in it. Her father had switched suitcases. He said her mother had packed as much as she would need to carry over. She had the photo of Aggie tucked safely in her handbag. Once it was returned to her at the home, she had no intention of letting it out of her sight again. Her mother could burn everything else for all she cared.

Norah boarded the plane for London, climbing up the last of the steps. Still in tears.

She turned around to look back, hoping to see her father on the viewing platform. He might have had a change of heart. No sign of him. People were waving, hanging out over the barrier, blowing kisses at their loved ones as they boarded the plane – but not to Norah. Raising her head, she wondered what Aggie would say if she saw her now. *"Keep your chin up, girl! Up, up, up!"* She could hear Aggie's laugh as she placed her suitcase in the overhead bin. She would write to her once she was settled in London. She would dream about living in a flat in London with Aggie.

Greta's soft Midlands accent reminded her of Martha, one of the girls she had met in the home. "You'll be fine, kitten. There'll be no tears once we take off, I can assure you of that. Just think! A whole new life awaits you. I take it that like most of us here you're on a one-way ticket?"

Norah nodded without opening her mouth. What could she say? That she was being shunted out of Ballygore. That she had given birth to a stillborn baby three weeks before. That she hadn't a notion how it happened. That she had prayed as hard as anyone had ever prayed that her parents would allow her to go home. That she missed her best friend Aggie Foley. No.

Forcing a smile, showing her large even teeth, she spoke.

"Don't take any notice of me, Greta. I'm just sad to be leaving it all behind. That's all."

Looking around her, she noticed the atmosphere in the plane had changed. No longer looking back at what they had left behind, people were looking forward towards the future, laughing and joking with each other, smoking their cigarettes. Norah's mood lifted.

Greta and Danny had kept their word, sitting in the seat just behind, arm in arm.

The man sitting beside Norah in the window seat looked shaken as the plane began to take off, clutching the curtain beside him. Norah smiled at him. Time to offer a kindness.

Wondering who else she had offered a kindness to. Wondering what Aggie would have said. Knowing full well that she would have had something to say.

The man beside her was nervous, beginning to make Norah feel uneasy, until she felt the nudge to her back. Greta peeped around the seat.

"Suck the sweet the air hostess gave you. It'll stop any pain in your ears, kitten."

Norah didn't ask what her new friend meant, but did as she was told. The man sitting beside her was still holding onto the curtain with his left hand.

Greta kneed the back of the seat throughout the journey to let Norah know that she had her back. Norah would never, for the rest of her life, forget the kindness of two strangers.

Norah entered the novitiate in London as a postulant, less than a month after James' birth. Being treated as a human being, without undertones, made her time in the convent more than bearable. Attending book-keeping classes with another postulant gave her just the focus she needed. On her own in her cell at night, she grieved for her youth. For her stillborn baby boy James, who owned no part of this.

The sisters in the convent had not been aware of her

situation. If they had, they'd kept it well-hidden. It had taken her months to settle in. But she had. Helped by her Aunt Celine who guided her patiently through her induction.

Walking to the convent school each day, wearing navy and white, she worked in the school office, honing her skills.

The tall Irish girl from Ballygore, who had left her home shrouded in shame and humiliation, having given birth to her poor stillborn baby was no longer recognisable.

She hadn't noticed the change in her in the beginning. She had always been a strong girl, as her father liked to tell her, but seeing the tall slim reflection in the shop window had taken her by surprise. Having lost so much weight, it revealed a face that she had never known to exist beneath the layers.

Her first Christmas in London had been difficult. Lonely. The scent of the pine Christmas trees lined up for sale along the street reminded her of happier times at home. Taking part in the festivities at the convent with the other sisters had made it almost enjoyable.

Helping the teaching sisters in the classrooms kept Norah busy, as preparations were due to be made for her transfer to the order in Alabama as a novice, where she would in time take her vows. Her life was mapped out for her.

There were twelve sisters in all, including her aunt, their ages ranging from ninety to her own age of almost nineteen.

What she had least expected had been the greatest

blessing. The comfort of being amongst women who accepted the differences between them. Days of silence, days of concealed rage, days of laughter and gaiety. Times when voices were raised and tempers frayed. Always changing, mostly forgiving, never taking one another for granted. The smell of cigarettes from one of the sisters as she swished by. No questions asked about the misplaced bottle of brandy from the parlour cupboard, there to be offered to the priest when he called. On evenings of celebration the small liquor glasses would be produced to offer a sherry to those who wished to partake. Norah was not unhappy. But she was beginning to falter.

Easter daffodils brought a smile to her face. Her time in the convent in London had been a welcome distraction for her. Her Aunt Celine had been kind, much kinder than she felt she deserved. The guilt of lying by omission made Norah feel uncomfortable at times.

Returning to the convent one evening from the school office, she was told that her Aunt Celine was waiting for her in the front parlour. She felt nervous.

"Norah, let's talk for a little while. These days we hardly get a chance to catch up. There's a few things I'd like to talk to you about, before we think about organising your passage to Alabama in June. Take a seat, dear."

Norah's face paled, unsure of what was coming.

"I just wanted to chat with you, Norah – to, I suppose, allow you the space to consider your future. I understand the way things were at home for you – that's why I wanted to have a word."

Norah remained silent, her heart pounding. She was waiting for her aunt to tell her that she knew everything. Uncomfortable in her seat, she steadied herself for what was to come. Her aunt leaned forward, taking her hand in hers.

Stop! Norah thought she was going to faint.

"Norah, your Aunt Statia and I joined the sisters around the same time. Statia in 1948, and myself the year after. Well before you were born. There was two years' difference between us, with your father Francis in the middle. We were inseparable back in those days and that was about the size of it. It had been Statia's wish to enter. And where Statia went, I followed. But, without doubt, Statia's vocation was far stronger than mine. I understood that she would be there to look out for me, so I came here as a postulant, as you're doing now, before the order sent me out to Alabama to join her. I hated every minute of it."

Norah blinked the tears away, relieved that the conversation was not what she had expected. Celine continued as Norah settled herself in her seat.

"As a trainee nurse on clinic duty, I remember my first experience of seeing a black-skinned person in Alabama, never mind that it was a young mother carrying her baby on her back. I was staring into the biggest brown eyes that I had ever seen. And she staring right back at me. The girl walked slowly towards me, just two inches from my face. 'Are you looking for something, sister?' she said. I nearly passed out. I said 'No, no.' And I never made that mistake again. But I learned a lesson for life. I hated every bit of it from the moment I arrived. The climate, getting eaten alive by insects and spiders and everything else that was crawling around the place. I was scared of my own shadow from day one and wanted to leave straight away. I was covered in bites and scrapes. It was Statia who kept me going, saying that it would kill our parents if I went home. And she was right. I imagined things would get better, but they didn't. Seeing the damage done by diseases frightened the daylights out of me. I wasn't a natural, Norah. No doubt I scared the poor women half to death, with the look on my face, as I removed the dressings on their ulcers, afraid to look at what was underneath. Your Aunt Statia had no such bad experience. She was a music teacher in those days. Merriment and dance, she took to the life in Alabama like a duck to water. And the people took to her. They loved her. And I hadn't a note in my head of course! As for rhythm – two left feet! She had the children singing and dancing in no time. She was always half cracked really. I suppose it helped her to be that way." Celine smiled at the memory before continuing. "I eventually became ill from it all. I was so sick they thought I was on the way out. So they sent me back here to the convent in London to recuperate. In my mind was the notion that at least in London I could ease my way back towards secular life. But I was scared that it would kill your grandparents. So … training as a teaching nun gave me purpose. And to make a long story short, here I am twenty years later, still looking for reasons to remain. Still questioning."

Norah listened to her aunt, scarcely believing what she

was hearing. Now was not the time to talk.

"And there was no coercion, Norah, from anyone. Nobody had a gun to my head. And I never opened my mouth about how I was feeling, not even to Statia, whom I missed dreadfully. So you see, my journey in life has been my own, and one which I continue to struggle with daily. And I mean struggle."

Norah was lost for words.

"I don't want that life for you, Norah. The guilt. And I can see it in your eyes every day. We're quite alike you know, you and I. But you must face your own truth and ask yourself is the religious life for you? Is this what you want, Norah, in your heart? If the answer is yes, then that's wonderful. Great. But if you're unsure or feel trapped, now is the time to say it. The life of protection offered to you inside these four walls won't always be available to you, and it certainly won't be easy out there. I suppose what I'm trying to do is give you my full support whichever route you decide to take. I'll be here for you in as much as I can be, because, I tell you now, if I had been asked the same question by someone who cared for me as much as I care about you, I wouldn't be here today, Norah."

Norah began to cry. Huge sobs of relief.

"But I cannot lie to your parents, Norah. So should you choose to leave us, at least do them the courtesy of telling them. It will take courage, but it must come from you. Sometimes the impact of not being open is worse than any lie. It hasn't gone past me this past year that there hasn't been post coming to you from home. And I haven't seen any letters bound for Ballygore in the outbox. It's OK, I won't ask."

Norah wiped her eyes, blowing her nose in the white cotton hanky handed to her by her aunt.

"I could see when I went back to Ballygore, when you were small, that Francis had you earmarked to follow Statia and myself into the order. I saw the innocence in your eyes along with your eagerness to please. You reminded me of myself in my younger days, agreeing to what others wanted, rather than upset them. Too young to know that once you stayed on the path of their choosing, there would be no escape. My brother was never the easiest – the only boy, he demanded his own way as a child. I watched how they sheltered you from the beginning, fearing that you'd be led astray by the loose morals of others. Norah, I understand. As I said, I see a lot of myself in you and, believe you me, I've seen your struggle."

Norah wanted to scream at her aunt. *"Yes, yes, you're right!"* To blurt it all out, to tell her about her baby, her beautiful tiny boy, that had no life in him when he was delivered. James, who had wrapped himself around her heart. Entwined forever. She wanted to tell her aunt how she hated her parents for what they did to her. But she couldn't.

"I wanted you to be ready, Norah, before we had this conversation. To give you the time to consider your future, outside of what others want for you. And, whatever you decide, I'm here for you. Always."

Norah continued to cry her tears of relief. At last. Someone whom she least expected to understand, had given her permission to listen to the thoughts in her own head. Hard to believe that Celine was her father's sister.

"Now that we're older, I'm sure your Aunt Statia would hold a more conservative view, which might distract her from being empathetic towards any difficulties you may be having. In other words, Norah, I strongly advise you to spent the next three months mulling it over in your own head, and come talk to me. And if you have doubts, act on them, don't let them fester until like me you become too afraid or too set in your ways to want to change your life. The world out there might be daunting, but you must grab it with both hands."

Norah watched her aunt remain poised, in control over emotions that she had learned over the years to conceal.

"Thank you so much, Aunt Celine," was all she could manage.

Three months later Norah thanked the sisters and left, hugging those whom she knew would be receptive to a hug. Accepting a hug from those who offered one. Having lived at the convent for over a year, she had become attached to some of the sisters. Seeing her name at the bottom of the scroll handed to her meant that she had prospects. A future outside of the walls of the convent. Outside the walls of her parents' expectations. Sending an open postcard home, the time had come to break free.

I've decided to leave the convent. It was never my vocation. Sorry that I've been such a disappointment to you both. I'm happy for the first time in years.

Goodbye,

Your daughter,

Norah

Chapter 32

The Vet

Julian Taylor had wanted to be a vet ever since he'd spent that first summer at his grandfather's farm, high on the hills in the north of Ireland. Helping out whenever an animal needed attention, moving sheep, corralling them into a shute for stamping – Julian proved his worth on the farm. Observing his grandfather making decisions – balancing whether to let a sick animal go or call the quack, or the vet, to intervene.

Julian had watched the vet on many occasions. Intrigued. Wellington boots and rubber apron, gloves up to his elbows, producing implements from a worn leather case which contained everything from sterilised implements to all sorts of medications.

By the age of sixteen, Julian was confident about what he wanted to do with his life. He would become a vet. His parents supported his choice when he told them that he wouldn't be applying to the bank after all. He would work hard to get his exams, and apply to study veterinary medicine in Dublin.

When the time came, his father had broken the sorry news to him. Times were just too difficult for the family. There would be no finance available for his studies in Dublin. The bank had refused the loan.

Julian had taken the news badly, deciding to empty his post office book and leave for England.

Working his way across Europe, he was determined to succeed. Taking whatever work he could find in the steel factories, he would find his own path into veterinary school, no matter how long it took him.

After spending four years in Germany, he had worked his way across the Atlantic on a cruise ship, taking full advantage of the generosity of wealthy Americans, who warmed to the charms of the Irishman. Heading straight for the mid-west, he was successful with his application to veterinary school. Having earned enough money to cover the first instalment of his fees allowed him immediate access to the course, once he had satisfied the entry requirements. The costs were manageable, more manageable than they would have been in Ireland. He would pay the fees over the duration of his studies, staying on campus, and working two jobs. Working long hours, deferring his studies at times when he felt overworked, Julian never lost sight of his goal. He lived frugally, in a carefully metered way. Julian was in control of his destiny, proving himself to be a diligent student.

Working out of hours, at the veterinary research farm on site under the jurisdiction of the college, he never complained. He showed no distress in seeing his fellow classmates overtake him, knowing that he had the end goal in sight. At twenty-eight, he was in no hurry.

Being offered a place on a research team at the university was all that he wished for. Ambitious to a fault, Julian was well on his way towards achieving his goal, advancing his studies, immersing himself in academia. Scanning within the broader scope of veterinary medicine, he steered himself towards veterinary anesthesiology, gaining himself a distinction in his exams.

Excited to be part of the entry team responsible for presenting a major research proposal to the university, Julian had made a lasting impression within the faculty. Having long overstayed his original timeframe, his latest project, researching the safest drug to allow emergency surgery to take place with the least side effects, had become his greatest work. Julian had no regrets. Having spent twelve years with the university, he had without a hint of regret found his niche. Initially he focused his studies on the drug Phencyclidine, which had been synthesised in America as an anaesthetic. Then his research led him to a more recent synthetic drug, CI-581, which was identified as a safer alternative to its predecessor, without the adverse side effects, such as emergence delirium, where patients had emerged from the previous anaesthetic distressed and delirious, suffering hallucinations. Julian was enthralled.

The fast-acting drug, which had been legalised in Belgium, had been reported on as being safe for humans, as well as being deemed safe for use in veterinary surgery. Research had shown that it could be administered in any number of ways, mixed with liquid by mouth, nasally or anally, or administered by injection. A large distressed animal could be fully anaesthetised within a few seconds, allowing the vet to examine it or perform full surgery. Julian's interest in the delivery of the drug and its use alongside other drugs continued to fascinate him. The wonder drug had the potential to be one of the most exciting drugs to emerge in the world of anaesthesia.

Tested on volunteers within the prison system, CI-581 was awaiting further research before it could be entered for legalisation in the United States. It was easier on patients' airways, shorter-acting, had lower potency and no disturbing psychotic aftereffects. A wonder drug. Julian engrossed himself in his research, experimenting, recording new facts meticulously as they emerged.

Aware of the huge interest in the drug in Europe gave him the impetus to look at returning home to Ireland, where he could continue with his research and work at the same time.

He had been more than pleased when he got word to say that he had secured an eighteen-month locum position in Ireland. The ageing vet in Kilnarick, three miles outside Ballygore, was taking time out for medical reasons. Gangrene. Julian's mother had seen the ad in the *Irish Times* and called him about it, but not before she had contacted the vet, to give him her son's credentials.

Eight weeks before his flight was due to leave for Dublin Airport, he had bumped into Darlene Fletcher, smoking her cigarette outside an Italian restaurant on the upper east side of New York City, where he had been visiting with friends. During the course of a quick conversation, he had become infatuated with the livewire.

Julian had never been interested in relationships up to now – casual relationships suited him better, given the intensity of his work. One-night stands, nothing too deep or complicated. Julian's dedication to his profession couldn't be faulted. Knowing where his future was headed, he didn't need the complications of a love interest and, if the letters from his mother were anything to go by, he wouldn't be short of meeting any number of girls on his return home to Ireland. Julian had no such dreams, his focus being to concentrate entirely on his research, leading to the legalisation of the drug for use in America, which would surely put his name alongside the greats in the academic journals. He had spent the last five years engrossed in the project.

Eyeing up the girl standing beside him, he wanted to get to know her. He wanted to ask her so many questions. He had come to the restaurant to meet a group of friends, but the girl under the canopy had captured his interest. He had to approach her.

All of his dreams and ambitions were put aside in that

moment, as the only thought in his head was to get her attention, before she had finished her cigarette and disappeared into the night.

"Sorry there, may I ask you for a light, please?"

She looked at him for a moment before replying.

"I don't have a light," she answered. "I got one from the bartender inside."

"Well, I'll just take a light of yours then, if I may?

She laughed. "Oh, of course. But where's your cigarette?"

"I don't smoke," he replied.

She had enjoyed the joke.

"Where are you from? That's certainly not a New York accent, I'd say.

You're Irish, aren't you?

Speak again, won't you?"

"What would you like me to say?"

"That you haven't just taken off a wedding band. That you're not married. That you don't have a girlfriend. And that you may just ask me for my phone number."

Laughing, they introduced themselves,

Darlene Mai Fletcher was the first girl in a long time that he wanted so badly to get to know. He had just eight weeks before packing up and leaving for Ireland. The same height as himself, with thick blonde hair and the greenest eyes he had ever seen. He could tell from what she was wearing that she was different, if her dress sense was anything to go by.

She wore a purple beret perched on the side of her head. Her cape was as green as her eyes, and underneath she wore a long flowing multicoloured skirt. He had just met his very own goddess, standing on the street outside a restaurant in New York City.

When he asked her for her number, she refused, telling him she had changed her mind. Before he had time to enquire as to why, she enquired if he had company inside, nodding back towards the restaurant. He said his friends were inside.

She said there was a bar next door. They could meet on the following night at seven. He agreed without thinking. He'd never met anyone like her. When he asked for her number once again, she wrote it on his wrist.

They met the following evening at seven, taking a table just inside the window. Julian had made it his business to be early.

When he saw her coming towards him, he knew that whatever happened he had just met the girl he would one day marry. She wore the same green cape, this time with white jeans. Without the hat, her blonde hair fell down her back. He was mesmerised by her.

Spending three hours, getting to know each other, had been enough for him. He had been around animals long enough to know when he had a good sense of them. And he had more than a good sense of Darlene.

Within two weeks the couple had pledged their love for each other. Julian had taken long overdue leave, to remain on in his friend's apartment in the city. Darlene insisted that she'd like to introduce him to her parents.

"I've told them as much as they need to know for now,

so come for dinner tomorrow night. They'll be fine once they meet you in person." She handed him a business card.

"Do they run a business from their house?"

"No. That card belongs to a friend of mine in an apartment on the floor below. He works in advertising. I carry his cards in my bag just in case. And if I happen to change my mind, as I've been well known to do, he'll send them on their merry way, telling them they've got the wrong address. Unless he likes the look of them himself, of course."

Julian couldn't think straight. He could scarcely understand her way of thinking, but it made her all the more interesting.

'I'm just kidding, Julian. Yes, that's my friend's card, he's moving out soon. I saw the cards and thought I'd grab a few. Same building. And see how useful they are now."

Julian entered the building having been shown to the lift by the doorman. Thinking as he walked through the foyer that whoever Darlene's parents were they certainly weren't short of a few bucks, to be living in a place such as this. Marble floors in the atrium, lots of brass and dark wood, with a huge crystal chandelier hanging in the centre of the ceiling. The doorman in top hat and tails. Once he was off the lift on the tenth floor, his feet sank into the gold-patterned carpet.

Pressing the bell on the apartment door, he could see a shadow shift behind the peephole at the other side of the door.

Then Darlene stood there with her a smile on her face, her eyes wide open.

"You found us, I see," she said, before jumping into his arms.

He adored her. Wearing a bright pink top, with wide flared trousers underneath, she looked like she had come straight from a photo shoot. Behind her stood a low-sized balding man with the same green eyes as his daughter. The apartment was what his own mother might call … ostentatious. She wouldn't have appreciated the Louis XIV furniture, or the embossed gold wallpaper. Or the cream sofas.

"Let the man come in, Darlene," a soft voice came from inside.

Her mother sat by the huge bay window at the far side of the room. A small frail-looking woman, who looked more like a sister to her husband than a spouse.

Having spent time with Darlene and her parents, Julian read the non-verbal clues. Her parents were more than pleased with their daughter's new man. Offering him food. Drink. Listening intently. Hanging on to what he had to say. Shushing Darlene every now and again when she broke in on everyone else's conversation. They seemed unfazed by the fifteen-year age difference between him and their daughter, and if they were fazed they passed no comment. The fact that he was Irish seemed to have a positive effect on both parents, once they discerned that he had a promising professional career ahead of him.

By the time he left with Darlene to return to his apartment in the Bronx, Julian hadn't mentioned that he had agreed to a locum post. In Ireland. That could wait. He adored this funny rebellious creature, the likes of whom he had never met before. He made up his mind that if he hadn't persuaded her to go to Ireland with him when the time came, he would cancel the locum position in Kilnarick and look for a job instead in the States. One way or another he was not about to lose Darlene.

Three weeks later he was back at the apartment, asking the judge for his daughter's hand in marriage. He had brought her back to the restaurant where they had met five weeks before. Going down on one knee right on the spot where she had been standing when he first laid eyes on her.

"Darlene Fletcher, will you marry me? And before you answer, I have taken a temporary post in Ireland in eight weeks' time. Will you be my wife and come with me?"

The ring he had bought in the diamond district proved to be the perfect fit.

"A good omen," she'd said. "Oh Julian! *Yes. Yes. Of course I will marry you.* And I've always wanted to go to Ireland. That's it, I'm going! We'll get married here and Dad can use his influence to fastback the paperwork. It's our destiny to be together." She snuggled close to him. "That must be what the fortune teller at the tea rooms in Boston meant, when she said she saw a green aura around me. I thought she meant my eyes, but now I know different."

"And did she tell you anything else I might need to know?"

"Well … she did say that the man I would marry would carry a dark secret. Oh Julian, I'm so excited."

Informing Darlene's parents of his impending move to Ireland had gone better than he had expected. He offered to forego the opportunity, should they choose to resist his request. They wouldn't hear of it. After the shock had died down, her father had consented, after he had received assurances from Darlene. Tears were shed. Brandy was poured. Cigars were smoked by the men.

They were married the week before they were due to leave. Her father hadn't been shy in mentioning that he had called in a few favours to speed things up. Insisting on paying for the flights, he handed Darlene a generous check to get them started in Ireland.

Chapter 33

The Project

1968

Julian hadn't enough hours in the day to complete his work, since coming to Kilnarick. Familiarising himself with the farms in the area had been taxing enough in itself. Paul Grogan had been a great help in showing him around, introducing him to the farmers in the area.

He tried to be at the surgery for half past seven every morning to prepare for the day ahead – returning home to Darlene, often at irregular hours, only to be called out again during the night.

As May approached, Darlene had been getting more restless with the stretch in the evenings. More unsettled than he knew was good for either of them. Finding time to concentrate on his research was proving difficult. They had been back in Ireland for just three months and no matter what he did for his wife, she complained constantly.

Julian began to feel the strain of her nagging. More often than not, she'd be waiting up for him. Waiting to have another go at him.

"Now what have I done, Darlene? Can you just leave it alone for one night? I'm covered in shit, blood, and God knows what else. And all you want to talk about is the way that Moira Kiely looked at you. Or the way Hilda Gorman in the shop spoke to you."

"Well, try putting yourself in *my* shoes."

"Well, tough luck, Darlene. Grow up and be the wife you promised to be. You knew darn well coming over here that life was never going to be easy as a vet's wife in rural Ireland. I've done as much as I can to help you, but you have to help yourself also. I'm working every hour there is and trying to keep the research going at the same time, and here you are acting like a spoilt bloody brat."

"But you don't understand … I miss …"

"Understand what, Darlene? What do you miss now? I'm sick and tired of your constant nagging. I told you – once I have the practice up and running, things will calm down. Just give me a break, will you?"

He had raised his voice at her again – he could see the tears welling up in her eyes. Feeling instantly sorry, he tried to console her. But he was tired.

Coming up with the idea of sending her home over the summer had changed everything. He had waited to mention it until things had calmed down between them – otherwise she would have said he wanted rid of her. She had immediately began to focus on her trip, leaving him alone.

With Darlene in America, he was free to stay in the surgery well into the night if he wanted to. Or all night if it came to it, aided by a little something from his drugs cabinet to keep his concentration going.

As each batch was delivered, the serial number was recorded, every minute gram accounted for. No room for discrepancies. Not an issue for Julian, who was looking forward to nearing the end of the project.

Paul and himself had become good buddies. The cattle dealer would arrive usually in the evening, or on a Sunday. Unannounced. And more often during times when Darlene was out of the way.

On his last visit, Paul had been more eager than usual.

"Julian, my man, how's it going? I hope I'm not disturbing you there?"

"Not at all, Paul, come on in, I'm just waiting for this little one to come around, before I get down to a bit of bookwork. I have twenty minutes or so, if you want to hang about?"

Paul had followed him into the surgery where a wild rabbit lay anaesthetised on the table, Idly picking up a vial of CI-581, Paul said,

"So this is the one you're working on, Julian, the one that has you here all hours?"

He nodded, telling Paul that the vial in his hand was nothing short of a miracle drug. He explained to him how he had been working on the drug for the past five years. Julian enjoyed explaining the diversity of anaesthesia to someone who showed such a keen interest in his work.

"Julian, I often wonder what would have become of me if I had stuck to the books. Maybe I'm in the wrong line of work."

"Give over, Paul. You're your own man, out there in your lorry on the open road, with no-one to answer to. Look at me here, working my ass off, alongside any spare hours I can find to put into the research. And then there's Darlene, but I have to say I've little to complain about these days."

Paul rolled his eyes.

"I was never one to take much at face value," Julian went on. "I get a notion in my head and I have to test it – so this research and experimentation suits me just fine. When it's all done and I'm back in the States, I won't know what I'll be at. Cats, dogs and parrots, according to Darlene, in a small animal practice outside of the city. But I'm glad of the opportunity to practise here in Ireland before I go back. I'd always said I'd come back for a few years, and when the opportunity came up I jumped at it. Funny how things turn out."

Paul had been hanging on to his every word.

"So what you're telling me is, this drug can be used on animals or humans to put them under in seconds."

"Precisely. And for un-cooperative patients – or animals. Of course, the animals can't talk but from what I can see there are no visual signs of distress. The vitals don't seem to be impaired – there's no respiratory or cardiac implications to worry about. Of course long-term use or misuse might be a different matter. There's any amount of research going on all over the world."

"And tell me, how come you're still researching it if it's already patented in Belgium?"

"It's been patented there for the past few years but not officially approved in the U.S. drug industry as yet. But nearly there. It's been around for a while, just in a different format. I'm mainly testing the drug's efficacy when mixed with other drugs. Refining the dosage, so to speak, according to the precise requirements of the surgery required. It's soluble in liquid for use as an oral drug, it can be given intramuscular or intravenously. Using the precise dose per ounce of weight of the animal renders the patient out of it within seconds, leaving enough time to operate. The control time is always under an hour and up they get and all back to normal. Magic."

"So this stuff can be mixed with liquid and drunk? Maybe I should give the mother a dose or two of that to tame her. She'd be classed as an uncooperative patient."

"Yes, my man," answered Julian, laughing at Paul's dry wit.

"This here is one of the most exciting advancements in veterinary pharmacology in years. Without giving you all the medical jargon, basically it's for putting a patient under quickly, with no side effects worth mentioning. Keeps the airways clear. No heart problems and no memory."

"*Hmmm* ... so if a young one was to get a bit stroppy, let's say, she'd be out cold for say, twenty minutes, and be none the wiser afterwards?"

"Exactly, Paul, exactly."

"Better not leave herself hear us talking like that. She wouldn't be too pleased, I'd say."

Julian didn't like it when Paul mentioned Darlene. It was never in a complimentary manner.

"I miss her, you know. She moved over here with me after knowing me for only a couple of months. She expected Ballygore to be like upstate New York. It'll work just fine as long as she goes back every few months – it'll give her something to look forward to and I can get my project moving ahead while she's away. All good, Paul. Now open up that bottle of Paddy there and we'll have a scoop. The cups are over there on the sink."

But the cattle dealer seemed interested in hearing more.

"So what you're telling me is that if I bring an animal back in the truck and find it in a bad way, you can administer the exact amount of this drug, per pound of weight, have it opened up and operated on and have the animal back up in jig-time?"

"Precisely, my man."

"Maybe I *will* get a drop of it from you, for Connie, to help her sleep."

Both men laughed. Then Julian saw the look on the other man's face and wondered if he was serious.

"So, for humans then? You could give me a few drop of that in my glass here and I'd be down under in seconds and I wouldn't be aware of a thing. Extraordinary."

"Of course I should have said that, taken orally, it takes

a bit longer to act. Fastest route is by injection. Seconds. Ten to twenty minutes orally, depending on dosage administered of course and the time frame required."

"Fascinating stuff, Julian. Just fascinating. Well, the mother is the same weight as say … a yearling, or a bull calf."

Both men laughed.

"Paul, no offence, but if I keep talking I might as well have Darlene standing there, as I'll get nothing done."

"Did you ever think about trying it out on yourself, Julian?"

"That'd be telling you too much, my man. I could be struck off if they knew the half of it. They used volunteer prisoners, you know, a few years ago to test it. There's a worry about it being used as a recreational drug, so they need to keep a tight control over it, and that's why I sit here at every spare moment accounting for every drop. Now, Paul, no offence, but knock that back and off you go. I'll get nothing done if I stay chatting with you."

"Right. I'll see you in a couple of days when I pick up the rest of the stock in Galway. There was a delay with the bloody TB test from their end and, you know me, if they haven't been cleared, I won't touch them with a forty-foot pole. The lower field at Black Post is there waiting to fatten them up, before they head off to the mart. It's the milk disease that's the bloody nuisance and the bloody red-water worse again. Right, see you soon then."

Chapter 34

The Cattle Dealer

1952

Paul Grogan had been interested in livestock since he was old enough to go to the fairs. Stick in hand, he proved himself to be natural. As the marts began to open up around the country, he made it his business to secure a seat in a lorry with whatever dealer would bring him along. He would offer to load the cattle on the truck, hanging around the mart with the farmers, watching money pass hands. Ears wide open. Eager. Listening.

He could spot disease in an animal's eyes well before the buyer had raised his hand to place a bid or agree to a sale. If there was a weakness in an animal, Paul had it spotted. There had been much demand for his sharp eye. The dealers would ask him to cast an eye around the sales enclosure. Those who were too tight to throw him a fiver, he'd refuse to help. By the age of fifteen he was much sought after by the cattle dealers to travel with them to marts all over the country. Paul would check the animal's teeth and tongue before money changed hands.

He got in on the game himself once he was old enough, buying one animal to begin with, slowly gaining the confidence to buy more, before selling them on at a profit. The game was profitable for Paul who had learned to rely on no-one but himself. By the time he was eighteen he was well known in the livestock trade around the country.

When he had enough money made, he put a deposit on a second-hand truck. He was good for the money. Cash. Paul Grogan wouldn't be under a compliment to anyone, least of all his father. *Paul Grogan Livestock* became a familiar sight on the road. He knew where to look for the animals he was interested in. What to look for. Buying up animals that came off poor land, fattening them up on the rich grass at Black Post before selling them on for a profit. Having a vet on call over the years had meant everything. And Julian Taylor was an expert. A man, not too unlike himself, who kept his head down, preferring to work alone. Paul trusted no-one. The vet was sound enough. And he'd learned an awful lot from him. But, if Julian was under the illusion that he was a push-over, he was sadly mistaken. Paul gave him all the chat, acting the fool at times, playing the eejit. Behind it all he knew he was far smarter than the lot of them. It suited him to let them think otherwise. The days of Paul Grogan the naïve schoolboy were long past.

The memory of long ago. The day that his childhood ended.

Creeping up the stairs, heading for his room, boots under his arm, careful to avoid the creaky steps, he had passed his mother's bedroom.

He could hear laughter. She had company. He went down on his knees to take a peek through the keyhole – sitting back on his heels immediately. His mother's friend from Italy was lying on the bed, undressed, in the arms of his mother who was also naked. He couldn't believe his eyes. Wanting to throw up. He looked again to make sure. He could hear music. *Thud.* One of his boots dropped from under his arm, falling hard against the floorboards. He stepped away from the door, just as it opened. His mother's head appeared around the door. Having a clear view of the bed through the large mirror on the wall of his mother's bedroom, he felt sick to his stomach.

Paul had seen enough.

He ran back down the stairs, clutching the other boot. Tears were running down his face. He jumped on his bike, cycling as fast as he could down the avenue. A shower of heavy rain had begun to fall. His stockinged feet slipping on the wet pedals. Getting off the bike, he threw it roughly aside against a tree just as he got to the gate lodge and run on. His mother had bought it for him for his eleventh birthday. He had been so thrilled. Now it meant nothing. He hated it. He hated her.

Banging at the door of the public house where his father stayed most nights with his aunt. He didn't know where else to go. His aunt had done her best to console him. No effect. Telling the headmaster at school that he had been sick, he had returned to his class. Knowing. He would never tell a single soul that his mother was a queer.

From that day forward, Paul Grogan taunted and bullied any boy he came across who appeared less than manly. He was all man. No room for weakness.

He never wanted to lay eyes again on the queer whore from Italy. Or hear her name. She wasn't a guest. She was a perverted bitch. A bitch he'd found in bed with his mother, in his own home.

As for his mother, she was dead to him.

Connie had acted as if nothing had happened when he arrived home from school at the usual time. He didn't know where the Italian had gone. But she had. Gone. Ignoring his mother, who was signing in a guest, Paul went to his room. From that day forward, he would address her only as Connie. Holding on to the image he had witnessed earlier that day. An image which sickened him to the core.

The following day, Paul Grogan had announced that he was never going back to school.

Paul didn't celebrate birthdays, as he had reminded his aunt every year since he had turned thirteen. What was there to celebrate? A lesbian mother who had tricked his father into marriage, to secure a life for herself in Black Post Inn.

Having a child for no other reason than to cover herself. A mother who proclaimed that he was the head of his father when he annoyed her. And a father who pointed out his mother's weaknesses to him at every opportunity, leaving Paul to suspect that he had more of Connie's ways than he would have liked.

Watching his father as he cowered behind the stairs, to avoid a blow from the sweeping brush, aimed at whatever part of his body she could land the brush on.

Paul had been ashamed of his father.

"Stand up for yourself, Mattie! Why don't you bloody well stand up for yourself?

Connie, leave him alone! Put down the brush!"

Running out the front door and into the yard, sitting on the ground, just under the window ledge in earshot of every word spoken through the open door.

His mother's voice raised. Shouting at his father to get out. His father shouting back at her, brave in the knowledge she couldn't corner him. Like a rat.

"I'm finished, Connie, as God is my witness. I'm finished. I've tried everything to satisfy you, but nothing ever will. The only time I saw you truly happy was when the Italian one came here a few years ago."

"Oh, 'tis all coming out now. Aren't you very brave all of a sudden – come on, say what you have to say, and don't do your usual running out the door. You're finished, did you say? Well. that makes two of us then. Twelve years of you making a holy show of me, inside in the bed in town with herself. And you acting like 'tis my fault. It wasn't all about my depression, you know. I wonder what triggered it in the first place?"

"There was nothing going on between myself and Johanna back then. And where else was I supposed to go to, and you here fit for nothing. With your ear stuck to the damn wireless!"

His mother was shouting. "I smelled her perfume on you every time you came home! *Soir de Paris*. It was me who brought it back to her from London in the first place. I had a hard time after having Paul and you damn well used it to suit yourself it. Gave you ample reason to go into her bed."

"At least she's not a trickster, Connie. Why don't you admit it? You tricked me into marrying you!"

Spotting Paul sitting underneath the window, his legs stretched out in front of him, had quietened Mattie, who stood in the front doorway, keeping his eyes on his son, leaving Connie to shout away at him from inside. Exposing her.

"Oh, the penny finally dropped, did it?" said Connie. "Yeah, I filled you up with whiskey, Mattie Grogan. And I landed you up to my bed. And no, we didn't do anything, and even if you had wanted to you couldn't, because you were too far gone. I pulled the pants half off you and got into the bed beside you. And no … I wasn't pregnant. How could I have been? But it didn't take too much to convince you all the same, did it?"

Paul didn't move. He had heard every word.

His father hadn't bothered to shut her up, to save his ears from hearing any more.

He hated them both.

"You know, Mattie, you've been the trickster here all along. I was more than willing to settle here with you. Did you ever once make an attempt to come to my bed after Paul was born? Even once, did you put your arms around me to comfort me during the tough years? And when I was breaking my back to make a go of the place here? Did you even recognise that some words of comfort might be welcome? You didn't! Because you were too busy with your lady love in town to even consider me. As for Paul, he'd rather be in with his aunt anyway. I've lost him and I've only yourself to thank for that."

Mattie had walked towards his son, offering his hand to Paul who pushed his hand away.

"Well, lad, you can see first-hand what you have for a mother."

Paul ignored him, running off through the fields.

It was teatime when he landed back at the house. Opening the door to the kitchen, he saw there was no sign of either of them. He finished the remains of a leftover rabbit stew. They were each as bad as the other. Paul would never allow another soul get close to him again. He would be the keeper of his own soul.

Mattie Grogan had sat into his truck, headed for town, parked at the old familiar spot at the back gate of Stapleton's public house. Ordering a pint and a half one, he was in the same spot three hours later, his head resting on his arms. He didn't return to Black Post for three days.

When he did, it was to pack a bag and tell Paul and Connie he was leaving.

"Paul, have you something to be getting on with outside? I'll see you out there once I've spoken to your mother. Go on now, good lad. Leave us talk."

Once he had finished in the house he met with Paul who was sitting on the low wall surrounding the wrought-iron sign. He told him he had made a terrible mistake by marrying his mother.

"But don't worry, lad, I've a plan afoot for you. You know how fond I am of your Aunt Johanna, so that's where I'll be, between the gate lodge and town. No more lies, son. And there's a bed inside for you, if you so wish."

Mattie had sat at the table on his return to Johanna, and cried like a baby. "Johanna, I've been such a fool. Why didn't I see what was staring me in the face all along? Connie has no more interest in me than the man in the moon. Nor I in her. I thought I'd taken advantage of her that night. Only you were smart enough to work it all out – she was never expecting in the first place and, by the time she was, 'twas too late. In order for things to change I have to become the kind of man I have always detested. From now on she'll be my wife in name only, and I don't care who knows it. I'll use the gate lodge to camp in, until such time as it all calms down."

"You'll do no such thing, Mattie Grogan. My bed has been good enough for you up to now. You'll stay here with me. Nothing will change that much – you're here with me most of the time as it is. And let them say what they like. That Bloody Black Post Inn is cursed, I'd say. There's no luck attached to it. Let herself stay in it. And Paul knows well enough where his bread is buttered. He's old enough at this stage to make up his own mind."

Chapter 35

Being Darlene

1978

Darlene Taylor walked determinedly towards the door of the police precinct on Fifth Avenue. She didn't know if she was doing the right thing or not, but she had to do something. She wanted relief. To feel that she had not been in any way responsible. At the very least she wanted information. She stated her business to the police officer at the desk.

"Hi, my name is Darlene. I hope you can help me, I may have some information linking someone I know to an unreported sexual assault, back in Ireland. Retrospective I might add, ten years or thereabouts. And I don't really know the victim too well, I'm afraid, so I haven't their consent to report this." The minute the words were out of her mouth she realised how futile it was.

The sergeant smiled weakly at Darlene. If the look on his face was anything to go by, he was not taking her seriously. He appeared to be waiting for her to finish, to hear for herself the absurdity of what she was reporting.

Darlene knew she was wasting her breath, but continued.

"Well. I'm here for information really. Say if I have information that I think may have led to a sexual assault, but I'm not sure, just a hunch really. Well … more than a hunch!"

The officer shifted in his chair.

"Well, ma'am, we'd need to know a lot more detail than you seem to have to offer. Such as, who are we talking about here? Names, dates, perpetrator, victim, witnesses, and so on."

Darlene sighed heavily.

"Why don't I help you, ma'am, by asking you a few questions, and you can fill me with the details as we go. Otherwise, we'll be here all day long and getting nowhere."

He was not taking her seriously. She nodded her head as he opened his log sheet.

"Look, ma'am. I'll go ahead and read a list of questions for you to consider. Are you ready? Darlene nodded.

"So … who's the alleged perpetrator and who is the alleged victim? Is there a victim statement to be had, or proof of the assault? Does the alleged victim have an idea that you wish to report this matter? Has it been reported in the jurisdiction where the crime was committed? When did this assault happen? Years ago? And hearsay is not enough. Was there motive, preparation? Is there a pattern here? Would you like to answer some of these and we'll see if we can help you out? And this all happened in Ireland, you say? Will I continue?"

Darlene stepped back from the desk. Overwhelmed.

"And after all that we have to consider the Statute of Limitations here in the state of Massachusetts."

She had heard enough. She had known it was a long shot. But something inside of her wanted her to hear it said aloud. To validate it. And now she knew what an idiot she'd been to think they would have taken her seriously.

"I'm not kidding you, officer! I know I sound like a mixed-up crazy person. But thank you! Perhaps I need to check up on a few things myself."

She ran down the steps in tears.

She would call Agnes when she got home, and handle it her own way.

Darlene had sat at her husband's desk, her heartbeat quickening in her chest. Knowing exactly where to find what she looking for, the key to Julian's bureau, where he kept his research ledgers. Her hands were shaking as she turned the key, flicking her finger along the dated ledgers, she withdrew the one she had been looking for.

The entry she had been searching for had not been difficult to find. All there in neat black print. Julian's handwriting. Using her forefinger to guide her down along the page. There it was. Her heart quickening, knowing what she was about to see would change everything for her. She had been distraught over the previous weeks, mulling it over in her head. Knowing in her gut that her suspicions had been correct. The suspicions that she had refused to allow surface from deep inside her imagination, since her time in Ireland. Now she no longer needed to push the ugly thoughts to the far corner of her mind. No longer having to scold herself for pointing the finger. It was there in front of her in black and white.

Dated: December 22nd 1968 at 8.45am. Black Post Farm. Batch number ci-12873 Administered test dose of CI-581 to Bovine calf. NG -168lb … the rest of the detail was irrelevant to her. Darlene had seen enough. She scanned through the page, her eyes resting on the last paragraph. **Animal recovered well within forty minutes. No distress. Vital signs checked.**

She felt sick. Her hunch had been correct. It all fitted. Too much to be a coincidence.

She had joked with Julian on many occasions, about him having obsessive compulsive disorder, when it came to logging details. Accountability he'd insisted. Citing instances where vials of ketamine had gone missing and been used in the underworld, Julian had always insisted that he was accountable from the moment he signed for his allocated consignment. Drugs in, drugs out. Batch number in – batch number accounted for. No discrepancies. Each vial labelled and accounted for. No room for mistakes, he had insisted. Well, he had made a mistake, a major mistake. Ownership. He had kept every last account of his research.

Julian had prepared and shipped his precious ledgers back to the States in a wooden trunk. Darlene had come across an old newspaper cutting during the move. Sorting through his papers, it had fallen to the floor.

It had been trying for him to have to confess to Darlene that he had been questioned by the police while in college, for being involved in allegedly drugging a female student before sexually assaulting her. The girl had initially alleged that she had woken up to find one of the boys on top of her. She said she had recognised the two students, but had been powerless to stop them. Having given an interview to the newspaper, the case was to be brought to court. But she withdrew her statement. Unfounded. Lacking credibility. Case dismissed.

Darlene had quizzed Julian about it. He insisted that it had been consensual, that the student had invited him and his mate to her room for a nightcap, knowing full well what she was doing. A group of them had been out drinking and smoking weed, and she had remained with the two lads after her friends had left. He had threatened to counter-litigate against the girl, but she had dropped all charges.

Darlene had no choice but to accept his word, given that there was no case for him to answer. He had often been distressed in his sleep, but not so much in later years. She had been left in some doubt, having questioned him until he had no more to say on the matter.

And she'd had thoughts, deep in the night, when darkness forced her to focus. Thoughts on the manner in which Julian had dismissed her questioning. His cold response, his lacking in empathy for the girl who had made the allegations, had remained with her.

Recalling the newspaper cuttings, Darlene felt that the old allegations against Julian might not been unfounded after all. He had been so wrapped up in his work that he never considered that someone outside of himself would have the mind to link it all together. Someone like Darlene, who had carefully worked it through. With one conclusion. *Guilty.*

Precision and detail were all-important to Julian. Recording each detail of his findings meticulously. He used to say that replicability, testability and precision were the hallmarks of good research. Each detailed entry in his journals had been precise to a fault. But the same precision would now destroy him, she would make sure of it.

Recalling the morning in Kilnarick when she herself had woken up feeling dazed. Stupefied. Sore. Confused. Having the feeling that something was not right. With Julian lying beside her, on his side, watching her, smoking a cigarette. Calm. They had made love the night before, it had been late. They had been out at the captain's dinner at the golf club. He had said it was the alcohol. But she hadn't been drinking that much and something had felt wrong. Darlene had told her husband she felt odd.

"I don't feel right. You know the feeling you get, when

you're asleep but you think you're awake and you can't move. What do they call it? Sleep paralysis. I've had it a few times here now and it's so scary. I hate it."

"Tell me exactly what you mean? You were awake or you weren't? Can you recall the moment or was it like a dream?" He had held her close in his arms.

"Oh forget it, I can't remember now. Just a dream, I suppose."

She had snuggled up to him, enjoying the closeness of his embrace but he had jumped out of bed, quickly planting a kiss on the top of her head.

"Ah, you'll be fine, Darlene. That's normal. Well, can't stay here talking all day, while there's work to be done."

Darlene hadn't dwelled on it at the time, even when it had happened again sometime later. Thinking it to be like Julian had said. Just a dream.

She had only ever experienced the feeling while they were living in Ireland. And now she knew why. Julian had a twisted fantasy and he had realised it. Tested on herself. Replicated on Norah Gorman.

After speaking with Agnes who told her about Norah Gorman's unexplained pregnancy, her suspicions about Paul Grogan drugging her all those years ago. It all came back to Darlene. Every niggling thought reappeared, consuming her. Once the thought had entered her mind, she could not let it go. Darlene would face what she had to face. Hearing what Agnes had to say, the cloud of fog had lifted.

"I was tidying the drugs cabinet, Darlene, and it hit

me, all of a sudden. Norah must have been drugged. That's the only way it could have happened – that's why she has no memory of having sex – he must have drugged her. And if he used what I'm thinking he did, she'd have woken up within a half an hour or so, oblivious to what had happened. With no memory recall. And the only place it could have happened is Black Post Inn, because it was the first night she'd had been away from home on her own outside of family. The dates fit. And there's only one man who could be responsible. Paul Grogan." Agnes had said it had hit her like a ton of bricks. "It had to have been him. He was always in the surgery, looking on, watching Julian operate on them rabbits and pigeons, small animals like, watching him like a hawk."

Darlene had been unnerved at what she was hearing. Knowing. Her stomach felt sick.

"It definitely must have happened the last time we stayed over with Connie," Aggie continued. "Remember the time I met you at Black Post? Connie had broken her wrist and couldn't balance herself properly. Well, it was soon after that. You were going back to America for Christmas. Remember?"

Darlene had trembled in horror, knowing what Aggie was saying to be true. In part.

Paul Grogan may well have doped the girl, and other girls. But those mornings she had woken up feeling the way she did, with Julian lying beside her on each occasion, a satisfied look on his face, with an empty cup of tea on the nightstand at her side, had caused her to wonder. He brought her a cup of tea every morning before he left for the surgery – he still did. She would drink it and fall back to sleep again, waking long after he had left to start the day. Apart from the mornings he had lain beside her back in Ireland. Watching her. Observing her. No doubt about it. She would not protect him.

The time had come to accept that her world had just turned upside down. Julian was a perpetrator of rape. Remembering Agnes's words.

"Think about it! Paul and Julian spend all that time together, with the key turned in the door. It was always in the evenings. Or on a Sunday. I remember, because I helped him out as much as I could, and blamed myself afterwards for not being there for Norah. Julian administering the ketamine, always having a second dose on the ready, in case the animal woke up. And the Paul fella taking it all in."

Aggie called Norah in London, from the phone box across the street. Having made a few attempts to tap the number, she had finally succeeded. She had intended to pay for the call, but had she done so she would have to have to go through the telephone exchange. This way she would be sure that there would be no third-party listening in.

"Norah, listen, you're not going to believe what I have to tell you, so you'd better sit down. Are you on your own there?"

"Yes, Aggie, what is it? Did something happen to –?'

"No. Not at all. This is about what we have been talking about."

"Aggie, what are you on about?"

"Black Post Inn, Norah. If you get me?"

"Go on, will you, please."

"Well, Darlene Taylor rang me this morning at work. She was asking me all sorts about the entries that Julian used to make in his ledgers. And about what happened to you, and the dates and stuff. She wanted to know the full details of when we stayed in Black Post Inn. When you found out you were pregnant. And she wanted to know about the doors in Black Post Inn and would they have been locked. She asked if Julian knew that you were on your own after I left for work. And then she blurted it all out."

"Why was she asking all that, Aggie? None of her frigging business at all, and you should have kept your mouth shut. I don't know what you were discussing me with Darlene for."

"It wasn't like that, Norah. Remember I told you that I had been talking to her a few weeks ago. And I happened to mention, that you were coming here for the weekend. And I was moving over to London with you in a few weeks' time. Then Paul Grogan's name came up and one thing led to another, and I was telling her about Paul's little issue, when I was with him. I just gave her the basics. I told her that we thought that Paul Grogan had slipped you something because he couldn't get it up if a girl was looking at him. But guess what? We have been blaming the wrong fucker, Norah, unless there was two of them in it. And I doubt that very much."

"No … no, Aggie, don't. I can't bear the thought of bringing it up again. Didn't you hear me at all? I thought I was going mad after it all happened, I was afraid to go out with a fella for years afterwards. Not knowing. But I've moved on, I told you, if I stayed in the frame of mind I was in, I'd have ended up in the Thames, or in a mental institution."

"Norah. Listen. You have to. Darlene gave me the go-ahead to tell you. Don't ask me why she told me. But she did. It's fucking Julian, girl. No second names, just in case. Yes, Mister God Almighty Julian. Her own husband, using the drug he spent years researching. He knew it like no-one else. And you weren't the first according to Darlene. He was accused of raping a girl on the college campus with another guy years ago. The charges were dropped by the girl, so there was nothing on him. But there's no smoke without fire, and Darlene is now certain that he even tried it on her during their time in Kilnarick. She opened her eyes a few mornings and had a strange feeling that all was not right. She found newspaper cuttings about him being named as a rape suspect years ago, and it made her wonder. And hearing about your pregnancy changed all that."

"Stop, Aggie, stop! *Please.* This is too much. I'm not comfortable talking about all this over the phone. It's not safe no matter what you say. We need to be face to face. So wait till you move over, we'll talk it through then. As long as Darlene keeps her mouth closed, it can wait. Two weeks after ten years of waiting can't hurt. Can it?"

"OK, Norah – but, Jesus, I'm in shock, that's all. Darlene only told me because she didn't want Connie to be all upset, if it got out about Paul. Don't worry, I won't tell a soul, but I better say it to Mam just in case. She already has an idea that we've Paul Grogan down as a rapist. But, sure, who will she tell? No-one."

"Aggie, you've some mouth on you. That's slanderous stuff, dangerous talk. Leave it be, will you?"

"OK, just one more thing. Darlene is guarded enough about it all, but willing to tell us what she knows. I trust her, Norah. And so should you. Look, I know it's a long shot and believe me I'd like nothing better than to take Paul down. But this is your call and now we have Darlene on our side. She's leaving him and she has no notion of going back. She says she'll get a divorce and sent him on the papers. She went to the police to report him but they wanted too much information before they'd take a statement, they wanted the why and the where of it all. So she walked out again and said nothing. Paul is a bastard, but I reckon Julian used him to make idiots of us all. Knowing that if we were to suspect anyone, it would be Paul Grogan. Darlene is convinced that Julian would have set him up if he was ever under suspicion. There's no end to it. And I working at the surgery all the time and never copped it."

Norah remained silent.

"Are you still on the line, Norah? OK … I'm done for now."

"*Good!*" answered Norah in a sharp tone.

"So we agree? No cops, no investigations. Let Darlene handle it?"

The line went dead.

Julian Taylor suffered a brain aneurysm three hours after being confronted by his wife at their home. His blood pressure when checked was at crisis level, resulting in the aneurysm which was more than likely caused by an undiagnosed weakness in one of his artery walls. At forty-nine, he might require assistance for the rest of his life. He would certainly need to be monitored over the coming months before his condition could be re-evaluated. But not by Darlene, whose mind had been made up to confront her husband before moving on with her life. The end result would be the same. She set about proving against all doubt that Julian had been somehow involved in drugging the young student on the university campus.

Locating the woman had not been difficult. She had been reluctant to come forward at first, until Darlene convinced her that she also had been drugged by her husband to satisfy his perverted fantasies. Once the woman heard about Norah and what she had suffered, she met with Darlene in Boston, telling her everything. Feeling powerless at the time to proceed with the case, she said she had dropped all charges.

Julian's heart was strong, they told her. Strong enough to live for years, as long as a stroke didn't take him.

Darlene returned to her parent's vacation cottage in Dennisport. Giving herself time to heal. Time to accept that the man she had spent thirteen years with had carried a filthy secret all the years that she had known him. His desire to control defenseless women. Coward. Unsure if he understood or not, she advised him that the divorce papers would be in the post as soon as she could arrange it. Karma had its own way of sorting things out.

Sitting on the deck, watching the flowers sway in the soft August breeze. Picking up the *New York Times*. Seeing his photo at the bottom of the page did little to sway her.

Senior veterinary partner removed from Register, retrospectively found guilty of unlawfully administering drugs to a student during his time in veterinary college. His conduct has been deemed unlawful and misleading.

The tears slipped down her cheek. A tear for Norah Gorman, who had gone on to live her life in London with Agnes Foley. A tear for Norah's stillborn child James. For Connie, back in Ireland, finally living her life in the gate lodge with her soulmate, Lucrezia. One thing was for sure. Julian Taylor would never hurt anyone again. Darlene had made sure of it.

Chapter 36

A Length of Driftwood

1973

Darlene had walked into the shop in Provincetown, browsing at first, before approaching the woman seated at her desk. She didn't have to ask the woman who she was. She just knew.

Handing a polaroid photograph across the table, the woman put her hand across her mouth before speaking.

"I don't understand. Please explain. Where did you get this? Is she here? Is Connie here? Tell me! How have you this? Please."

Darlene explained to Lucrezia that she had lived in Ireland five years before, with her husband, in Kilnarick, just outside Ballygore. She had met Paul Grogan through the practice and later befriended Connie, whom she adored. Connie had told her all about Lucrezia. Not at first. But before she had left to return to the States.

Having busied herself for a couple of years after she

first moved to Sandwich, further west on the Cape, she had recently been back in contact with Connie and Agnes Foley in Ballygore.

"I wasn't sure if I should be interfering at all. It was my gut that brought me here today. I haven't seen Connie for four years now, but I call her from time to time. I live in Sandwich and we have a cottage in Dennisport, so I'm well familiar with the Cape. And I've been coming here to Provincetown since forever. I noticed your shop some time ago and when I saw the driftwood with your names on it, just like Connie had told me. I knew it was fate. But I had to check with Connie first, if I could come and say hi."

Lucrezia stood there, unsure at first. Walking to the front door, she closed the shop.

"Come, come with me to the back, where we can talk. Please."

Darlene told Lucrezia as much as she could remember. She explained how she had known since back then that Paul had been unkind to his mother. That he wasn't nice to her. Controlling her. Punishing her. Darlene disclosed that Connie had told her that he had been locking her in the bedroom for years. Keeping her contained. Making up all sorts of trash about it being all for her own good.

"Did you know that Mattie, her husband, has remained in town all these years living with her sister? He barely passes Connie the time of day."

"She said nothing of this in her letters, why? Oh why? Dearest Connie, why didn't you feel able to talk to me?

Why?" Lucrezia laid her head on her arms, resting on the table.

She had broken down in tears, comforted by the blonde American with the green eyes, whom she had never laid eyes on until two hours before.

"Oh Connie! Why didn't she tell me how cruel life was for her? Are you sure of what you've been telling me? The few times I did speak to her on the phone she seemed guarded, unable to express herself. But that's always been Connie. Writing letters should have been easier in some sense, but she has never complained. And on the phone she ... Are you sure?"

"I'm sure all right. It was Agnes Foley, a local girl, who filled me in when I first met Connie. I believe one-hundred-per-cent that all these years she has been bullied by Paul. Connie told me herself that she just wants a quiet life. She said she wanted to keep her ties with you, on a separate track to her life in Black Post Inn. She didn't want you to be upset, or tainted by her family. Connie told me that your own life hadn't been easy. She puts up with the crap from them, knowing that you're safe here in Provincetown, living the life that you two had planned together. Living her dream."

"Does she not know that it never mattered where we were – we have always belonged to each other?"

"You know Connie better than anyone. She has kept quiet about her troubles and battled on. She has been controlled for years. Mattie and Johanna have ignored it all, facilitated the poor treatment of her in many ways.

But Connie is much better these days, I can assure you of that."

Lucrezia had a lot to think about after Darlene had left. Feeling the fury build inside of her she picked up the telephone to call Connie before banging it down again. No point in overacting and she did not want to alarm Connie by opening up to her about Darlene's visit.

It had been almost twenty years since she had left Black Post Inn in such a hurry. Another few months wouldn't matter. The important thing was that she knew where her life was headed.

Over the following three months Lucrezia worked out her lease on the store on Commercial Street. Spending her evenings penning letters, organising herself.

Refusing to be daunted by Mattie's delay in replying, she sent letters to him by registered post. Finally calling him, to put her proposal to him, warning him that if any one of them caused Connie one more hour of suffering, she would see them both in court. Adding that she was aware that Paul had been cruel to his mother. Lucrezia left Mattie in no doubt as to the lengths she was prepared to go to expose them all.

Calling Connie afterwards. Sensing the relief in Connie's voice as she told her that she would be coming to Ireland quite soon.

"Connie, it's our time, *amore mio*. We have waited over forty years. We have overcome every obstacle that has been put in our way. And now there are no more. No more demands and expectations on either of us. We have survived for each other. We have been the wives and the mothers to our children. From here on we can live our own lives. I will explain all when I see you. But first I have to sort out a few details."

Chapter 37

Lucrezia in Ballygore

1973

Lucrezia had put her bag down on the floor of Stapleton's pub on Mill Road, waiting for the landlady to notice her.

"Yes, dear, what can I get for you?"

"I'm here to see Matthew Grogan. He's been expecting me. We've spoken on the telephone.

"And may I ask who wants to see him?"

Lucrezia squinted her dark eyes.

"You certainly may not ask me anything. I take it you're Johanna. But I'm sure you know damn well who I am. I'm here on business with Matthew Grogan which has nothing at all to do with you."

"That's him over there at the fire. There's no-one else here," Johanna snapped.

Johanna continued to dry the glasses with her dishcloth, staying as near as she could to eavesdrop on the conversation.

Lucrezia offered her hand to Matthew who recognised her immediately.

"'Tis yourself. I see you haven't changed much. What is it? Twenty-five years or thereabouts?" Showing her to a table by the window, he invited her to sit.

"Sit down, sit down."

Coming straight to the point, Lucrezia said what she had come to say. No small talk. Mindful of her accent, she spoke slowly.

"Mattie, you've had plenty of time by now to consider my proposal. As I said to you on the phone, I feel it's time to do the right thing. My boys are mature men now, with their own families, so they no longer need me. I've been living in America for years. As it happens the lease on my business has run out. I'm not short of money, my late husband has made sure of that, so it is my intention to spend the rest of my days here. With Connie. And I believe the best place for us to do so is at the gate lodge, as we discussed. None of us are getting any younger, and there's been more than enough hardship from all sides."

Lucrezia turned around to look directly at Johanna.

"Paul cannot be allowed to bully his mother to her grave, because that is what he has been doing all these years, and as far as I can see you have turned a blind eye, as has that excuse for a woman behind the counter. I'm sure that Connie's papa would turn in his grave at the treatment of his daughter. And at you, for the hand you have played in all of this."

Lucrezia had his attention.

"Hold your horses now, Lucrezia, Connie hasn't exactly been innocent in all this. She hoodwinked me into marrying her when I had too much drink on me. When my eye was only for Johanna there."

"And the vows you took the day you married her meant nothing to you? I married my husband, Marco, and remained with him for over twenty years. I had thought about leaving Italy years ago when I had the chance, but I couldn't do it to him. He had been partially blinded by thugs after the war. Did I abandon him? No. I didn't. I remained right by his side until the day he died."

"Ah, that's all water under the bridge now. You did what you had to do. But I'll give you one thing – Paul hasn't much time for his mother. No one tells me anything and I don't ask, so what's in the past, leave it there."

Johanna turned away towards the far end of the bar as Lucrezia moved closer to Mattie.

"You see, I have so much in my life but I do not have Connie. My dearest, dearest friend." Quickly adding words in Italian she expected he wouldn't understand.

Mattie sat back into his seat, upset by what this woman was saying.

"You do know that she never wanted Black Post Inn for herself? Whether you acknowledge it or not, Connie loves her son, she always has. If he thinks otherwise, then it is not in Connie's power to convince him. He'll have to work that out for himself in his own time. That's why I am offering to buy the gate lodge from you in Connie's name. Only in Connie's name. So, it will never be a separate entity to the farm. I could put an offer on a dozen houses, and believe you me I have tried to convince her to leave Ballygore, but I know that she wouldn't settle. Not now, after giving her life to the place. If I should die before her, she'll have her comforts. As for me, it'll be time enough to go back to my home country, in the event that Connie goes before me. I want nothing out of this, apart from assurance from you that we play it straight, legally signed by all parties. Whatever the relationship between herself and Paul, she is his mother, and no one has a right to cross the golden bridge of emotion between a mother and her son. No-one. I have no wish to upset Connie any more than she has been upset this long time. Give her these last years of freedom with me and I will give you my word she will want for nothing. Time to let go of the misery of the past, Mattie. Time to let old wounds heal."

Mattie nodded. Indeed, it was time to let go of the past. He was tired of it all. James Stapleton would have wanted it no other way. Mattie had been in the firing line between the Stapleton sisters for long enough.

"I'll visit my solicitor and have the paperwork drawn up so. I don't have too much to say to Connie these days, but I wish her no ill. It's a pity in many ways the way things turned out. But you know, I think Layla, the mother, might have had something to do with it. Always putting the sisters up against each other. Paul got caught up in the middle, with a mother who didn't have a maternal bone in her body. And myself? I was just as bad, never knowing a mother or father. But herself over there was always cracked about the lad." Mattie pointed over towards Johanna. "I was never one for talking and all this thinking business has taken its toll. But I know one thing for sure. James Stapleton would indeed turn in his grave at the way the two of them have turned on each other."

"Maybe in time, Mattie. Maybe in time."

"I'll sell it to you at the market price so that we're all clear, and Paul will have no crib. At the bottom of it all he cares for his mother, no matter how it seems. He's just forgotten how much."

Chapter 38

What Goes Around Comes Around

Connie didn't need help in packing her bag, even though Agnes Foley had offered. Reaching in under the bed she pulled out the old suitcase covered in dust. Using the palm of her hand to wipe away the dust, she glanced around her bedroom. The bedroom she would never again have to set foot in. The years of isolation were behind her. She wanted nothing more from the room which had held the last memory of Lucrezia for over twenty years. No time for regrets, no room for blame. Agnes had arranged the weekend trip for her at the Gresham, where Lucrezia had filled her in on the arrangement that she had made with Mattie. Guilt, Lucrezia had insisted, raw guilt. They had shopped in Clery's, Arnotts, and Brown Thomas on Grafton Street. Money was not a factor according to Lucrezia, who insisted on paying for everything.

"It was Marco's dying wish that I come to you and believe me I earned every penny. Marco has made me a very wealthy woman. I spent too long without you." Lucrezia had laughed, the old familiar laugh. "Connie, it's not as if we need so much. Just enough to please ourselves. Like the old times."

"I won't hear of you providing for me. I have my post office book, which I have kept hidden since the day I got married, adding to it every chance I got. And I have my pension. So, let's see how we go."

"Haven't we each suffered enough, *amore mio*? It's time for us to live our lives, unhindered by those who are too narrowminded to understand. *"T'amo!"*

"Ti amo anch'io!" answered Connie.

Lucrezia cried softly on hearing Connie's brave attempt at speaking Italian.

"Yes, Lucrezia, I have been studying that Italian phrase book you gave me all those years ago in London. I love you too."

Packing the boot of Lucrezia's small Fiat car, Connie walked out of Black Post Inn, leaving the hurt of the past years behind her. The newly renovated gate lodge would be perfect for them both. The driftwood sign over the front door, which Lucrezia had brought from the shop in Provincetown, had caused Connie to gasp in delight. *Lucrezia and Connie* – the letters were etched into the wood and painted in white, just as they had talked about all those years before. Lucrezia had thought of everything. They were free to live their lives, signed and sealed. The lodge was in Connie's name, to be passed back to Paul upon her death. Lucrezia wanted nothing to do with Black Post Inn, if Connie was no longer there to share it with her. A deal was a deal. She would return to her beloved Napoli, if that happened.

Connie sat lazily in her armchair by the open fire, the brightly coloured cashmere shawl that Lucrezia had brought back from her latest trip to Naples around her shoulders. Contented. Smiling to herself, she watched Lucrezia conduct an imaginary orchestra as she listened to Vivaldi on the record player, which she had ordered from a store in Dublin. Neither spoke. They had long since let go of the past, no need to be wasting precious time discussing what might have been. Each contented to have the other in their place of peace. No need for conversations about the betrayal of lost years.

The End

Printed in Great Britain
by Amazon

82661929R00222